INTO THE
MACRO COSM

Written by: Konn Lavery

Edited by: Robin Schroffel

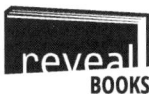

reveal BOOKS

Ebook ISBN-13: 978-1-7771640-1-0

Print ISBN-13: 978-1-7771640-2-7

Published in Canada by Reveal Books.

Book artwork and design by Konn Lavery of Reveal Design.

Photo credit: Nastassja Brinker.

Printed in the United States of America.

First Edition 2021.

Find out more at:

konnlavery.com

AUTHOR MESSAGE

Into the Macrocosm is part of an on-going universe creation housing many stories. The large-scale expansion spans across genres and varying literary styles. Most of the short stories in this book have been previously published in some form. They have been revised from their original state, enhancing the narration and reinforcing the expanding macrocosm.

PREVIOUS STORY PUBLICATIONS

Crusaders: Featured in Constellate Publishing ZINE, May 2019, originally edited by Ellen Michelle.

Mr. Super: Originally a featured live reading on Author Assist Radio Show Sept 13, 2019.

Inspirer: A new story.

All remaining short stories were previously published on the blog at konnlavery.com from 2018 – 2020 as part of the regular monthly short story feature.

THANK YOU

The conception of the monthly short stories on my blog was dual purposed. They provided readers with strange new worlds every month and ultimately let me compile them into a collection. Every story has allowed exploration of the human condition and improving upon my craft. They have drastically enhanced my writing from when I first started in May 2018 with *Runner*.

I'd like to thank you all who have been reading the short stories on the blog, newsletter, or listening to the audio versions online over the past couple of years. I adore the comments. *Into the Macrocosm* is for you, hence the second person overarching narrative with Malpherities. New short stories continue to be featured on konnlavery.com, in the newsletter, and in audio, exploring more of this strange universe. So, thank you again.

I'd also like to thank my mother, Brenda Lavery, for the countless years of love and support. Thank you, Lindsey Molyneaux, for encouraging me and listening to my earlier drafts – letting these stories thrive. Thank you to my brother, Kyle Lavery, for the many years of feedback. Thank you to my editor, Robin Schroffel, for continually providing tremendous insight into the written word. Lastly, but not least, thank you to my family, readers, and friends. You all have helped nurture this growing macrocosm.

Now, let's see where it will take us next!

SYNOPSIS

Explore a strange universe where time and space blur. Being dead or alive no longer matters as the afterlife and the real world intertwine. A talking goat head, sleep paralysis, genetic freaks, killers, and celestial beings are just a handful of the weird found in this growing macrocosm.

Observe through the lives of 22 souls as the Nameless One attempts to discover the lost memories of how they died. A ghoulish companion in the mysterious Midway aids in the search, where one can witness any time, at any place, for clues. Yet, they're not alone in this post-death realm. Even in death, danger lurks, and it is not too fond of visitors.

Award-winning author Konn Lavery's Into the Macrocosm dives into an on-going large-scale story expansion. The short story collection magnifies on previous connecting suspicions found in his horror novel *Seed Me*, thriller *YEGman*, and the dark fantasy series *Mental Damnation*. These interconnected tales bring them all under one, obscure, unsettling, cosmos.

TABLE OF CONTENTS

01

WELCOME TO THE MIDWAY

An explosion. Wait . . . no. A car crash? Stabbed, or hanged? The details are muddled and are impossible to recall. You've moved so far away from the living. Everything is cold. So cold, right after the brief moment of shock. The one thought that passes through your shutting-down mind is, *I'm dead.* At this moment, your brain floods with a blast of chemicals. It is trying to cope with the fact that the body is indeed turning off forever. Life doesn't end, though. You're now seeing that the flesh isn't you, as you experience weightlessness. The chill. The dark. An abstract sense of space, yet you have no body. Time is entirely still as the world fades away.

Linear thoughts are becoming more mangled. You try to pass a statement through your mind, tempted to ask, *What is this?* But ultimately, you feel no need to do so as dozens of expressions run through you. These ideas aren't made up of the linear form of language, giving them more flexibility and potency.

Love. Peace.

Warmth. Wait a minute. Warm—that's a refreshing change from the iciness of death.

Light.

An array of post-death colours blast by you, moving in waves outward, intricately overlayed with geometric patterns. The more closely you look at them, the more you discover tinier designs within them, continuing endlessly. The rays themselves are so vibrant you wonder if you could ever explain them. Your vision is seeing more within the spectrum of light than any human eye could. So many colours! In a strange sense, despite being so far away from everything and everyone that matters, you feel at home. It's as if everything is going to be okay. Your consciousness has risen, broadening your understanding of life, the universe, and how everything so closely connects on a molecular level. The warm feeling is inviting, overpowering, and it pushes everything else aside as you experience the euphoria.

Call it Heaven, Nirvana—whatever human-bound word you choose matters not.

Life after death. Beautiful.

What's that? There's a black spot in the centre of the colour array. Strange. It's growing. Even without a body, you feel a harsh vibration, like an earthquake. Disturbance. The black spot pulls apart, ripping the colours like fabric. It spins as it tears even more space, twisting around and around, sucking the colours into the unknown. Deep purple and blue smoke seeps from the centre of this new blackness. The rumbling you feel shifts into a sucking force, pulling you into the unknown. You can't control yourself, helpless, being pulled into the black as all colours twist into thin lines until they're nothing.

The welcoming feelings of peace, home, and oneness are foggy. You are stuck on this horror roller coaster of darkness, descending deeper into the abyss with no way out. The expanding consciousness is closing. The oneness you felt is gone as the regular, direct, word-based thoughts of your mind return. It's as if you are alive once more. The black-and-blue spirals seem to go on forever. Lightning, purple clouds, and loud crackling are all around in this strange vortex. You swear you can see faces in the storm. Hands of lost souls reach upward, trying to pull you in.

New—or familiar, depending on how you look at it—senses come to you in the form of a body. Smell: rotten. Taste: stale. Touch: bitter breeze. Sound: groans of death. Vision: unfathomable. The spiral comes to an end with a loud thundering *BOOM*, pushing the clouds away, bringing the haunting ghost hands with it. You fall a few feet onto a rocky grey surface with a heavy thud, nose-first.

Nose first. A nose . . . *yours*. The body has returned to you. It's healthier, at prime age. You're able to push yourself up with arms and stand upright. The form is familiar, but so much better, making you wonder how this could be. You must be alive; otherwise, you wouldn't have a body. Perhaps this is some strange form of reincarnation. If it is, we humans got it all wrong because this grey landscape is no part of Earth. You gaze out into the scene of nothing, reinforcing your thoughts. Everything fades to blackness beyond the edges of a strange oval-shaped plateau. The dark goes on forever, just below the not-so-ordinary sky. That black-and-blue vortex of spiralling faces is directly above. The damned vacuum that pulled you from euphoria is now hovering overhead, mocking you.

"How unexpected," a growly, reverbing voice echoes. The voice is doubled, like two beings talking simultaneously. It comes from the dark, all around, and it is impossible to pinpoint the origins.

You want to respond, but are petrified. Everything is beyond confusing. One moment you were alive, and now you're here, in some form of life after death.

"No mortal ends up falling into *and* out of Death's Vortex," the voice continues. "This may even be a first."

Lightning and thunder erupt from above, catching you off-guard. You take a step back, walking into a light blue smoke channelling below your feet. You move. It follows, growing larger. You try to shake it off as it spirals up your limbs. Maybe swatting will work. Nope, your hand goes right through it, and you hit yourself in the junk. It looks like you can feel pain again, too.

The animated fog swirls away from your lower region and into open space. Dark blue-and-black smoke follows, appearing from the unknown as the elements clash together, moving through and around each other. They compress and mould into a torso, lean arms, and a skull with an extended muzzle; sharp teeth, white eyes, and tentacle-like black hair form. The being's inner core contains the bright blue vapour, while the other smoke transforms into a translucent outer layer, like the white of an egg. Even without pupils in the glowing white eyes, the being is undoubtedly looking right at you. There are no legs. It floats effortlessly from the dissipating smoke below, endlessly channelling from the body. The tentacle-like hair flows up and down in a zero-gravity state, unlike your body, which is clearly bound by gravity.

"Well?" the being says, folding its arms, exposing the crosses scarred on his wrists.

You are speechless, uncertain how to reply, and you say, "Am I dead?"

The being laughs. "Am I dead?" it repeats. "I'm guessing you were a comedian in your past life."

"I . . ." You pause, thinking about the question. Were you a comedian? Now you're uncertain. You try and think back to the jobs you've had. Blank. Nothing. There is a giant gap in your knowledge. This is disturbing. You try and recall anything else about your past. Loved ones. Your first kiss. Family. Places you've been. The food you like. All of it—gone. You've forgotten every memory and everything you knew. Yet, you're *you*. You know it.

"I . . ." You look down at your hands. Yes, those are yours. "I don't remember . . . anything?"

"No, you wouldn't," the being says.

"What do you mean? I know I had a life. I was there."

"Yet you can't recall a single memory."

The thought annoys you. Lacking memory is frustrating. It's there, like a dream fading away while waking up, leaving you with nothing but vague feelings. "What is happening to me?"

"You are dead. You got that right. So keep observing your surroundings."

Dead. The being confirms it. You had a life, one that has slipped from your memories. A brief moment of sadness washes over you, for all the things you cherished in life are now gone. You can't recall any of them, no matter how important they once were. You want to freak out and scream in horror. Your lungs tighten as you forget to breathe. Your hands are shaking. Energy hums through you as you're about to have a conniption.

The being speaks, pulling you back into the moment. "What interests me is how did you end up here?" the being asks, coming closer to you, only an arm's reach apart.

"This . . . this can't be. I'm dead?"

"Yes, we just discussed that."

You rub your fingers together, feeling the texture and pressure of your skin. "How?"

The being extends one of its long claws, poking your forehead. It hurts. The skin is punctured. "That is what makes you a fascinating anomaly."

You touch the pierced spot on your head. There's a small bead of blood. You can feel pain; you have to be alive.

"I'll ask again," the being says. "How did you end up here?"

You scratch your head, trying to breathe calmly. "I don't know. There were colours, brightness and—"

The being interrupts you. "Yes, yes. Home. Warmth. Broadening of the mind. All that typical nonsense that you experience when you die. Every mortal feels it. I want to know what was different, because that was supposed to continue until you've become one with it."

"I was supposed to?"

"Yet you were pulled into and out of Death's Vortex."

"Death's Vortex?" you ask.

"Yes." The being points above. "An endless spiral moving inward; the resting bed for souls once they've lived out all their needed lives."

"Those are souls . . . people?" You take another look at the vortex above, examining the wraith-like faces coming and going through the spirals. You'd think they would be in fear, but their expressions are neutral. Those hands are still trying to reach for you.

"Observant," the being says.

"What happened?" you ask. "Who are you?"

"I should really have a welcome brochure," the being mumbles to itself. "Even if I did, you're no normal case. Your soul's trajectory was interrupted."

"What? Who would do that?"

"Might not be a who but a *what*," the being says.

"Okay, so, what did it? Where are my memories?" you ask.

"Gone. Perhaps it is related to how you died, or your soul was in mid-transition of entering its next life, which would have erased them. Memories are always wiped when your next life begins. Let's see if there's any drop of knowledge in that primitive brain of yours. Answer me this: were you practicing any forms of magic?"

"I don't think so."

"Dark arts?"

"Not sure what the difference is."

"Quantum experiment? Particle smashing? Wave manipulation? Deal with a demon?"

"No. No. No. No. I can't remember anything."

"Most interesting." The being strokes its long jaw, staring at you, not blinking.

Many questions run through your mind. Where are you? What happened to your memories? Who are you? What is the meaning of all this? They spin around in your head until you finally blurt one out, saying, "What's your name?"

The being breaks from its thoughts and introduces itself. "I am Malpherities. Seeing how useless you are, you probably don't know yours."

"No, I can't say I do," you reply.

"All right, then we'll call you the Nameless One."

"That doesn't have a ring to it," you say.

"Come up with a better name then," Malpherities says.

At the moment, you can't. It's tough to think of a new name when you're completely flustered with not knowing anything about yourself. So, you say, "We'll work on it. Anyway, what are you?"

"I am a ghoul, a being birthed of Death's Vortex. Unlike your carbon-based life, I come from the nether."

"The nether?"

"Here, where we are. I'm one of many ghouls. We're the conscious state of Death's Vortex, expressed through individual entities."

"What? This just gets more confusing."

"Let me explain in a way you'll understand. What period were you alive in?" Malpherities asks.

"I don't know."

"Of course, useless. All right, judging by how you talk, you probably were alive during some technological advancements. I am a piece of a *hive mind*. A projection of a larger consciousness with a twist of my own. Do you know what the Father, the Son, and the Holy Spirit are? In human religion, Christianity?"

"I think so."

"Think of me like that. All three are one, yet each has their own personality, or ego, if you will."

"Okay, so if you're this Death's Vortex, can you take me out of here?"

"If only it were that simple. You see, you're now encased in a body again. You have flesh. I could kill you if you'd like; that would work."

The thought passes through your mind. Considering you died once and don't remember how, dying doesn't seem too bad. Then again, experiencing the pain at the moment doesn't sound appealing. You scratch your head, unsure what to say.

Malpherities raises his claw. "But you'd be thrown into Death's Vortex. It's a magnet for souls when you're here. You won't go back to the soothing colours that will transcend you into a new life."

"Reincarnation?" you ask.

"Quick learner."

"Fair enough. What is 'here,' anyway? You said 'the nether.'"

The ghoul hovers away, presuming you will follow. So, you do. With each step you take, the darkness moves away from you. The vortex above behaves like a spotlight, beaming directly over you and the ghoul.

"Here is the Midway," Malpherities says.

"Like purgatory?" you ask.

"You do have some knowledge in that brain of yours, after all. But no. Purgatory is a simplified explanation mortals have come up with for multiple realms you can end up in post-death."

"Dimensions?"

"Sort of. Not overly relevant right now. Dimensions make things too complicated. What we're interested in is knowing what happened to you."

"What about realms?" you ask.

"You're mortal; therefore, you're from the mortal realm. It's simple," Malpherities says.

The two of you reach the edge of the oval plateau.

"What else is in this realm?" you ask, looking out into the vast darkness.

"Don't bother. This plateau is all that matters," Malpherities says, hovering towards a stone spiral staircase off to the side, leading down. Over the edge is a vast black sea thousands of feet below. The water is so still, it almost looks like a mirror. One can only wonder what lies beyond, if anything. You stare at the ocean for a moment and shake your head, realizing you'd best follow Malpherities until you have some grasp of what is happening. You hurry to catch up to the ghoul, following him down the stairs and into a vast cavern where large stalactites hang from the dome-like ceiling, covered in condensation. The sandy ground inclines to the centre of the cave, where a matted black pedestal rests, topped with a smooth golden bowl. Droplets fall from the large stalactite directly above, dripping into the dish. The distance of the droplets' fall is so precise that nothing splashes outside of the bowl.

Malpherities moves up the hill and to the bowl, saying, "Come. We must find out why you're here. If you did something in your mortal days to pierce through the soul's natural passage, that is an extraordinary power that is unfathomable."

"I'd have to be pretty smart to be the first to do that."

"You would, which seems unlikely. I propose it is a series of events that managed to jolt you from your soul's trajectory. A freak scenario of the cosmos, if you will. Or, someone else has unlocked an exceptional power."

"I did see the center tear apart before coming here."

"Interesting, and it brings you here," Malpherities says.

"The Midway," you say.

"Correct. The Midway was built by us ghouls, to allow us to phase in and out of space-time."

"Space-time?"

Malpherities sighs. "You are a puddle of uselessness, aren't you? We aren't going to have a science crash course. Time and space are interchangeable. We ghouls shift through them, letting us feast on the dead, bathe ourselves in the dying."

"So, you're like the Grim Reaper?"

Malpherities snorts. "Grim Reaper. No, I'm not."

"Sounds like you are," you say.

"I am only an observer of death; it feeds my life force. Despite being connected to the larger hive mind, we ghouls possess our own personalities. I, for one, relish in schadenfreude."

You reach the shrine beside Malpherities, who is standing directly beside the golden bowl. The ghoul looks into it. "For your overly simplified thinking," he explains, "this Midway lets the users enter and leave periods. You can exist within the space, or simply observe through the mind of another."

You lean over the bowl, looking into the black liquid that sits peacefully within. How strange, for you just saw a droplet land inside. It seems like there are more otherworldly mysteries to be discovered. You point at the bowl and ask, "Through this bowl?"

"Exactly. Dunking your head right in will send you into a specific time and a precise space. Depending on the potency, you may be a spectral, like a ghost, or a fully-formed being. Sprinkle a few droplets over your eyes, and you'll be an observer."

"An observer?"

"Well, we can adjust where and when you end up observing. This will aid us in trying to figure out how you died, when you died, and who you are. These answers will give us a sense of how you ended up here."

"And you want to help me?"

"Whatever means that got you here disrupted a delicate balance for souls. I for one, don't want any more of you showing up in the Midway. Or if someone did do this, they may be a threat. This place is for us ghouls, not mortals or anyone else."

You look around the cavern, unsure about this whole bowl concept. The space is large, and the cavern descends deeper into darkness. At the edge of shadows, you see another sandy hill with a matte red pedestal and a golden bowl resting on it. "What about that bowl?" you ask.

"Again, we don't need to get into dimensions. Everything gets . . . sticky," Malpherities says.

"What if something from another dimension did this to me?"

"Let's start with the practical, shall we?"

"And there's no way you can put me back to that peaceful state?" you ask.

"No, unfortunately not. Your soul is here now. Death's Vortex awaits."

"But this bowl sends you to different places?"

"Yes," Malpherities says.

"So I could just dive into it and live a new life, forget all of this?"

"You could, but you're inexperienced and have no knowledge of controlling the Midway. You could end up in a torture chamber, or maybe on a planet filled with flesh-eating man-rabbits, nibbling away at you."

"Gross."

"Very. Let me control the bowl." Malpherities dips one claw into the black liquid, scooping up a small amount. He uses his other two claws to rub the fluid around his palm, gently poking it. It's unclear what he is doing. Maybe he is adjusting that space-time thing he talked about. Malpherities stops, then rises above you. "Open your eyes," he commands.

"What?" You take a step back.

"We're going to find out what happened to you. This will let you observe another's life. We'll shift between time and space to find out who you are."

"You're just going to make me observe someone's life? Will I feel anything?"

"You will. You'll experience everything the other soul does, as an observer. We'll throw you into a person's experience, letting us gather any sort of clue that will spark your memory, if there is any. A simple process of illumination."

"How many times are we going to do this?" you ask, looking up at the ghoul. A droplet of the black liquid dangles from the tip of his claw, soon to fall on you.

"Hopefully, not many. Human minds are frail." Malpherities taps his claw, forcing the droplet to separate. It falls directly into your eye, followed by a couple more drops in the same socket. You close your eyes, feeling a sting, now a burning sensation. You try to rub them, but it makes the pain worse.

"This hurts!" you shout.

"Embrace it. Let go of yourself," Malpherities says, his voice fading. "Accept the passing and become the witness of another."

Your eyes fly open. The cave, the shrine, and the ghoul begin to dissolve into white. Weightlessness returns to you. This time, it's different, for there is no cold or warmth. You're losing your thoughts as you enter a trance—an observer of another place and time.

GOAT WISDOM

IN HELL

Today was one of those days at school. A day you wish you could just stay in bed because the teachers breathe down your neck about everything you do, and the other normie-kids talk about the stupid music they like and the lame TV shows they watch. Not to mention you see your crush hitting it off with her new boyfriend—the quarterback of the football team. Honestly, a day like this is a typical day at school. I can't ever recall a good one. Oh well. Cheers to the best times of my life.

I fiddle with my pencil, carving the sharp lead into the wooden desktop, following the grain, and leaving behind a trail of graphite. It is a mundane, pointless activity that I like to do while I am in the classroom. Carving is better than listening to Mr. Patton ramble on about physics. Where am I even going to use this stuff? I don't want to be some sort of Einstein. Apparently, we're supposed to take all types of sciences in grade ten, so we can decide where we want to go. I know where I want to go: cloud nine.

"I want you all to turn to page twenty-seven," says Mr. Patton. "Read the assignment. You can do the first portion for the rest of the class and the second half when you're home."

The whole class—about thirty kids—pull out their pencils, turn to the page, and begin reading. Some of the keeners in the front are the quickest, probably because they are following along with Mr. Patton. Nerds. I just flip open to a random page to look like I am paying attention.

"Hey man," whispers the boy next to me.

I turn to look at the kid, Marcus, one of my good pals. For the first time today, I notice his Goat Lord T-shirt—a kick-ass death metal band we enjoy. They're raunchy and forward-thinking. My favourite track is them warning us of Y2K; it's going to shut down the whole world! How metal is that? Marcus and I actually have the same shirt and make sure we don't wear it on the same day. He can wear his on Wednesdays. I wear mine on Tuesdays. The last time we matched shirts, the jokes about us being a couple were aplenty. Now we avoid that risk of embarrassment. What girl is going to show interest if they think Marcus and I are dating?

"Yeah?" I ask.

"You want to get out of here when we're done class?" he asks.

"Damn right, I do," I say.

"Word. You got some green in your locker?" Marcus lowers his voice.

"Sure do," I say with a grin. "We should get Felicia in on this too."

"You just want to try and stick your hands down her pants," Marcus says.

I tighten the grip on the pencil. Marcus's words irritate me because they are right. He's a good friend and is entitled to remind me when I am doing something stupid. I just don't want to hear it. I can't understand why she would go for someone like Don. I suppose being the quarterback makes you cool, despite being a complete dud. Don't even get me started on his goofy horse-face.

"Well," I say, "if I run into Felicia, I will talk to her. If I don't, we can just head to the ravine."

"Sure, whatever you say," Marcus says. "As long as she is cool with my music."

"Totally, she's into metal."

"Yeah, the mainstream pussy-ass stuff," he mumbles while staring down at his book.

Confusion paints his face as he reads the text—probably similar to my expression throughout the class. Neither of us is interested in physics. Gotta love that forced education system. We're not going to use any of this shit when we graduate. For the rest of the period, we stare at our assignments, pretending to work. Marcus is trying while I'm doodling around the edges of the paper. Unfortunately, Mr. Patton watches everyone like a hawk, waiting to strike his prey. He loves catching students misbehaving and making them an example in front of the rest of the class. That's why we pretend to work. Later, we can pay off one of the smarter kids to help us with our assignment. Smart kids like drugs, too.

Eventually, the heavens hear our agony, and the bell rings. Finally. That class could not have ended soon enough.

GATHERING THE GOODS

Marcus and I pack up our things and hurry out of the classroom. We have our exit strategy on routine and are often the first ones to leave, despite being in the back of the room. Today we're slow, splitting when we exit the doorway. Our lockers are in opposite wings of the school. It's kind of a bummer, but we always know where to meet up when ditching school. Physics is dull, but the next period is social sciences. God no.

I hurry through the hall to get to my locker. My route while leaving physics class takes me right past Felicia's locker. She has math during this period. On most days, I can see her making out with Don. That buck-toothed ass always has his hands groping her body. The rage I feel comes from jealousy. Truthfully, all I want to do is fondle her up and down. Just like every other day, she's at her locker. Lucky for me, Don isn't here. It looks like Felicia can have some fun.

I slow my pace to a relaxed stride. Damn, her red hair is hot. I approach Felicia as she fumbles through her locker. I gather my cool attitude and nod at her, saying, "Hey, sup?"

"Hey!" Felicia jumps, smiling at me. There it is, that deadly smile of an angel, pushing her right cheek higher. An expression that freezes even the most willful of boys. The snake-bite piercings just add to the rock-and-roll charm. She has a way with her grin, and maybe her whole mouth—I'd love to find out. Either way, I sometimes wonder if she is friendly to everyone, or if she actually likes me. We've known each other since junior high. My feelings for her have just multiplied over the years. Probably something to do with teenage hormones.

"Marcus and I are going to the ravine to have some dope. You want in?" I ask.

"Fly!" Felicia shuts her locker and adjusts her backpack. "We bouncing now?"

"Yep, going to meet Marcus just out by the east wing."

"Think we have some time to grab Don?" Felicia asks.

"Uh, as if," I say. "Doesn't he have to go slap some boy-ass on the football field?" I smile to make sure she knows I'm joking.

Felicia giggles and brushes her red hair aside, exposing her pale neck. I want to kiss it. She says, "So how was Mr. Patton? Is he still running that dictatorship of a classroom?"

"You betcha," I say as the two of us walk. She's close. I can smell that gentle aroma, a mixture of freshly washed hair and her natural feminine scent. We brush shoulders. Oh man, I'd better not get a boner. "How about you?" I ask.

"Oh, you know, math is math. The teacher is clowning, but I don't mind it. I just can't wait to get the hell out of here."

"Two more years," I say.

Felicia and I reach my locker, where I snag the small jar that contains the joint. I always try to reduce the smell by hiding it inside a glass container with a cork. The method isn't perfect, but as long as I keep it at the bottom of my backpack, no one knows. With the joint obtained, Felicia and I leave my locker and head for the east wing. We chat during the walk about the same stuff we usually do: movies, music, and video games. Time is a blur with this girl.

BLOW THIS POP STAND

Felicia and I exit the school, finding Marcus outside, leaning against the brick wall of the building. He perks up, saying, "There you are, fart-knocker."

The words are obviously directed towards me. Marcus is not too fond of Felicia. He sees how this girl has me wrapped around her finger—whether she knows it or not. Plus, Marcus is kind of a purist when it comes to music. If someone doesn't fit within his criteria of taste, they aren't cool enough to hang. He probably tolerates Felicia just because I like her a lot. Again, he's a good friend.

"Yeah, man," I say. "I was just grabbing my stuff."

"No duh," Marcus says, heading over and walking with us.

"I'm so glad you guys can get your hands on weed," Felicia says. "My dad would kill me if he knew I was into this."

"Mine too," I say. "I just don't give a fuck."

The three of us laugh while walking across the grass. Felicia's eyes stray to the football field. The team is training together in their deep blue uniforms. Their coach directs them to perform specific tasks that never look fun. But I know Felicia isn't thinking about that. She is trying to see if Don is there. That douche. I wonder if his dick resembles a horse like his face does. That'd explain why Felicia can stand his ugliness.

Eventually, the path takes us to the fence at the end of the school property, right beside the river valley, down a dirt path mostly worn down by students over the years. It isn't paved or covered in gravel, which makes roots stick out everywhere. The bumps and ditches are whack with roots sticking up every which way, muddy patches, and steep dips, making us pay close attention to where we step as we descend deep into the ravine. We find our familiar spot, just off the beaten path. It's difficult to see due to the thick foliage and dense trees, making it a perfect crib for getting high.

CLOUD NINE

"Secluded enough?" Felicia asks.

"Well, we don't want to get caught," Marcus says as he pulls out his portable mini boombox from his backpack.

"This is the usual spot Marcus and I go to start trippin'," I say while taking the glass container and a lighter out of my backpack.

Felicia plays with her hair. "Boy, I feel special." She smiles. That deadly smile. It catches me, and I can't look away. The moment lasts forever. Her green eyes. Those lips.

FUCK YOUR WHORE MOUTH!!!

The lyrics blare from the mini boom box, metal music shooting me back to reality. I look away from the girl. Damn it, Marcus! Oh well, at least he put his Goat Lord CD on. I hadn't even realized how long I'd been staring at Felicia. Strangely enough, she was gazing back at me. She still is. Wicked. I have goosebumps. She's into me, I think. Oh, how I would love to make some kind of move on her.

Felicia leaves her trance and looks at the boom box. "What is this?" she asks. She seems a bit annoyed.

"Goat Lord," Marcus says with pride, sitting down beside us.

I take the joint out of the glass container with a rush of confidence. With a flick of the lighter, I bring the joint to my lips and take a puff, embracing that sweet taste of green. The pungent marijuana cloud fills my lungs and the air around us. I pass the joint to Felicia. She inhales the green and exhales slowly, letting the smoke ease its way out of her mouth.

"That's smooth," Felicia says, passing the joint to Marcus.

"The best," Marcus says while taking the joint.

We continue to pass the weed around, embracing the wonderfulness of the drug. Each puff we have increases the weed's effect on our systems. We laugh, joke, chat about school, complain how stupid our parents are, and so on until there is nothing left of the joint. At this point, all three of us are feeling pretty blitzed. Each of us gazes off into different directions, submerged in the blaring double kick drums, shredding guitars, and demonic growls of Goat Lord. Felicia begins to play with her hair while using a stick to draw in the dirt. Marcus is lying on his back, looking up at the leaves. His head rests on his hands. He has a funny smile on his face that doesn't go away. That's what makes weed so awesome—it always puts you in a good mood.

As for me, I'm trying not to stare at Felicia. Man, she is so hot.

My mind wanders from the girl and into bigger-picture stuff, like what is the purpose of school? Society forces the youth to work so hard at pointless subjects. They want us to learn things we don't care about. We barely even know ourselves, and we are trying to understand how particles move? What is x, anyway? It's ridiculous. The other part of my mind gets sucked back into the Felicia fantasy. She sits close to me. I'm not sure if it's the weed, or if she is leaning a little closer. It's a bit hard to tell while high.

"KISS HER," comes a whisper.

I look around, trying to see where the voice had come from. It had to be Marcus. The voice was raspy and male.

"DO IT NOW," the voice says.

The voice is coming from Marcus's direction, yet his lips aren't moving. Where is it coming from?

"KISS FELICIA," the voice says again. This time I can see that the sound is coming from the Goat Lord T-shirt Marcus wears. The animal's mouth moves as it speaks.

No way. This is the most intense trip I have ever had on weed. That goat is talking to me.

"KISS HER NOW, OR YOU WILL REGRET YOUR ACTIONS ALWAYS,"

the goat says. The illustration of the goat looks directly at me while talking. The mouth moves as if it were human.

I'm not a fool; I know that T-shirts can't talk, let alone give pretty good advice. Even though I know it is the drug talking, I like what the goat has to say. Just look at Felicia. Her red hair, green eyes, smooth legs, that ass . . . everything about her. The goat is a reflection of my deepest desires coming to the forefront, confronting me. All I want to do is take Felicia into my arms and start playing suck-face. It's all I ever wanted to do. From what I can tell, she is into me, too, despite being with horse-face.

I lean in slowly towards the girl and pause. A moment of clarity hits me: if I kiss Felicia, what would that mean? Felicia is seeing Don, and things seem to be going well with them. I'm already not in the football team's good books. How much more difficult could they make my life? At the core of my relationship with Felicia, I am her friend. I genuinely care about her. What if she isn't giving me hints, and I did kiss her? She would feel betrayed and creeped out, and Don would kick my ass. I should step off.

"DO IT NOW!" the commanding voice of the goat illustration booms. "DO IT NOW, BEFORE IT IS TOO LATE."

I freeze. This is a dilemma I never thought I would have to experience. On the one hand, the girl I want is right beside me—getting questionably close. On the other hand, I can't tell if this is all just the weed. After all, I'm getting advice from a talking goat drawing on a T-shirt.

"YOU MUST," the goat says.

"No!" I say.

My shout catches the attention of Felicia and Marcus. Hell, I startled myself too. The sudden sound throws us off, killing the good weed-vibe. Felicia scoots away from me while Marcus stands up, brushing the dirt and grass from the back of his shirt.

"What time is it?" Felicia asks.

"Probably getting close to the end of the period," Marcus says, pressing stop on the boom box.

I stare at Marcus's T-shirt, my eyes fixated on the static goat illustration. The eyes are as lifeless as they were before the weed. Its mouth doesn't move, and there are no voices. Damn it.

REGRET

I get up and scratch my neck, feeling nervous about the fact that I shouted out a word to my friends who have no context to the situation. I know I must look like a total weirdo.

"Smoke much, man?" Marcus says with a grin.

"Word. Shit, I had some whack thoughts," I say. "I'm wondering if that thing was laced with something else."

"Worked wonders for me," Felicia says.

"I doubt it's laced," Marcus says. "I think you just tripped some serious balls."

Felicia giggles. I blush, wanting to tell my friends about the ridiculous experience I just had with the auditory hallucination. The rational part of me says no. It is a stupid story, and it might weird Felicia out. Maybe I can tell Marcus later. For now, this stays with me. With that, the three of us exit the ravine and return up the path to the school property. We walk across the grass until we near the football field, where the team is just finishing up their training routine.

One football player notices us, and he steps away from the group, waving. Right away, I know it is Don, the goofy horse-face of a douche. Felicia waves at the boy. He jogs— Sorry, he trots towards us as Felicia hurries to him, leaving me with Marcus.

"There goes your girl," Marcus says.

"Dope," I say with zero enthusiasm. There really isn't much else to say. Felicia has the most popular guy in school for her boyfriend. I am just her stoner buddy, watching in disgust as she and Don embrace one another. Her arms wrap around his neck. His hands firmly grip her hips. The two of them make out disgustingly with tongue and all. I just can't look at it anymore.

"Man, she was such a flirt with you today, hey?" Marcus says.

I didn't need to hear that. I sigh, saying, "Let's get something to eat."

The goat had been right. In that doped-up state of existence, I'd heard words of wisdom from an unlikely source. Instead of listening to the strange goat's words, I froze. I wasn't bold. I took a coward's way out. With a clear head, I recall the scene in the ravine: Felicia's knees nearly touching mine; she played with her hair while leaning towards me, brushing it aside so I could see her pale, smooth neck. She was just too shy to make a move—just like me. The goat was the clarity, trying to guide me into something that could have been hella fly. The goat wisdom that I had not listened to. I should have never doubted the Goat Lord.

02

Lightness.

Fading.

Darkness. Cool air. The tingling of fine sand between your bare feet amplifies. The senses of the flesh—all are returning as you regain conscious thoughts. The stinging feeling in your eyes is now gone. Your head is groggy as you rub off the crusties from your eyelids. They're black. The liquid from the golden bowl. The path of the observer is gone. You're you once more, in the Midway.

"You're back," Malpherities says, hovering beside you.

"Yeah," you say, blinking a few times. You take a breath, realizing you're in control again. The passiveness of the observer has melted away. "It was like a dream," you say. "I could watch and feel, but I couldn't do anything."

"Yes, as is the role of the observer, watching the ego play out."

"What?"

Malpherities lowers to your level. "Do not overthink it. Tell me, Nameless One, what did you see? What did you *feel*?"

"I was some young kid, a teenager," you say. "A boy."

"Yes, you may have been a boy in your past life. Maybe not."

You pat your body. "What do you mean? I'm me."

"This body you have now isn't you, as you learned while flying through the colours before coming here. This body you have now is just an accumulation of what you're familiar with."

"I'm familiar with this body? It feels better than I have ever felt."

"Have you ever noticed how everyone sees themselves differently in the mirror? Or how your voice sounds different in your head compared to any form of recording?"

"Yeah," you say.

"Your mind and ego play an important role in how you perceive yourself. They manipulate and distort the real you. So this body you have now isn't accurate to the version you had while you were alive."

"Great. So I could be anyone?"

"Yes, which makes this a challenge. Judging by how disconnected you seem with this teenage boy, I'm going to guess you weren't him at the moment of death. Tell me, what else did you experience?" Malpherities asks.

You scratch your head, trying to recall all of the details. "It was maybe the mid-nineties. They talked about Y2K. I had a crush on a girl. It was all I could think about. Jealousy. Angst. Rebelliousness."

"Did these things feel familiar to you?" Malpherities asks.

"No, not really. I didn't die, either. Was I supposed to?"

"Not all experiences will be death-based. We want to find strong memories that will jolt your mind. The Midway lets me detect powerful emotions expressed by mortals while they're alive. Dying is a strong one, so it pierces through space-time, letting us ghouls sense it. Other emotions can do the same. Whatever you experienced while observing this teen's life was profound."

"I guess," you reply. "He just got high and was worried about getting a boner."

"Huh, well. . . Adolescents tend to make a big deal about nothing due to their immaturity."

"He was pretty focused on his queer jokes, too," you say.

"As teenage boys are. You said the nineties?"

"Yeah," you say.

"Interesting. Your comment there may have given us a clue." Malpherities strokes his jaw, looking at you like you're just a puzzle game.

"What do you mean?" you ask.

Malpherities soars up to the bowl again. "With that type of observation, you may come from a more progressive time."

The clue is small, but it gives you a slight feeling of hope. Malpherities is quick, and perhaps the two of you will be able to figure out what happened faster than you first anticipated. You walk up to the bowl and lean closer to it. "Are we going again?" you ask.

"Yes." Malpherities dips his claw into the black liquid, causing it to ripple. "Open your eye."

"Where are we going this time?" you ask, stepping back from the bowl.

Malpherities hovers above you. "Far from the previous time." He taps his claw, causing a droplet of black to fall onto your eyeball.

The cool liquid has a slight sting but it's nowhere near as intense as the first experience had been. You're building resilience. With a deep breath, you blink a couple of times. Each motion coats your eye with the liquid. The cave begins to fade once more, leaving you in whiteness.

Thoughts go.

Lightness.

HARVESTERS

DUTY

We're on the trawler vessel heading to the harvest world, just like any other job. I manage the equipment in the docking bay while we are en route. Two others in our unit are with me. We herd the cattle once they are harvested from the ground squad. I never thought much about the job. My father did this before me, and now this was my role in The Society. That's all there was to it. The Society keeps things structured and ensures humanity's survival by improving our wellbeing. So why mess with a good thing?

The trawler vessel rocks side to side as the ceiling lights flash—a sign we are entering the atmosphere. I hold onto the emergency handlebar with my right hand, awaiting the oncoming catch. My two comrades do as well. The adrenaline hits me every time. I know what is coming. The ground squad will bring the cattle here, and our role will begin. The cattle always act up. Our unit has to be extremely focused on coordinating the beasts in the cage for the safety of everyone on the ship.

The ship stabilizes its motion. My grip on the handle relaxes as we enter the planet's atmosphere. Six units armoured head to toe—the ground squad—march into the chrome oval shuttlecraft, holding their black pulse cannons. Glowing purple lights hum from the chambers. Safety mode is off, and their weapons are ready. The craft's door closes up as the last unit enters, letting it lift off the ground with a blue light projecting from the exhausts of its underbelly. The trawler vessel opens the docking door, giving us a view of the grey atmosphere of the planet.

A question enters my mind—what is the surface like? The ground squad knows. From what I learned in school, I know it is infested with disease, rubble, and pollution. No wildlife survives there, except for the cattle. But they seem to flourish, luckily for us. The cattle are vital to The Society. Their biological makeup is a crucial component of our scientific progression. Their genetics help us understand our past and improve our DNA. That's all I know, but it's enough to make me ponder useless thoughts.

The shuttlecraft roars as the bottom thrusters rotate, letting the craft zoom out of the trawler vessel and into the cloudy grey atmosphere, where it disappears. The harvest has begun. One time, I did get a view of the planet beneath that foggy sky. It's blue and brown. I saw it from the cockpit, although only for a few moments. I had to return to my station shortly after as we were entering orbit. It's probably for the better. I need to keep focused on my job if I want to live up to my family's name.

ANTICIPATION

Now, I wait for the ground squad to return. My left hand clutches the black electro-spear, waiting to shock any cattle that act out in the cages. It makes my heart race thinking about potential action. They have hands; they can operate basic tools. Even though my curiosity about the planet torments the back of my mind, I know I don't want to be in the ground squad, gathering the beasts. They're dangerous if not harvested carefully. I've seen the footage in school. The paintings. The portrayals in the media. Filth riddles their hair, and their nature is violent. As much as I'd like to be a part of the ground squad and partake in harvesting some of the cattle, I can accept my duty in The Society.

The ground squad doesn't take long to come back to the trawler vessel. The docking station had remained open for the duration of their absence. Soon, the intercom erupts, with the pilot's distorted voice coming through the speakers, saying, "Ground squad arrival. Shepherds, initiate."

The lights above turn blue. The other two shepherds march forward. I follow after them as the shuttlecraft comes into view. The craft carefully lands back inside the trawler vessel as the docking door moves upward to close.

"Positions," the shepherd to my left—our squad leader—says through our helmets.

SHEPHERDS

I grip my spear with both hands as the shuttle lands. The engines underneath the craft turn off, leaving us in a moment of silence. The back of the ship hisses and the hatch continues to close. Three ground squad members are on each side of the interior, with a large steel crate in the center. It levitates off the ground. Small holes wrap around the middle of the cage, underneath the semi-translucent forcefield surrounding the container. The ground squad marches forward, and the cell hovers ahead with the unit. Groaning echoes come from inside the cage. Snarls and roars. They are in there. Angry. Hateful.

A dark silhouette appears from behind the last ground squad member. The motion is too fast for me to see clearly. The black blob is crouching. It moves closer, yet there isn't a seventh squad member. That is cattle.

"Free run!" I shout, rushing forward.

"Free run!" the other shepherds say, joining me in the pursuit.

The ground squad spins around, raising their pulse cannons, the purple orbs glowing brighter. The three on the opposite side hurry around the cage to face the threat. The others fire pulses from their weapons, missing the silhouette by a fraction. The plasma blasts soar past the being, highlighting a humanoid creature standing upright, wearing pants. Muscular arms end in five-fingered hands that hold a crude metal pistol, firing the weapon at the closest ground squad unit. The scene lights up as a bullet rips through the gun's chamber and into the chest of a ground unit. It bounces off the armour, leaving no indent.

Time slows down as I run. My body's motion is in autopilot, while mind is left in disarray as I glimpse the scowling face of the cattle in full light. The beige dirt-covered skin. Two eyes. Blue irises. Long black hair. It's human.

The cattle fires again, missing the ground squad in front of him. They fire back. One of the pulse cannons' plasma blasts hits him in the chest, throwing him back and knocking the gun from his hand. The two shepherds and I arrive directly in front of the cattle. Our squad leader lunges his electro-spear into the being's chest, causing his entire system to jolt and fall lifelessly.

I stare down at the cattle. No. It can't be. I am looking down at a fellow human. The physique is less toned, and it is slightly smaller. That aside, it is undoubtfully human—an unmodified version.

03

What? you think. That's your thought. You're separating from the observer once more, returning to your new body in the Midway. You take a few steps back as your vision returns. Your heart is racing while you catch your breath. The tenseness of the situation dissipates, and your muscles roar to life, sending your arms flailing wildly.

"What was that?" you ask, gaining full control of yourself once more. Your breath is fast as you try to comprehend the strange world you observed.

"What was what?" Malpherities asks.

"Space ships, plasma guns, I don't know. People were being treated like cattle. They killed them."

"Not everything you see is going to be light and fun," Malpherities says. "You're going to see horrors that will rattle you to the very core."

"I . . . that's too much." You rub your head, thinking back to what you saw—those poor people.

"Anything else?" Malpherities asks.

"No, I can't think of anything. It was so alien."

Malpherities dips his claw into the bowl again. "So we went too far into the future. Let's dial it back."

"Can we take a break?" you ask.

Malpherities blinks, seeming startled by your words. "For what?"

"It was so intense. I don't know."

"Exactly. Accept the fact that what you are seeing is happening, has happened, and is going to happen. A chaotic mess of the now."

"More space-time stuff?"

"Precisely," Malpherities says, hovering above you. "Open wide." He smiles a toothy grin.

You sigh and look up to the droplet as Malpherities taps his claw, giving you no chance to collect your thoughts. What you saw was just another's life. You were the observer, seeing some unknown distant future. Where will the ghoul send you now? You wonder if knowing your past is even worth witnessing these horrific events. It's too late to think about it. The liquid falls. Your eye stings, and down the rabbit hole you go again.

INSPIRER

A beeping noise erupts from the smooth chrome smartwatch that wraps around the man's wrist underneath the cuff of his white dress shirt. Its flashing LED screen and the desk lamp highlight the man's aging, worn face in the dark office. The watch's noise is indicating that it is now 10 p.m. That's the second alarm for the meds. Usually, the sound would be of high importance to the man, but today is different. It's Friday, and he would normally have been home at this hour. Instead, here he is, at the office. Friday is a day celebrated amongst the working class. After hauling ass for eight hours, five times a week, Friday paves the way to the glorious weekend where you can finally spend time doing what you enjoy and seeing the people you love—presuming you have such people. That's an important note.

"Douglas, how could you not see this coming?" A man's raspy, smoker's voice pierces through the silence from the other end of the large office. The window blinds are open, giving a high view of the other downtown skyscrapers, and he sits cross-legged on the leather chair, the moonlight reflecting against his polished black shoes.

The man named Douglas taps his smartwatch to stop it from beeping and leans against his wooden desk, looking over his shoulder toward the metropolis night.

The second man is too difficult to see in the dim room. "You knew that Allen Oil Site Solutions was downsizing. I am unsure why you worked so hard, considering the direction of the economy, too. You thought you could somehow *prove* your worth?"

Douglas grits his teeth, knowing exactly what the man is referring to. He swallows the thick saliva building in his mouth from the tension, recalling the sharp plummet of Alberta's economy. Many people lost their jobs and became homeless, and families are starving. Douglas had believed that if he put in the extra time at work, he'd be irreplaceable.

"You've spent your whole life *religiously* working, and working. Dedicating yourself to the plans you've made for the future. So focused on the endgame."

Douglas clenches his fists and snaps, "What's your point?"

The second man's voice softens. "It's not fair."

Douglas looks down at the table where a third of a bottle of Scotch remains beside some sticky notes, prescription bottles, and his laptop. Well, technically, now it's the company's computer. He exhales heavily while shaking his head. "How could I have let this happen?"

"You gave it your all, Douglas. But hey, on the bright side, they liked you enough to let you clean out your stuff. Imagine how embarrassing it would have been being escorted out by security?"

Douglas's head pulsates with frustration as he tries to piece together how he managed to get himself fired. "If I had worked just a little more each day, maybe I could have proven to them I was worth keeping."

"I admire you, Douglas. It is why we have had such a good relationship. From an early age, you were always determined, good grades, worked hard, and got what you wanted—nothing stood in your way. Men desire that kind of ability."

Douglas presses his lips together, eyeing the stack of documents and proposals he had yet to get to. "But was it worth it? My job . . . Ashley and the kids." His voice trembles when mentioning his family. After focusing his life on work, this is what he got.

"I've been your friend for as long as I can remember, and I hate to see you go through this."

"I-I-I don't understand what I could have done differently." He wipes his face and extends his hand to the stack of papers. "What were they thinking, firing me? These will never get looked at."

Douglas determines he needs to wash away his emotions. They're no use now. He snatches the bottle of Scotch, tilting it back and consuming a large gulp of the strong liquor. The liquid burns from his mouth and down to his stomach. "I gave Ashley everything she ever wanted."

"You sure did, bud."

Douglas slams the bottle down, turning to look up at the stars. His left hand holds the cross pendant on his neck. "Why would God do this?" he mumbles.

"God? I ask the same question, Douglas. It has to make you wonder, does it not?"

Douglas presses his eyes shut, squeezing the cross pendant. "I've been a supportive, loyal husband to Ashley."

"Yes, but she's not the same as you. Her eyes wander. Hell, even to me. You know it."

Douglas says nothing.

"Don't worry, I never fucked her. Women are complicated creatures. Their mystery is what makes them so desirable, if you ask me. However, one thing is obvious: Work isn't sexy, Douglas. And Allen Oil Site Solutions? Your wife is basically sandpaper down there."

Douglas clutches the pendant harder, feeling the metal edges press into his skin as he shakes his hand.

"I swear, I never did," the man says.

Douglas brushes the disgusting thought of them plowing aside and says, "I've brought in more revenue in one year than this company has seen in two."

"Agreed. If anything, you should be praised as a hero. Look at how they repay their heroes—take the profits and boot your ass to the curb. You're a good man; companies take advantage of good men. Especially this place. Allen Oil Site Solutions eats people up."

Douglas looks down at his right hand, a tan line revealing where his wedding ring once was. He stares at the strip of pale skin, recalling how Ashley would yell at him for months for working too late. The yelling turned into silent aggression and, eventually, a handwritten letter outlining that she was filing for a divorce. She took his boys. Douglas's lips begin to tremor, nostrils flaring. Energy seeps through his core, containing sorrow and rage. The blood pumps to his head, making his face pink. It looks like the booze is kicking in. He tries to stay calm, with little luck.

The man speaks. "You were more than willing to spend your time making money to improve your family's way of life. Maybe even have the peace of mind that you became the son your father wanted."

Douglas's father flashes before his eyes, recalling what the man had said to him on his deathbed.

"You never learn." The memory is as real to Douglas as standing in the office. The words strike his heart heavy—a beat skips. For years, Douglas tried to make his father proud, but it never seemed to be enough. His father passed away shortly after his wife, Douglas's mother, left him.

"Your father went through the same hurdles as you—"

Douglas cut in. "Which is why he said what he did. You don't need to remind me."

The man shrugs. "History repeats itself. It must have broken your father's heart to see you take the same steps as him."

"I thought it was what he wanted. I thought it was what my family needed. I thought it was what *I* wanted."

"You can keep skulking around asking yourself if it was what you wanted or not. Nothing is going to change anything. The truth is, you got yourself here. Fired and on the way to a divorce."

Douglas turns to look at the man. "I didn't know . . . I didn't think it—"

"You didn't put any thought into anything at all, dimwit!" The man's voice booms as he stands. "You just made a bunch of assumptions about what you and everyone else wanted."

Douglas shakes his head, looking to the ground. The weight of shame makes his limbs weak and his shoulders shrivel. The other man takes several steps closer to the light, exposing his white suit, pale lean jaw, and frowning mouth.

He speaks. "You were so blind-sighted with assuming you were making the right decisions that you never stopped to ask yourself if you were."

The words sink Douglas's chest. His heart pounds heavily, begging to escape. The comments are thoughts that have long resided in the back of his mind, and yet Douglas never actually put them together into a complete idea. Now, hearing them spoken to him, he can't grasp how he never realized it before.

"With your career down the tube, honestly, Douglas, what do you have left?"

Douglas turns around and rests his head against the glass window. His eyes close as a single tear runs down his cheek. "Nothing. I can try and start over." He opens his eyes, seeing a faint reflection of his now wrinkling face and the several dozen grey hairs sprouting from his balding head. It has to be the lighting.

"You're old, Douglas."

"I am forty-seven. I can start anew."

The man laughs. "Look at yourself! You're speaking more lies to reassure yourself that your first impulsive thought is the right course of action. That attitude is what brought you here. You can't start again. The stress you endured from this job has aged you far more than you think."

Douglas's work had always been his passion—he relished in spending repetitive weeknights wrapping up the last email of the day, weekends dedicated to side projects to get a raise, downing four to six cups of coffee a day, and eating endless amounts of takeout food. Oh, he was so blind to the drive he had that he was oblivious to what it was doing to his wellbeing.

"Don't even get me started on what your dating life is going to be like now. Fuck. Look at your lard-ass." The man sighs. The grim silence is strengthening his words. "You blew it, Douglas. You really did. As I said, I have always admired you, but the irony is that, through all your success, you managed to be unsuccessful in your happiness."

Douglas hears the man take a couple more steps. He dares not look back. What would be the point? He is an ashamed dog. Each word the man speaks unravels more truths that Douglas has spent the years trying to cover up by working harder and keeping his eyes on the prize—pay off his home, a retirement plan, and funds for his sons' college.

The man slaps his hands together. "So, what's the plan? What could you possibly do to revive yourself? You're looking at divorce papers, legal fees, maybe seeing your kids once a week. Losing the house, debt, probably half of your shit, too."

"What can I do?"

"That's what I am asking you, Douglas. You said you wanted to start over."

"There's nothing left," Douglas says softly.

"Nothing but decades of headaches, if not the rest of your life," the man says.

Douglas raises his head, forehead smearing against the glass. He looks at the man in the reflection, seeking guidance. The man shrugs.

"I know if I had caught myself in this predicament that you're in, I'd ask myself . . . What are my options?"

Douglas bites his lip, trying to think of what he has. His hands are sweaty, but his body is cold. What cards can he draw to pull himself out of this downward spiral? The more he thinks, the more he realizes his hands are tied. He has no savings. The chances of him getting a job are slim with the way Alberta's economy is.

"I messed up . . . I know that now. I had an amazing life, and I pushed it aside to work more, thinking I could get the life I wanted." Douglas sniffles, stopping some mucus from escaping his nostril. "You're right—that is irony. I did have the life I wanted . . . What would you do?"

The man sways his head side to side. "I've always believed that drastic situations call for drastic actions."

Douglas nods, waiting for more words of wisdom.

"You and I are not so different. We're both men of action, which is the one thing that gives results. Talk is cheap."

Douglas turns towards the man, eying his extended hand, which points towards the bottle of Scotch beside the prescription bottle. Douglas jumps—his smartwatch is beeping again, another reminder to take those damn pills. He silences it and rubs his hand across his eyes, feeling them burn from the lack of hydration. He sure will feel a hangover tomorrow. "I've drunk enough. It's not going to solve anything for me."

"The bottle is a tool for a more . . . permanent solution, my friend," the man says, nodding towards the window.

Douglas's eyes widen, realizing what the man is saying. *Could I?* he thinks. Based on the conversation, his future seems rather bleak. Is his life worth going through all the effort? It could so easily come to an end, right here, right now.

"Just to keep your head above water is far more of a struggle than what *I* would want. There's comfort in an eternity of silence."

Can Douglas go through with this? He's unsure and clenches his teeth. The years of headaches could end so quickly. *I could stop it all . . .* he thinks.

The man speaks. "Look at it this way—do you honestly think anyone would miss you? Your dad is dead, and the extended family is halfway across the country. When was the last time you heard from them, anyway?"

Douglas's family is torn, an obvious fact that they didn't need to discuss. Douglas grabs hold of his cross pendant again. This is crazy. "I can't end it all. Psalm 34:17 clearly says when the righteous cry for help, the Lord hea—"

"Don't give me that bullshit! Come on, if God honestly existed, do you think you would find yourself in this situation? You've been rehearsing his commandments for as long as I've known you, and yet here you are."

"God works in mysterious ways."

The man laughs. "That's a copout if I ever heard one."

Douglas has no ammunition. The man is right. All the worship has led him into a corner with no way out. Trying to convince himself more than anything at the moment, he asks himself, *How can God turn his back on me like this?* Now he is alone. *No one is here for me,* he thinks.

"You have no one on your side, Douglas. Your beliefs, your family, your work, and your whole life has all been chucked aside in one giant swoop."

Douglas scowls, snapping the necklace holding the cross. "Everyone has fucked me over," he mutters.

"They truly have, except for me. I've always been a voice of reason, and it doesn't come easy for me to give such honesty. I care about your wellbeing, and you rarely trust me or even return my calls. Now, who is with you in your darkest hour?"

"I'd be starting from nothing, and for what?" Douglas says, clutching his hair. He paces back and forth behind the desk, tugging on the sparse grey strands so tightly his eyes water. What the hell is he doing? His heart races. The headache pounds relentlessly. "Can I go through with this?"

"The better question, Douglas, is why do you keep trying to hold on to this joke of a life? You have nothing, and you have no one!" the man says.

Douglas releases his hair and hugs his arms, adding up all the challenges that are ahead of him. "It's just a void."

"Maybe stop trying to live a life based on your impulsive choices and make a rational move for once by doing yourself a favour." He points at the bottle with a stern finger.

"This is insane!"

"Insane? Wasting your life the way you did with repetitive action was insane! You could have had a life worthwhile, but it's too late for that now."

I threw everything I ever wanted away. I'm a fuck-up. Powerful energy surges through Douglas's whole body—energy accumulated from the years of buried stress, frustration, and lack of fulfillment.

These suppressed emotions force their way to the surface of his consciousness, expressing through his shaking body. "I've wasted my life for people who don't care."

"Exactly, fuck them! Do something for you this time."

"Fuck them!" Douglas shouts.

"Do it for you, Douglas!"

Douglas lets out a howl at the top of his lungs, face burning red, grabbing the liquor on his desk. He knocks over the container of pills chucking the bottle from his hand. It spins a couple of times before the thick bottom collides into the glass window, shattering it on impact. Gusts of cold wind funnel into the room, blowing documents from the desk and into the air. No more thoughts. No more reasoning. No more projects, work, disappointed father and family. This is for Douglas. He dashes towards the window, still shouting in a blind rage. With no hesitation, he leaps from the window. His stomach lifts upward as he leaves the ground, seeing that the next surface is now hundreds of feet below him.

As Douglas falls, his smartwatch beeps again. He forgot to take his pills. The cool air and gravity blast him with sobriety—he didn't take his pills. The damn pills. His mind had worked against him. Douglas knows he fucked up this time. He glances back up to the window where the man stands laughing hysterically. The night sky casts enough light, revealing Douglas's balding face on the man's body. The reflection of himself. His mind lost the mental battle. The man vanishes like smoke. Those damn pills.

Through the gushing winds, Douglas hears the man's voice loud and clear as if he were beside him. "I look forward to your permanent stay, Douglas. I've waited for this day for a long time."

Douglas's stomach sinks deeper than the pressure of his accelerating body. Was it those damn pills?

His mind works frantically. What is life after death? Did he just jump off a building because he forgot his pills? Is that man a figment of his broken mind, or something supernatural? He decides to try and reason with anyone listening. Maybe this can all be reversed. He shouts, "No.

I didn't mean to. I'm sorry! I'm sorry! God, plea—"

Too late.

04

"Help!" you shout, reaching up to the sky. The closeness of death was so real. Your heart is pumping, sweat drizzling along your skin, breath fast. Vision and control return and you find yourself staring at the beading stalactites above, gently dripping black liquid into the bowl.

Malpherities raises his brow, watching you return to a relaxed state. "I presume that wasn't a pleasant viewing?" he asks.

"No, it was horrible. The man killed himself. The other man wasn't . . . a real man."

"Was the first man you?" the ghoul asks.

"No, I don't believe so," you say. Come to think of it, you're not even sure *what* you were, but are too flustered from falling off a skyscraper to think about it any further. You close your eyes and take a deep breath. You're okay. You're only an observer.

"We'll see if we can mix it up." Malpherities dips his claw into the bowl. "Shall we go again?"

"Let's," you say, mentally preparing yourself. As you've learned, anything can happen as an observer, and you feel everything. If you genuinely want to know who you are, you're going to have to be brave and fearless. Possibly the most daring you've ever been. With your lack of memory, you don't know if you were ever courageous, or perhaps you were the most. Either way, it's time to keep searching through observations. Keep yourself still, wait, and watch through the eyes of the flesh.

LISTEN TO ME

BUSINESS AS USUAL

Clicking keyboards, ringing phones, and working machinery filled the room with noise. Stacks of paper and large commercial printers were housed in the backroom behind the lobby. Beeping from the front door came every quarter of an hour or so as customers entered and left the shop. The busy season, summer, had begun. Every individual was looking to get their posters made, wedding invitations prepared, or some other side project done. The giant corporate cheeses were looking for trade show displays, brochures, and booklets. It was a lot for everyone to keep up with at the shop. It also didn't help that they were understaffed, and their boss didn't want to hire anyone.

A lady let out a sigh while staring at the computer screen. There was a graphics software open with a business card photo and some basic shapes overtop of it.

"Still tracing that logo?" called a man from the other end of the room. His puffy, frizzy black hair bounced as he turned to face the lady.

She put on a closed smile. She knew the man, Ceagan. He liked to start small talk, something she was not too fond of. She just wanted to get the job done and go home. The man sipped on his coffee, creating elongated slurping noises. Then there was silence. She didn't want to do this mundane tracing task, but seeing that business card holder with cards neatly angled upward was flattering. It made her look like some sort of professional. At the same time, the card design itself was hideous, making her feel incompetent at her profession.

I would love to fix up that typeface—that colouring, awful. The logo needs work, too, she thought, eyeing the Mega Speed Print logo just above her full name: *Haideh Harkovitch.* Her title, *Graphic Designer,* was just below her name. Perhaps one day, she could convince the boss that their whole visual communication needed improvement. Then, she could have a decent portfolio piece and get out of this dead-end print job. Haideh could apply to a design studio and take on some actual challenging projects. Until then, she knew she'd be stuck tracing other designers' work. Like today. And tracing it from a photo of a business card, no less. A monkey's job.

REAL-WORLD STUFF

High heels clicked as a shorter, middle-aged woman came into the office from the front lobby. It was Candice, owner of Mega Speed Print. She looked up at the mounted TV in the far corner of the room. "You getting a look at this?" came her croaky voice.

"What do you mean, on the telly?" asked Ceagan, adjusting his thick-framed glasses.

"That's what I am saying," Candice said. "It's completely bonkers, look!"

The TV showcased the news, where a reporter and a cameraman riding on a helicopter overlooked the streets below. Crashed cars and civilians lay on the ground, and debris covered the pavement. The people that could move were running in all directions. Closed captions typed out as the reporter talked on the muted TV, saying:

"THERE ARE HUNDREDS OF PEOPLE MOVING IN A PANIC HERE IN

DOWNTOWN LONDON . . ."

"My God," Haideh said, wide-eyed. "It's like it is out of a movie or something."

"What is happening?" Ceagan asked.

Candice pointed at the TV. "That!"

Several people walked calmly down the road as civilians hurried away from them, like fish trying to escape a whale. There were a man and two women. All were wearing ordinary clothes: jeans, T-shirts, blouses—nothing obscure. The three each had one hand extended outwards, palms facing the crowd; blood ran from their fingertips, drizzling down their skin and onto the pavement. They had blank stares on their faces, eyes completely white.

"Where are their pupils?" Ceagan asked.

"WE CONTINUE TO FOLLOW THE THREE FIGURES THAT WERE REPORTED MERELY MINUTES AGO. THEY SEEM TO BE FOLLOWING THE CROWDS, CAUSING DISORDER FROM THEIR PRESENCE . . ."

"What are they? Terrorists?" Ceagan asked.

"I don't think so," Candice said. "They just seem to be walking down the street."

WHISPERS

A man on the TV dashed out from behind a wrecked car, holding the hand of a lady, trying to get by the three blood-fingered people who were slowly approaching. As a single unit, the three stopped walking and moved their hands, palms upward, towards the man and woman. Their target stopped dead in his tracks, and his hands began to shake, then his head. The lady tugged on the man's arm, trying to get him to move with her. She shook her head, crying and pulling on him with all her might. The man didn't budge, like he was glued to the ground.

"What is wrong with him?" Haideh asked, watching in disbelief. *This isn't like anything I've ever seen,* she thought. She blinked twice, checking if she was still in control of the situation. She'd had pretty realistic dreams in the past and wanted to be sure she was awake. Yes, she was.

"THE POLICE ARE ATTEMPTING TO CONTROL THE SITUATION . . . WAIT, WE'RE NOW WITNESSING WHAT THESE THREE ARE CAPABLE OF."

The cameraman adjusted the lens, zooming in on the five people. The closer view revealed the blood from the fingers seeping endlessly out from the cuticles of the three beings. It was an unnatural amount of blood. Their lips were moving, yet it wasn't clear what they were saying from the helicopter's height. As they talked, the targeted man began to shout erratically, looking up in the sky, arms coiling into fists. Red liquid oozed from his clenched hands, drizzling onto the road. The lady gently grabbed his arm, face drenched in tears. He relaxed his hands, shoulders lowering. His face released all tension while glaring at her with wide eyes, gently touching her face. She smiled at him and held his hand.

The three blood-fingered figures each took a step closer to the man and woman, reaching their hands out as far as they could. The motion caused the man's eyes to twitch. He clutched the lady's face with force, and she screamed. She tried to pull away with no luck. With his free hand, the man forged a fist. Letting out a roar, he slammed it into her face.

"Christ," Haideh said, looking away from the TV. She couldn't dare witness the intense violence. She never did handle it well and preferred to watch some reality TV for a few chuckles, or spend the night at the pub, maybe get lucky with a man. To her, violence was just disgusting—especially real violence like this.

"He won't stop hitting her!" Ceagan exclaimed. "Does the prime minister have anything to say about this?"

"I'm not sure. I haven't looked," Candice said. "I saw this and came here to ask if you two had seen anything about it."

Haideh looked up at the TV again, watching as the man continued to assault the lady, her face now unrecognizable.

"IT IS UNEXPLAINABLE, MAT. WE ARE SIMPLY REPORTING INFORMATION AS IT COMES IN. THE POLICE ARE BELIEVED TO BE ON THEIR WAY . . ."

REMORSE FOR THE UNKNOWN

The blood-fingered three directed their hands away from the man. Their lips stopped moving, and they returned to their calm walking.

"OUR RESPECTS GO OUT TO THIS TRAGIC LADY'S FAMILY," the reporter said.

"Now, why'd he go and do that for? Running out in front of those three?" Ceagan asked.

"They didn't even touch him," Haideh said. "He went completely looney. Are they using some nanotechnology?"

Ceagan snorted. "Nanotechnology? Lay off the TV, Haideh. It could be some sound-based hypnosis."

"Why are their hands bleeding?" Haideh asked. "Can we switch the channel, at least? This is making me uncomfortable."

"Sure," Candice said with a sigh. "The remote is around here somewhere. With all this commotion, business is sure to slow down."

"That don't matter much, I think. Look at what is going on!" Ceagan said.

"We rely on the busy season, Ceagan. As you should know, that keeps you employed. You should be worried."

"I'm sure I will be tomorrow. Today, I want to know what the hell is going on here." He took a sip of his coffee and said, "Can we change the channel to see if there are any other reports on this?"

"Look for the remote!" Candice said.

"Candice!" came a young man's voice from the front desk.

"Yes, Mark?" Candice replied with a groan. Haideh knew that Candice was testy with questions. Mark was the new guy, and he didn't know Candice's wrath yet. He was brave in his naivety.

"This invoicing software is being funny. Can you come take a look?" Mark asked.

"On my way," Candice said. "You two keep working—don't let that rubbish on the telly distract you," she said before leaving the room.

Another beep came from the front entrance—the front door was pulled open. More customers. Perhaps Candice was wrong about the day quieting down.

AN EPIDEMIC

Ceagan watched as Candice left the room, waiting until she was gone. Then he spun his chair around to face Haideh, saying, "Funny, ain't it?"

"What?" Haideh asked.

"The boss can come by and chit-chat with us, but when she's gone, it's back to work. This is some history-in-the-making stuff the news is reporting!" He stared at the TV, watching the chaos.

Haideh looked up for a moment to see that the cameraman had shifted the view to the news reporter. She gripped the microphone tightly.

"WE'RE GETTING INSIGHT THAT THIS IS NOT THE FIRST CASE. THERE ARE MULTIPLE REPORTS ACROSS THE COUNTRY JUST LIKE THE THREE WE ARE WITNESSING BELOW . . ."

"Across the country? Are we under attack?" Ceagan asked, now fiddling with a pencil against his lip.

"We should get back to work," Haideh said, spinning her chair around to look at the graphics software again.

A scream erupted from the front entrance. The sound of fumbling and crashing followed. Grunts. Another crash, and a prolonged gurgle. Haideh stood up, mouth open, looking at the doorway. It was impossible to see anything other than the walls and the entrance door.

"Candice?" Ceagan called out while getting up from his chair. He looked over at Haideh as he walked towards the front entrance. "Stay

here," he whispered.

Ceagan crept up to the wall, getting closer to the entrance as more fumbling came from the front lobby. He took another step, glancing back at Haideh, then at the entrance.

"Help!" came a worker's shout from the backroom where the printers were. "Somebody, please help! Mark . . . wait . . . what? Mar—!"

A thumping sound came from beyond the office, silencing the worker. Another beep from the front door came. The door was pulled open.

Ceagan swallowed heavily before leaning forward, peeking around the corner, then bringing his head back.

"What do you see?' Haideh asked.

"Nothing. No one is there," Ceagan said.

Haideh hurried over to Ceagan and whispered, "Who was calling for help? Dan?"

A scream came from the other room.

"Maybe?" Ceagan whispered. "Or Daniel. It's hard to tell."

"Think this has anything to do with what we heard on the telly?" Haideh asked. She knew it was a stupid question. From what they'd heard, it was. She just wanted reassurance from someone.

"I'm going to guess so. Come, let's call the police," Ceagan said while getting up.

He quietly walked over to Haideh's desk—the closest to the entrance—and picked up the phone. He punched in the numbers and brought the receiver to his ear. Haideh crept over to Ceagan, keeping her eyes on the entrance, just in case someone was to come into the room. She couldn't help but wonder what had happened out there.

"The line is busy," Ceagan said coldly.

"What do you mean?" Haideh asked.

"I can't get ahold of them. There's nothing there," Ceagan said. "We're on our own."

Haideh felt her heart race. Who had yelled from the back room? Who else was in the print shop? There were no answers, and no rescue from the police in sight. Ceagan and Haideh would have to fend for themselves.

BACKUP

The two stared at one another for several moments while the sounds of screams came from the back of the print shop. If anything about the television report was right, then only two rooms away, someone's life was being taken from them. Their co-workers, people they saw every day, were now fighting for their lives, and Ceagan and Haideh just stood in their office, listening.

Haideh wanted to run and get as far away from this chaos as she could. She also knew that there was nowhere to go. The TV showed that the streets of London were far worse than the print shop, and the police weren't picking up the phone.

"I want to try my mum," Haideh said, snagging the phone from Ceagan's hand.

Ceagan scratched his neck and looked towards the entrance of the office room. "We might want to focus on what is right in front of us."

Haideh ignored his comment, punched in the numbers of her mum's home line, and waited. The phone rang for several moments before a crackly old voice picked up, saying, "Hello, you have reached the residence of Lacey Harkovitch . . ."

"Voicemail," Haideh muttered while pressing on the hook to dial a new number. She had friends, ex-boyfriends, and family. She wasn't alone in this situation and wasn't going to give up just yet.

"Haideh," Ceagan said.

Haideh snagged her smartphone, thinking perhaps the print shop's line was the issue and tapped her cousin's number. She listened to the phone's ringing again.

"Haideh," Ceagan said once more.

Haideh raised her index finger, hoping it would silence Ceagan so she could try and get anyone on the line. She didn't want to listen to whatever Ceagan had to say. He liked to ramble. The phone continued to ring with no answer.

"No one is picking up!" Haideh said. "I'll try Reeves." The word ended in a groan. The thought of her recent ex made her sick. But at this point, she was willing to try anyone. She needed to hear a familiar voice.

"Haideh!" Ceagan said sternly as he placed his hand over her phone. The abrupt action from Ceagan caught her attention. He never acted out so intensely. This was serious. He pointed to the other room. "I think whatever we saw on the telly is happening right now in the print shop. We'd best jet from here for our safety."

"I know," Haideh said.

"Then why are you still trying to dial numbers?" Ceagan asked.

"I want to know if my loved ones are safe, I think."

"So, you tried Reeves?" Ceagan asked, raising his eyebrow.

Haideh let out a sigh and looked to the ground. "All right, all right. I am scared! What the hell is going on, Ceagan?"

Ceagan pushed his thick-framed glasses up with his finger. "I don't know, but we probably shouldn't stick around here much longer. Whoever is in the back room is still here." He glanced around the office, looking at the different desks. His eyes locked onto a hole puncher and he rushed over to the desk, snagging it. "We need weapons," he said, shaking the hole puncher, causing paper fragments to fall out of the bottom.

"That's not much of a weapon, Ceagan," Haideh said.

"Better than anything we have right now," Ceagan said. "Come stay behind me. There are two of us and one of them. I think."

THE GREAT ESCAPE

Ceagan was the brave one, creeping towards the office entrance. This was real—Ceagan was going to investigate, and Haideh had to follow. She wanted to hide under her desk and hope for the whole damn thing to blow over. At the same time, she couldn't just leave Ceagan to fend for himself. Whoever was out there had taken out at least two people on their own. Who knew what type of madness was out there? Ceagan needed her to back him up.

Haideh took a deep breath, thinking, *You got this.* She mustered up the courage and grabbed her purse from her desk—couldn't leave that behind. She took a step forward, feeling every thread of her clothing's fabric move against her skin. The adrenaline buzzed through her, amplifying all her senses, and she even picked up on Ceagan's musty smell.

The two reached the entrance. Ceagan took a step forward, exposing himself to the other room. He continued to move, keeping the hole puncher held high, ready to strike. Haideh entered the lobby, looking around to see that the space was empty. No customers were in view. The chairs were left as they always were. The entrance and the back room were eerily quiet. Usually, phones were ringing, clients were talking, and the loud machinery of the printers was going on throughout the day. Now, there was only silence.

Haideh took another step into the new space and spotted a pool of blood oozing from behind the front desk, where an older lady's hand lay limp on the ground. That had to be Candice. The front desk monitor was missing. The keyboard, mouse, and various papers scattered the surface area. There had been a struggle here.

Haideh lightly tapped Ceagan's shoulder. He jerked. "Look," she whispered, pointing at the hand.

The two reached the counter, leaning over to see that their boss was on the ground with glass shards in her skull. Blood oozed down her face beside a broken monitor. Her neck was red and blue, and some of her clothes were torn.

"Is she alive?" Haideh asked.

Ceagan looked at Haideh with a cold stare, saying nothing. His silence was enough for her to know what he was implying. Candice, their boss, was indeed dead.

"Should we check the back room?" Haideh asked.

"Yeah, let's see if anyone else is alive," Ceagan said.

"Do you think? There was Candice, you, me, Mark, Daniel, and Dan."

"Don't forget about Richard."

"Was Richard working today?"

"I believe so."

"Okay, okay." Haideh looked at the front entrance. "Okay," Haideh said while unbuckling her purse. She searched through it and pulled out her keys, feeling them jingle in her hands. "I can drive around back?" Haideh said.

"What for?"

"So we can approach it from the other end?"

"Maybe the killer is out there," Ceagan said.

"I'd prefer if we didn't run into them," Haideh said.

"We have to if we want to save who's left."

"What is our plan here?" Haideh snapped. "Honestly, I want to get my car and get the hell out of here."

"I say we go check on the others. Besides, I parked in the back," Ceagan said.

"What?" Haideh exclaimed.

"Hush!" Ceagan said.

"Why would you park in the back?" Haideh asked.

"Because Candice was getting upset that the staff were taking up all of the front parking and leaving none for the customers. I was just trying to keep the boss happy!"

A crash came from the back room. Ceagan held the hole puncher up high, glaring towards the entrance behind the front desk. From the doorway, the printers and shelves stacked with empty paper stocks were visible. Everything else in the back was a concerning mystery.

COMPANY

"Someone is still back there," Ceagan said. "Come on, let's go check it out."

"Ceagan, no, please. Can we just get to my car?" Haideh begged.

Ceagan shook his head and took a step forward and then another. Haideh glanced back and forth between the front entrance and her co-worker, who walked around the front desk, approaching the back room. She couldn't leave him behind.

"Damn you, Ceagan," Haideh whispered under her breath, hurrying to catch up to him.

Ceagan carefully crept around the front desk and Candice's body as Haideh caught up. He gave her one nod of confirmation and stepped into the back room. The printers were still on. They weren't processing any of their jobs. The workers in the back were nowhere to be found.

"Let's check behind the next shelf," Ceagan said while walking towards the next aisle separated by shelves of paper stock and completed print jobs.

A bludgeoning sound picked up as they approached the new aisle. Ceagan slowed down, coming to the side of the aisle, one step away from standing out in the open. The pounding was louder now, dull, like flesh. Haideh took a deep breath. She wasn't sure what she was supposed to expect on the other side of the shelf, but she knew they were going to find out, and it wasn't going to be good.

"Careful," Ceagan said. "As one."

The two synchronized their movements, both poking their heads around the shelf to see that a tall, gangly man with dark hair was on his knees, forehead against the floor. He raised his head slowly, blood dripping from his face, and then slammed it back down onto the concrete, causing his face to crack and blood to splatter onto the floor. Blood seeped from his fingers, just like on the TV.

FRIENDS ARE CRAZY

"Mark?" Ceagan whispered.

"Look," Haideh said, nodding to two bodies behind the man. "Can you tell who those are?"

73

"That red sweater, Dan, for sure. I think the other is Daniel from his height."

"Where is Richard then?" Haideh asked.

"I don't know," Ceagan muttered.

"Those blood-fingered freaks got to Mark," Haideh said.

"It appears so. They've made him crazy."

Mark let out a loud shout and stood up from his kneeling position. He continued to shout, throat tensing up and face crunching as he clenched his fist. He repeatedly slammed his fists into his bloody face, coating his hand in a mixture of blood and saliva.

"Why is he doing that?" Haideh asked.

"It's like a child, but violent," Ceagan observed.

"Possibly."

"Maybe we can check the security camera? See what happened," Ceagan whispered.

"Do you know how to access them?" Haideh asked.

"No, Candice always has the key. Maybe it's in her office."

"I say the hell with it," Haideh said. "Let's get out of here."

"What about Richard?" Ceagan asked.

"He's not here. We checked the lobby and the back room."

Mark let out another loud shout and picked up speed, running in their direction.

"Look out!" Ceagan said, ducking back, pulling Haideh with him.

The shouts grew louder, footsteps thundering. Ceagan tightened his grip on his hole puncher, ready to attack. Mark dashed from the aisle and away from Ceagan and Haideh, charging straight into the nearest shelf. The impact caused the structure to wobble, toppling down onto him, burying him in paper stock and wood. Pieces of paper flew off the shelves and into the air, scattering in all directions. Haideh and Ceagan took a step back. Mark was buried entirely by the paper and rubble.

"What was that about?" Haideh asked.

Ceagan shook his head. "He has no brains left. I've never seen anything like it."

"Is he dead?" Haideh asked, taking a step closer.

Ceagan grabbed her wrist. "Don't. I think it's safe to say we have time."

A knock came from the exit leading to the lobby. They both jumped, spinning around to see a larger man with a neckbeard raise his hands.

"Guys!" he said.

"Richard!" Ceagan said, relaxing his arms. "Where the bloody hell were you?" he asked.

"In the washroom." He shook his head. "Jesus, what is going on? I locked myself in when I heard all the screams."

"You chickenshit," Haideh cursed.

Ceagan and Richard looked back at her, squinting at the sudden harsh language.

"I mean, it's good to see you," Haideh said with a forced smile. The words even surprised Haideh. She wasn't usually one to lash out at people. Perhaps all the stress from work and this epidemic was making her a little loopy. Regardless, here they were, the last of Mega Speed Print.

They still had no idea what was happening, nor who the blood-fingered three were. Fear was a guarantee. The future was unknown. For all they knew, things were going to get worse.

One thing was certain: they could finally leave work. It wasn't like the boss could give them grief for leaving early. The country was in chaos. Not to mention, she was dead. They didn't need to listen to her anymore, even in the busy season. Now Haideh could get a better graphic designer job, presuming the blood-fingers didn't get her next.

05

The brightness fades, and the darkness returns. You look at Malpherities, slightly underwhelmed and confused. What you saw wasn't anything you've seen before. Bleeding hands, people acting like wild animals, and an entire country in disorder is a lot to take in, let alone what you saw in the previous observation. You cannot help but wonder how much stranger all of this is going to become.

"You're a little calmer than the last witnessing," Malpherities says. "Anything of value in this one?"

"I'm not sure. I recognized London. It, along with all of England, was under attack, like some apocalypse. Is England gone?"

"Gone? I suppose no more than it isn't."

"Right, we jump time. So does—or *will*—England fall to those . . . things?"

"Oh," Malpherities says, looking down. "Right, you were there. Don't worry about it."

"Does humanity eventually split off into The Society?" you ask, recalling the strange futuristic world you observed. The sight of herding humans through genetically altered eyes wasn't going to be something you could shrug off easily.

Malpherities sighs. "Explaining the entire human history is a broad stroke, and, truthfully, it's boring. Events are far more exciting."

"Why'd you send me to that time just now? With people going crazy and the bleeding hands?" you ask.

"I'm making educated guesses on how you might have died. That event in England was pretty tragic, as you saw. They eventually recover."

"What caused the hands to bleed, and people to go crazy?" you ask.

Malpherities thinks about the question for a moment and then says, "Something to do with a cult, if I'm not mistaken." He reaches for the bowl. "You're not recognizing anything we throw at you. This may take a bit longer than I first anticipated."

"Great." You rub your head. "So, what's next?"

"We'll cast a wider net," Malpherities says, rubbing his black liquid-covered claws together. "Open wide," he says with a toothy grin.

You press your lips tightly, ready for the passing into the observing-state once more. The droplet hits your eye. Instinctively, you try to wipe some of the stinging liquid from your face. Too late. The effects are potent. You are the observer.

VOID WATCHER

REDISCOVERY

Goodnight, I love you. Zea heard the phrase every night during her childhood. She would get a kiss on the cheek and a tight hug before being dismissed. The ritual was cute as a kid, but as an adult, it makes her sheepish. Even through the embarrassment, Zea wants her mother to be happy. The woman was never quite the same after Zea's dad passed. Her mother wants to be directly involved in Zea's life, so the least Zea can do is say goodnight to her. Hugs and kisses are a lot cheaper than rent, even if it makes her feel like an adolescent. Zea's mother is far too lenient. She let Zea move back home after college—a blessing and a curse. Mom's kindness made it too convenient for Zea, who still hadn't found a job. Dinner was made every night, and laundry was taken care of. Moving back home was a permanent bed-and-breakfast—Goodbye, ninety-nine-cent mac-and-cheese meals.

"Tomorrow is a brand-new day," Mom says with a warm smile.

"Thanks, Mom," Zea says.

"Oh! Before you go to bed"—Mom leans down below her office desk. She lifts an old cardboard box onto the desk with a heavy thud—

"I was looking through the basement earlier and came across these gems."

"What's that?" Zea asks, stepping closer.

Mom flips the box open and pulls some sheets of paper out. "You know these."

"No way." Zea folds her arms. "You kept all of this?"

"You were such an artist, even then!" Mom says, flipping a sheet of paper over.

Zea stares at the paper, looking at the crude crayon figure of a ghost with an upside-down triangle for a head.

"I have no idea where you came up with these ideas," Mom says, handing the drawing to Zea. She sifts through the box, saying, "There was that tiger in here that I liked too."

Zea swallows heavily, staring at the triangle-headed drawing. *The watcher*, she thinks. The grim memories are still here, deep in the forgotten chasms of her mind. The watcher followed her every night before her dreams. It was the reason why she had a nightlight well into her teenage days. Its words. . . Its . . . teeth. She shakes her head, pushing the thoughts back to the depths whence they arose, and forces a smile, saying, "This stuff is so bad!"

"Nonsense! You've always had talent," Mom says.

"Talent doesn't get you employed," Zea sighs. She hands the paper back to her mother.

"You'll find a job, dear," Zea's mother says, taking the drawing and placing it back in the box. "You are exceptionally gifted."

Zea rubs her arm. "Thanks, Mom," she says. "I'm going to bed."

"Of course," Mom says. "Goodnight, I love you."

Hugs and kisses.

A NEW RITUAL

Zea leaves the home office and heads up the stairs to her childhood room. She flicks the light on and closes the door. The room is exactly as it was before she left for college. When she first came back, she wanted to remove the boy-band posters and the stuffed animal toys but purposely avoided changing anything in the room. Keeping the childhood items convinced her that she wasn't going to be here long. Nine months later, here she is.

She turns off the lights and undresses. The blue nightlight automatically turns on, projecting enough brightness for her to find her pyjamas and slip into them. She swipes her smartphone screen, unlocking it, and sets the alarm for the next day. After months of bad sleep, Zea has finally decided to set a timer to get up early each day. Her unrestful slumbers had been making her sleep all morning and well into the afternoon. By early evening, she would have a heavy nap, ruining her sleep cycle for the night, and would repeat the cycle the next day—an unhealthy pattern if she ever wants to get a job. She's ready to break that pattern.

Zea notices a dating app notification at the top right of her smartphone's screen. The icon indicates there is a match. *It's probably another dick pic,* she thinks. She places the phone on her dresser, telling herself she will check the notification tomorrow. Zea isn't in a rush to meet a man; she can barely get her own life together. No one will want anything to do with an unemployed deadbeat like her. Well, then again, there are a lot of "fuck bois" out there, as she learned from college.

Zea jumps into her bed, sliding under the covers. She takes a deep breath and lets out a sigh, trying to brush away the constant pressure of being unemployed. Zea knows that her mother is patient with her situation, but she only feels guilt for being here and not having work. She can't even land an interview. Her portfolio was top of her class at that. Hell, even her instructors were impressed! *What am I doing wrong?* she wonders.

"Tomorrow's worries," Zea says through an exhale.

Her mind drifts. She takes deep breaths in through the nostrils and out the mouth. Supposedly, this is the better way to breathe. Zea's brain always runs a thousand thoughts a second before bed. The moments just before sleep is the one time she is not doing something. The downtime gives her brain a chance to play catch-up, reflect upon the day, the regrets, the observations, and think about the wishes of tomorrow. This is why she practices deep breathing. The stillness helps calm the body.

Nose in, mouth out.

After what seems like a good eight dozen breathing cycles, Zea's thoughts turn fuzzy, and her body relaxes. The worries of today and the uncertainty of the future fade; the guilt of staying with her mother and not paying rent wash away. The stress of being single and making no use of her college degree is of little concern now. There is only Zea, the bed, and the blue glow of her nightlight. With another exhale, the walls dissipate. Her eyes lock on to the blue-tinted speckles of the ceiling. Her limbs are jelly, and her breathing pattern enters autopilot. At some point in the process, the room goes dark. Her body lightens, as if she has left this reality. Her thoughts dissolve into the abyss, leaving her to observe the dream world. She begins to drift through the empty, black space. She is weightless and free. The physical constraints that bound her during the day cease to exist.

"Welcome to the other side," a raspy, deep voice says in her mind.

THE VOID

A loud thud comes from the bedroom door.

Zea's eyes twitch open, and she attempts to move them to the sound's origin. They don't budge in their sockets. She can only see the upper half of the door frame from her peripheral view, due to the angle of her head. Zea tries to move her eyes again with no success. Despite her best efforts, she can't adjust the position of her eyes in her skull.

What the . . . ? she thinks. The words in her mind are supposed to project from her mouth, but she only makes caveman groans from her throat. Her jaw and lips do not respond. Some saliva oozes down her chin. Zea attempts to use her tongue to grab the liquid. No luck. Her tongue is as useless as her eyes. The door to her bedroom creaks open, revealing a black hallway beyond the frame. The blue glow from her nightlight shines abnormally bright, increasing the contrast of light and dark. An immense invisible force pushes onto Zea's chest and limbs, sinking her deeper into the bed. She tries to scream, only to make more caveman sounds.

I can't breathe! Zea cries in her mind, feeling a lack of air enter her burning lungs. Her voice is nothing but gurgling gibberish, despite the clarity of her thoughts. The force on her body continues to press into her being, pushing her deeper into the bedframe. The mattress morphs into a tar-like substance, absorbing her.

A white shape enters the room, gliding closer to her. From her peripheral view, it looks like a body draped in a white robe. The head, on the other hand, is an upside-down triangle with glowing blue orbs resembling eyes; these orbs hover above the two higher points of the geometric shape. The triangular head floats on the body as a mouth appears from the lower point of the triangle, stretching up to the blue orbs.

Someone help! Zea attempts to talk again, but gurgling is the result. Her limbs fail to respond as she tries to spring from the mattress. She is in an unresponsive body, watching while the being glides towards her bedside. The elongated mouth reveals razor-sharp teeth and a red snake-like tongue.

"We have watched you from the Void since your childhood, Zea," the being says, the skin moving like rubber.

Help! Zea cries.

The being leans closer, multiplying the invisible force. No air enters her lungs as she helplessly stares at the triangular head.

"Your mind remains intact with this world and the next. You are attuned through your two-dimensional visions. You are awake. This is why we remain in contact throughout your realm's years. The Void has waited for your visions to grow stronger. The All-Being Entity awaits you, my Oracle."

An arm-length form pushes from underneath the being's robe, followed by three sharp grey claws. "The time is now, Oracle. I have come to open your mind to speak with the All-Being Entity directly," the creature says in a cold tone, the claw reaching for her.

She can't move—more caveman noises.

The claw—inches away. "You will initiate absorption."

"No!" Zea screams as the mattress rises to its normal state. Her body becomes hypersensitive, a chill creeping across her skin as she springs from the bed in a sweaty mess. Her eyes widen to see that the blue nightlight has returned to its normal value. The pressure on her body ceases as her motor functions return. She kicks the white sheets away. The triangle-headed being is gone. No one is in the room, nor is the door open.

Zea rubs her forehead, feeling an intense headache pulsate throughout her skull.

Some things never change, she thinks.

Breathe through the nose and out the mouth.

Sleep paralysis, she tries to reassure herself. But she sees the small scratch on her arm.

06

The burning ends; the observer is gone. You are your flesh once more, chilled, but calm. You blink a couple of times and reflect on what you saw.

"Less apocalyptic, Nameless One?" Malpherities asks.

"Yeah, but unsettling," you say. "Seeing someone fall asleep after coming and going as an observer is . . ."

"Deja vu? Familiar? Repetitive?"

"Yeah, I guess."

"Maybe these sleep states have some relevance," Malpherities says. "Sleep is a powerful state that aids in dropping your ego. It lets the subconscious take the wheel, providing wisdom and insight beyond the mind's conscious limitations."

"Right," you say.

Malpherities rolls his white eyes. "Heard of the expression *sleep on it*?"

"Yeah, I understand that," you say. "You think sleep is triggering my memory?"

"Possibly. It's worth a try." Malpherities once again dips into the black liquid as you stand below him, ready for another go. "Let's find out," he says, tapping his claw, sending you to observe through new eyes.

MR. SUPER

I am on my way to bed like any other day. Mom makes sure that I stay on a strict schedule with finals coming up. I don't want to challenge the wrath of my parents. If I don't listen, Mom will tell Dad. Let's just say Mom is the nice one—it's that simple. After brushing my teeth, I go into my room, hop into bed, and fire up my laptop. I have that stupid test tomorrow, and it's best to review some of the notes I took.

The joys of high school. I'd rather be out with my friends, hanging out at the graveyard, casting a spell, or checking out new music online. There are all sorts of cuties making darkwave music. No luck for me. I get to be the nerd, thanks to my airheaded arrogance of denying the Good Lord. It turns out you shouldn't burn Bibles in front of your parents.

The door to my bedroom closes slowly, making my laptop the only source of light. This is strange. No one is in the hall that I am aware of, or in my room. I flick the on light on the nightstand and take notice that by the door is my old teddy bear, Mr. Super, with his little red cape.

"Hello?" I ask. Someone has to be in this room.

"Roger," comes a deep voice. A familiar one. I know I've heard it before. Wait . . . that is . . . can it be? "Roger, you don't need anything else," the voice says. It hits me—the voice is coming from Mr. Super. It is the same voice I made in my head when I was a kid, but now it's coming from the bear itself.

"Who is there?" I ask. I don't believe it can be Mr. Super. Maybe I am more tired than I realize.

The lamp flickers. Darkness. It jolts on. Mr. Super is at the end of my bed. "Roger, you abandoned me," says Mr. Super. His stitched mouth doesn't move. The stuffed toy's beady little eyes look right at me. His felt eyebrows are slanted inward. They were never angled when I was a kid.

"Wh-wh-what are you?" I ask, gripping onto my laptop tightly. Sweat builds up on my palms. A moment of clarity hits me—I'm talking to a stuffed toy. The moment passes as Mr. Super speaks again.

"Roger, I am your best friend. We did everything together."

"I was a kid," I say. Now I am reasoning with the toy? This is all crazy.

"You promised we'd be together forever. You put me in the closet, Roger."

"This is stupid," I mumble, getting up from my bed.

The laptop flies out of my hands and smashes against the wall by an invisible force. I gasp, watching it fall to the ground in a dozen pieces.

"You can't replace me with technology or other humans. They don't understand you as I do," Mr. Super says.

"Help!" I shout, running to the door. The same power snags me by my ankle. I fall with a thud—chin-first—slamming into the Ouija board and burnt-out candles my friends and I used last night. The force drags me back to the bed as I put the pieces together. Shit. I really should have kept that Bible.

"No one can hear you, Roger."

I look around the room for a way out. My eyes land on the window—outside, the neighbourhood is gone. It is pure blackness outside.

"We'll be together once again," Mr. Super says. "This time . . . forever." The bear's stitched mouth morphs upward into a wicked smile with pointy, sharp teeth.

07

*N*onsense. The thought breaks you from the observation, and you mutter, "What the . . . ?" Speaking out loud makes you realize you're back in the Midway.

"That was short," Malpherities says.

"Yeah. There was some demonic teddy bear," you say.

"Humans do strange things when opening doors to the otherworldly, especially when they don't have the proper barriers to protect themselves."

"Apparently. I got nothing from this. It's too far out there from what I feel my life was like."

"A dead end, then. Let's try to find something more grounding— closer to death itself."

OPTION THREE

Being alive is not a concrete concept. Sure, you can feel with your senses and experience joy or sadness, and that might be the definition of *alive*, but that's not what I'm talking about. Maybe I am coming from a philosophical standpoint. What does it mean to be alive? What are we? I do not know. Some days I find myself questioning my mortality. Like, my mind lives inside of my brain—according to science—and that is where my thoughts are. The brain is where *I* am. With that logic, my mind is just a series of electrical neurons buzzing around some organic tissue. Take the mind away, and the body is not me—according to science. Or if the brain stops shooting neurons, I'm dead—according to science.

It's a bit crazy to ramble on these tangents of the self. I feel mad, going through these answerless questions. They seem to come daily now. There isn't much else to do in a butthole of a town with a population of under a thousand people. Your options for activities are limited. The other kids smoke up, drink, fight, and vandalize. I do too. They're my friends, some of them, so I join along and get high and drink to excess. Then the grizzled after-work drunks yell at us from their porch, seeing us barely walking, inebriated. They threaten that they'll call the RCMP, but they don't. They have nothing to stand on because we don't have any weed or drinks on us when we're walking down the road. We're not stupid.

Don't get me wrong; I like getting wasted like anyone else and getting yelled at by the townsfolk, who tell me to take off the spiked collar and the makeup, and focus on school. It's a real good *fuck you* to the prudes when we stay up until the sun rises. It's fun, and it is the only activity you can do here. Still, at some point in the day, you are done all of that. You can only drink and do drugs so much at any given time. Even for only a few minutes, you'll find yourself at your most vulnerable. You might be waking up in the morning, or walking to school, or in the shower, and you'll find yourself alone in your thoughts—the most frightening experience of all.

Ideas run through my mind, like wondering if I will ever get out of this small town. No one likes to talk to me. I mean, talk, talk to me. The adults are either rambling about the government being a bunch of lib-tards taking oil money away or telling me to stop dying my hair and help my folks. My friends want to get drunk, break shit, and poke fun at the nerds. No one wants to *talk*. When I say talk, I mean getting into the nitty-gritty of ourselves. Introspective, if you will.

My gramps had a lot of books. We have them now since he blew his brains out. I read through them, not understanding everything. He had a wide range of books, like some on religion, philosophy, social sciences—all the good stuff. My parents don't read them. They watch the tube, drink, smoke, and then fight over the dishes or about that waitress my dad banged over a decade ago. They don't have time to learn, let alone pay attention to their kid. The books just stay in Gramps's old room, left untouched since the day he died. They've become my teacher. I ignore the odd bloodstain I find every now and then.

Maybe these books are what separates me from everyone else. I've asked my teachers if they've heard about them. Some have, others haven't. In short, they tell me to focus on my grades that are slipping. Whatever. If an academic facility is not the place to talk about ideas, where is, then? I don't know. Thus, I find myself wandering inside of my mind, puffing on a cigarette alone, watching the sun go down from the rooftop of that old abandoned butcher shop. I do enjoy the sun. The warmth and light bring a sense of stillness. It doesn't judge my outfit or my thoughts. The giant fireball only watches before it vanishes behind the horizon. Then, I am left in the beautiful blackness of the night while the world slumbers.

I get stuck on the question of who we are. If science is right, then we are just a series of neuron links accumulated together to create consciousness. Take a single neuron out of the equation and examine it, and that is not you. With that reasoning, how many neurons does it take to make up *you*?

These are questions with no answers. The more I read, the more I wonder. Religion offers different solutions, also with no conclusion, other than we are the abstract concept known as a soul. Dig into any of those books, and you'll find they can't answer some of the tough questions with anything more substantial than saying that's the way it is, and to have faith. I have discovered one thing, though. The more questions you ask, the more it alienates you. My friends have started to talk to me less. Whatever. They were boring to me, anyway. We still chat at school and stuff, but I don't have much else to say beyond that. My mind is too troubled by my mortality. My interests have made me an outcast amongst the rejects. No amount of spikes or layers of black nail polish will convince my friends to see me in any other light—or darkness, if you will.

Now that I am not off getting high or drunk every moment I can, it has given me more time with the self. I am wondering what defines me. Where do I go when I die? The body and the brain stay here. The neurons die. Then is that it? Does the consciousness fizzle out? If so, then why does any of this matter if we eventually end up in the nothingness? The joy in life is so short-lived, only to be met by misery. We wait for another wave of happiness, and then the cycle repeats itself the following day, over and over again. I wonder if experiencing life with others is what gives living value. Then is it your memory that lives on through others that matters? I chuck the idea aside. That has no place for me—not in this small town. I don't want to share my time with these hicks.

I wonder if I will ever get out of here. I'll graduate high school in a year, and I don't have a lot of money to skip town and head for the big city. It's not like I have any aspirations. I just read and get myself tied up in theoretical knots. Skipping town to be homeless in a big city doesn't sound appealing, either: escape the suffering here for new pain. It's all pointless. Whatever.

Did I mention my gramps blew his head off? Yeah, he was a bit of a gun freak. My folks cleaned out his collection. They didn't check his bookshelves—because they don't read—and I found an old revolver tucked inside a dummy-book. Man, did that ever shock me. There is so much power in something so small. One bullet can end all thoughts inside of someone's head. Sight, smell, touch, hearing, and taste all go away. The emotional sensations cease to be with one pull of the pistol's trigger. The everlasting slumber.

Back to the mortality and life-after-death stuff. If this is all we have, and our consciousness dies inside of our mind, then we do return to some state of neutrality when we die. We can't experience loss, sadness, or misery because our neurons are toast. It's kind of the closest thing to isness, that thing that monks try to do. Death is the answer. The eternal peace.

We all end up in the grave at some point. It's up to you how long you want to gamble in the game of life. Roll another dice each morning, hoping something will get better. The years go by, you keep trucking along, and eventually, you turn into my parents—drunk and fighting. As you get older, you could end up like Gramps and finally call it quits anyway and take your own life instead of rotting away in a rocker.

Now I sit here on that same old abandoned butcher shop rooftop, puffing on a smoke and watching the sunset. I think about my quality of life. I have a choice to make. I could be isolated from everyone with my intellect. I could swoop back down to drinking, smoking, and vandalizing with a real punk-rock attitude. The third option is I could end it. The revolver in my sweaty hand is loaded. I suppose it doesn't matter what choice I make. At some point, I will eat the dirt. It's really up to me if I want to try or just take the shortcut. No one will miss me, anyway. Over half the time, I am alone. I don't talk to anyone anymore. I have no one to touch. Death sure would make for some talk around the town.

Option three is one I've been considering heavily today. That's why I have the revolver in my mouth as I stare out into the sun. The fiery ball is looking back at me, not judging, only watching. The neutrality of the star is the one thing I would miss. It has a strange sense of isness. Now I second-guess my gramps and myself. Maybe the sunset each day is all I need. Hey, there's something worth living for, or whatever. It's probably a good idea to take the gun out of my mouth, then. Maybe I'll give life a go for one more day, enjoy this setting sun, and embrace the slumber of the night.

08

The warmth of the sun cools into a chill. Goosebumps rise on your skin, making you shiver. You blink; lightness blooms over your vision and fizzles into the dark cavern in the Midway. The brief experience was grim, soul-touching, sad, and joyful, all jumbled into one big mess. At least there were no demonic teddy bears or bleeding fingers.

Malpherities leans against the black pedestal, looking bored. "And?" he asks.

"The girl . . . or boy . . . I don't know, it was sad. I just felt sorrow, like I was trapped deep in the person's soul. It wasn't quite as in-the-moment as some of these other witnessing experiences."

"Interesting," Malpherities says. "We still don't have much to go on, other than you didn't die in the nineties, you know of England, and spaceships scare you."

"Pretty much," you say, realizing the past few witnessing events hadn't given you any clues.

"Let's throw you into a distant land—one that I hold dear."

"Really? Where is that?"

"Human history is muddled up, and has many wide gaps of knowledge." Malpherities dips his claw into the bowl, as usual. "We'll bring you deep into the forests of Zingalg."

"Zingalg?" you ask.

"The lost continent. We'll take you to a specific time, when it was near the end of its lifespan."

"What happened to it?" you ask.

"A tale for another time." The ghoul taps his claw. The droplet falls, hitting your eye, sending you back as an observer.

OTHERKIN

ALL FUN AND GAMES

Normally I don't find myself wandering through the forest at dusk. The sun setting means it is about to be dark, and that has everyone fearful. Being in a forest at night, hearing, "Catch me, catch me. Don't think you can. Guess I'm free! Hee! Hee! Hee!" sung softly, echoing through the trees, is enough to send anyone running. No one good is in the woods as the day reaches its end. Luckily, I know whose voice it is, and I cannot just leave him for what lurks at dusk. What kind of brother would I be?

"Quit playing around!" I call out. "Mother is going to be mad at us. It's past dusk." I step over the slippery ground, carefully avoiding the creek, so I don't fall into the cold water. My boots are covered in mud; overalls, dusty. This was a trio of all the things that put grey hairs on our mother's head.

"Edmund!" I call out again. This is downright childish. Edmund knows the dangers of being out in the dark. He is a child, but that doesn't make this any easier. A splash comes from the creek, catching my attention. It is too dark to see what hit the water, but the ripples are coming in my direction. "Edmund?" I ask, taking a step closer to the sound. With another step, I spot a half-wet rock in the water. In the dim light, the narrow shape looks like a strange mask.

"Cut it out!" I say.

Rustling comes from the nearby shrubs. That has to be Edmund. I step away from the creek and hurry over to the noise. The sound continues, and I can make out branches of a bush shaking around. Gotcha. I slow my pace, creeping up to the bush as the plant continues to move. It's an arm's length away.

"Edmund!" I shout, jumping over to the other side of the bush. Nothing. The bush continues to shake. Is Edmund inside?

"*CAW!!*" A high-pitched scream erupts as small hands snatch my forearm.

I spin around, gasping. Beside me is a small blond kid in a tattered knitted shirt—my brother.

"Edmund!" I slap his head. The bush stops moving. "What the hell is wrong with you?" I ask.

Edmund smiles, raising one hand, which holds a string. "I got you good." He pulls on the thread, causing the bush to move.

"Very funny. We're so late. We have to get home, come on." I snag my little brother's hand and march down to the creek.

"We're just playing," Edmund says. "Look how far we got today!"

"Yeah," I say. "We can explore more tomorrow, just before dusk. This was way too risky."

I understand my brother's enthusiasm for going farther up the creek. Our goal is always to see how far into the forest we can go before dusk. Since we are on a strict time limit, the game of exploring the woods is a real thrill. He just took it too far today.

"Mother is going to be boiling with rage," I add.

"No, she won't," Edmund says.

"Yes, she will. For all we know, they're prepping a search party for us."

"They've never done that. The otherkin would get them," Edmund says.

My brother has a point. No one ever seems to do much when

someone goes missing in the forest. Once darkness hits, it is too dangerous to try and send in a search party. In the eyes of the village, the lost turn into the deceased. Victims of the otherkin.

"All right," I say. "You got me there. Just please don't pull that kind of stuff again. Otherwise, the otherkin will get you too."

BACK HOME

The two of us follow the creek back down to the village, leaving the thick forest to enter the rocky wilderness. A couple of lights come from the houses down below, while the rest is dark. Lights off by dusk is the wisest thing anyone can do. We reach the gravel road and walk into town towards to our home. I cannot help but think how mad Mother is going to be. She will have my head because I was the older brother. 'Little Edmundie' cannot possibly do anything wrong.

Edmund scratches his head. He says, "I've seen one."

"What?" I ask.

"An otherkin."

"That's a big pile of horse crap," I say.

"It's true!" Edmund argues.

"No way. You'd be dead."

"Nu-uh."

"No one has survived seeing one. People simply go missing."

"Then how do you know they're real?" Edmund asks.

"Because we can hear them. They imitate human voices. Plus, we've found their nests and feathers. Oh, and then there's the obvious fact that people go *missing*," I say.

"Not all of them," Edmund replies. "They're not much different than us. They're like 'kin' more so than 'other.'"

I shake my head. There is no point in arguing with my little brother. He has a mind of his own, hence the fiasco tonight. He is convinced he's seen an otherkin. The boy has an active imagination, and there isn't much else to say about it.

"You'd have to be out super late," I say, still humouring him. I am not sure why—probably because he gets under my skin. "You couldn't have seen one."

"No, sometimes they are awake during the day."

"No, they're not."

Edmund and I hike home. Our home is one of the houses with the lights on. By the time we reach the front door, it opens. Both my mother and father step out.

"Darold, Edmundie!" my mother says, rushing up to us. She gets down on one knee and takes Edmund by the shoulders, examining him thoroughly. "By God, what were you two doing?"

My father puts his hands on his hips. "Do you have any idea how late it is? You could have been killed!"

"Yes," I say. "I am aware. Edmund wandered a little too far again."

"Heavens, no!" Mother says. "This was well past sunset. Edmund, you got lost." She wraps her one arm around Edmund and the other around me, bringing us both in for a tight squeeze. I look up at my father, who stares down at me, saying nothing. With a glare like that, I know he is blaming me for this stunt.

A distant chatter clucks through the skyline. It is high-pitched, almost like the sound of a little girl laughing.

Father exhales and waves his hand. "Let's get inside."

"That's earlier than normal," Mother says, standing up.

"We haven't seen much other wildlife over the past few weeks," Father says. "They're hungry."

ROUTINE

The four of us hurry inside. Father locks the door and reinforces it with planks of wood. Mother extinguishes all the candles, leaving us to wander in darkness. This is the usual routine. We make sure everything is off the floor so we can quickly get to our shared bedroom. It is much safer sleeping in a group than in separate spaces because otherkin are cowardly and prefer easy pickings. Father keeps his musket with him. Mother is by his side, with my brother and me between them.

Muffled shouts and cries pick up outside. They are the usual sounds we hear most nights when the otherkin come out. They try to mimic people, hoping to lure someone out.

"Don't do that again," Mother whispers.

"Yes, Mother," I say.

A thud comes from above—we look up. Dust falls from the ceiling with the heavy thumping as chattering and laughter pick up. The sounds bring back the memory of when I first heard the haunting chirps of the otherkin. Now, it is just another day in my life. Today is just another day of survival. The thumping stops as several big gusts of wind pick up, then the sound fades. They had to have flown away.

My father exhales deeply. "I hate when they peck the roof."

The rest of the night is uneventful, and the four of us get some sleep. We usually get up at about sunrise, when the otherkin return to their nests. We attend to our daily tasks at the village's farm, eat, and continue our work throughout the afternoon. After dinner, my brother cannot wait to get out of the village, go to the creek, and see if we can make a farther hike up to the forest. Maybe this time, we can find an animal corpse—leftovers from an otherkin's meal.

"Darold," Mother says, "please don't stay out that late again. Come back *before* dusk."

"We will," I say.

"Promise?"

"Promise."

After that, Mother approves and we hurry outside, following the road into the forest.

NEW RECORDS

Edmund and I walk up the creek as usual. This time, I keep a closer eye on the kid, making sure he doesn't get any wise-ass ideas. The last thing I want is to get another lecture from my father about responsibility. Edmund is lucky. He is the baby in the family and doesn't have to hear about responsibility. The two of us wander through the creek to where the long, mask-like rock rests in the stream. Today, it's just a rock. In the daylight, the shadows don't cast the same visuals. Either way, this was the last point we reached. We've made good time.

"I need to pee," Edmund says, stopping in his tracks.

"Just go behind that tree." I point to a large tree behind us.

Edmund hurries from the creek, carefully stepping around the slippery mud and up to the tree. He moves around the trunk and out of sight. A whizzing sound follows. Then silence.

"Edmund?" I say. "Come on out—no games this time."

"Catch me, catch me. Don't think you can. Guess I'm free! Hee! Hee! Hee!" he sings.

"Cut it out!" I hurry up to the tree trunk as my brother peeks around the other side.

"Hi!" Edmund says.

"Don't sing that song. I'm so tired of your jokes."

"I didn't."

"Excuse me?" I ask, eying my brother. He has to be lying.

"I didn't sing that," Edmund repeats.

"You mean, right now? Don't mess with me."

"No, it's the otherkin."

"*C-a-ch me, c-caw-ch m-m-aw . . .* " A voice picks up in the forest.

Every hair stands up on my skin. "Edmund," I say. "That song was never you, was it?"

A branch snaps loudly in the tree above, causing debris to fall. I brush leaves and wood splinters from my face until my hand comes into contact with something soft. I snag it off my face. It is a grey feather.

THE OTHERKIN

Instincts kick in. I snag my brother's hand and skid down from the high ground. Scraping comes from above as bark tumbles down onto the dirt behind us. We reach the creek and sprint down through the forest, carefully avoiding the mud and slippery rocks. A thud comes from behind as a large squawk roars through the woods. Thumping echoes our footsteps; the sound is heavier and is accelerating.

Don't get us, don't get us. My heart is racing while I tighten the grip on my brother's hand. My knees ache as my legs slam down the slope towards the village.

"*C-C-AW-TCH M-AH!*" a high-pitched scream screeches behind us. "*C-C-AW-TCH M-AH!*" It sounds so close.

Please don't. Please don't. Is it right behind us? I honestly don't know. The trees ahead are farther apart. We are on the outskirts of the forest but still too far from the rocky wilderness and the village. The stomping increases and I can hear the sound of ruffling feathers. I cannot help it. I have to see what was behind us. If this is it, I need to see my nemesis.

Ahead, a man appears from around a tree on the shore of the creek, musket in hand, pointed at me. I quickly tumble to the ground to avoid the gun, still holding onto my little brother. We splash down into the creek.

A deafening pop roars, and the being behind us squawks. Several gusts of wind pick up as I roll onto my back in the shallow creek bed, wiping my face clear of the mud and water. A silhouette of a humanoid with wings and sharp talons for feet is right there in front of me. The sun is blocking any details as it flies above the trees, further into the forest, eventually disappearing.

My little brother cries. He is beside me, on his knees, covered in mud and water.

Further down the creek, the man with the musket stands as smoke escapes the chamber. Father: Victor of the otherkin.

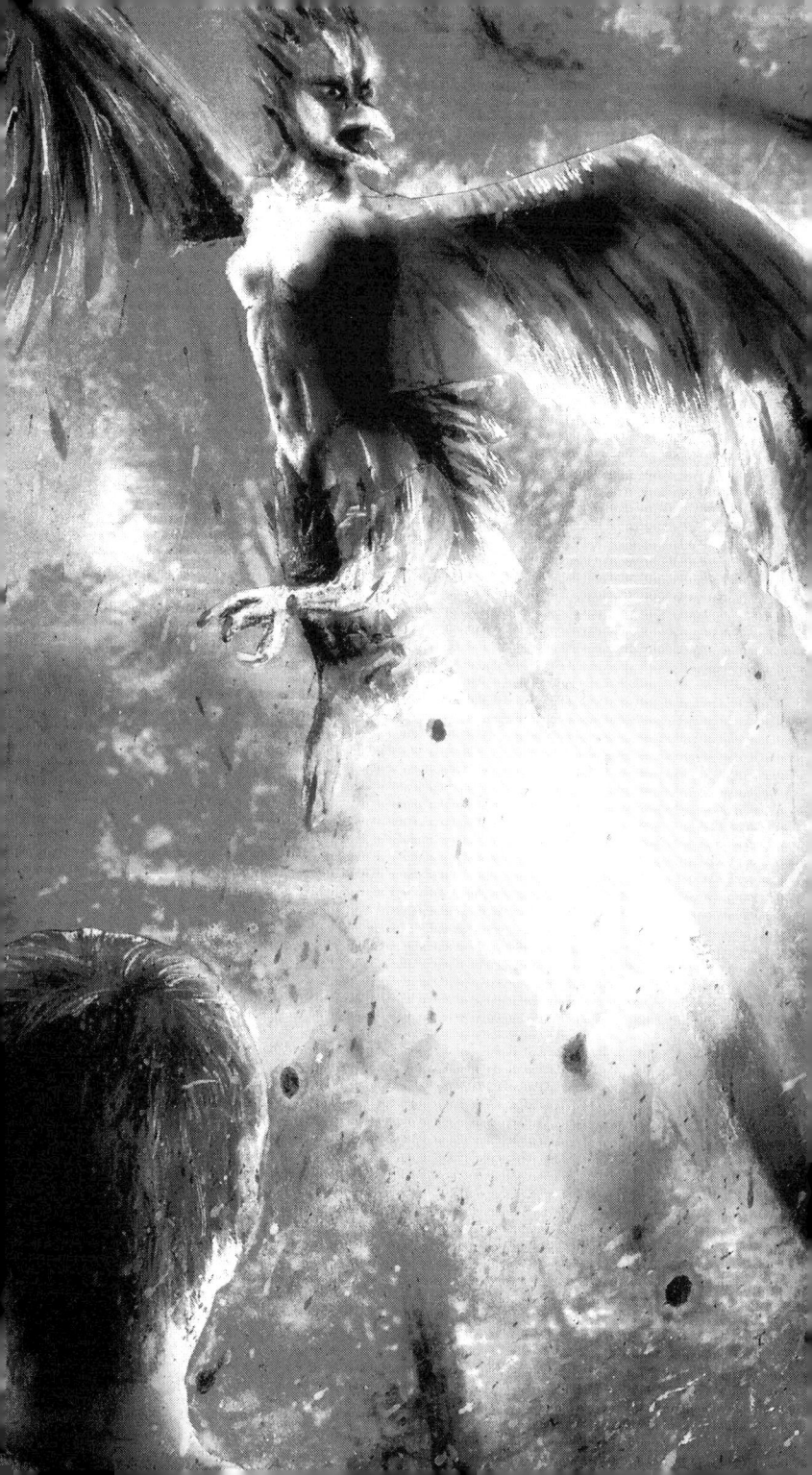

09

Man-eating birds . . . that's something new. One perk of being in this strange Midway is that no one is chasing you. You have to solve your memory problem, which is frustrating since you haven't made a ton of progress, and these witnessing experiences are starting to exhaust your mind. The memories all seep in like they're your own. The emotions . . . senses . . . all of it is now in your thoughts. Stronger than a dream.

The otherkin experience dissolves, and you wake up, collapsed on the sand.

"Welcome back," Malpherities says.

"Thanks." You get up, brushing the grains off yourself. "I fell. I thought you said I was an observer?"

"Yes, you are. You fell before this one started."

"Oh. So that was the lost continent, Zingalg?" you ask.

"A portion of the region, yes," Malpherities says.

"Man-eating birds?"

"The lost continent has many wonders, some never to be discovered by humans," Malpherities says.

"And it's lost?"

"Depending on when you died, yes. Eventually, the continent

collapses on its mystical forces, taking all of the fantastical creatures with it, sinking into the oceans."

"What? Land doesn't work that way."

"Yes, it can. Tectonic plates move."

You scratch your head. "Well, those bird-people weren't familiar."

"Back in you go, then," Malpherities says, reaching for the bowl.

"Can we take a break?" you ask.

Malpherities squints. "You're so keen on breaks. Why?"

"Just to process everything I've seen and felt. It's too much."

"Nonsense. Everything has already happened, is going to happen, and is happening. Your idea of time is constructed by the linear thought process you humans use."

"That's how time works, though."

"No, that happened due to the creation of language."

"Is that so?" you ask.

"Yes. The trees nor the animals worry about minutes or hours. Their time in life is in the now, the closest thing that is tangible to being real. Then, eventually, they pass and return to the dirt. Relish in their spirit, for you have nothing to fear. Besides, feeling them is only temporary, as you experienced in your death. Another memory that doesn't matter since you are here at this moment."

You sigh, choosing to humour the ghoul. His words of philosophy and space-time are not helping. You're not sure if you even grasp his strange explanations. "Fine. Maybe pick something less thrilling."

"Let's see what we can do," Malpherities says, scooping up another droplet of the black liquid from the bowl.

You take another deep breath, preparing yourself for the unknown. The droplet falls, hitting your eye. Into the observer state you go.

SCRAPPERS

BIG PICTURE

We try to stay hidden by staying underground. People like me have to go to the surface, though. When we do, we do our best to keep noise levels down and stay light-footed. You'd be amazed at how well satellites can pick up the alteration of the landscape from the skylines. Even the smallest detail—like a footprint—can be detected by their drones. Stealth is all we have until we find a better way to fend them off. There are probably a dozen names given to them. Everyone has a grudge for something they did or someone that they took. The Godly, Gene Freaks, Anti-Sapiens, or whatever your choice of phrase is, we all know them as the Harvesters. The Harvesters always return to Earth. They come for us. They find us. No matter how well we hide.

"Angie, get with it," came a croaky voice.

My eyes shot up at the sound. A man was looking over at me, the orange hue from the setting sun casting sharp shadows on his leathery skin. The neon green LED lights from his goggles shined right at me. Ruggy, my partner. We had a mission: gather scraps.

"Sorry," I said. "I wasn't really here." My thoughts had dragged off into big-picture nonsense about the world. Our attempts to survive.

Stuff that Ruggy wouldn't care about hearing.

"Keep your mind on why we're on the surface. I don't want to be here, either, but there aren't any options." He adjusted his rifle under his arm, holding the gun at a forty-five-degree angle, gaze forward. "Magnify your map and stay on course. The operator said there is an amplitude of metal not far from here."

THE LOST

I adjusted the interface display within my goggles. With a twitch of my eyelid, the goggles change the glass to project night vision. Another subtle eyelid movement caused the UI to zoom in on the map that displayed at the corner of my view, showing a detailed landscape as we walked on the rubble. Well, a map of what everything *used* to look like.

"These maps aren't helpful," I said. "They're well over a century outdated." I looked at the top-down view of the geographical location of the map. It showcased skyscrapers, roads, and complete pathways. With my naked eye, all I could see was a charcoal skyline, rubble-covered ground, and nature attempting to grow new green life in between the concrete cracks.

"It's the best that we have to work with," said Ruggy. "Us Scrappers always get the low-tech stuff."

"Isn't that the truth?" I said. There wasn't much of a point in discussing the topic. He was right. Scrappers were a low rank; that was why we stuck together. Plus, I knew what Ruggy was thinking: shut up and do your job. It was tough to do just that. We were in the middle of a long-forgotten civilization trying to find old metal scraps, praying that we wouldn't be detected by the Harvesters—not exactly motivating.

"This seems like a waste of time for us," I said. "We've never gone this far out into The Lost."

"Yeah, well," Ruggy said, "we've raided the closer past cities. We don't have much choice but to go farther in."

I scanned the ground in front of me, squeezing the rifle tight. There were washed-out yellow-painted smooth stones mixed in with grey rocks. These were once roads, and this was what was left of them. I'd seen complete streets in the archive photos before. Never had I seen such large chunks of remnants in person.

"All of this seems surreal," I said. "These people used to live in peace before it all went south."

"They didn't think so. Spoiled pricks arguing over trivial things," Ruggy said, taking a turn down an archway. "Down here," he said.

I followed behind him, looking at the massive archway. It was large enough to house a twelve-man transport shuttle. "What makes you say that?" I asked.

"They weren't happy and tried to change the world, which got us into this mess," Ruggy said.

"I suppose." Ruggy had a point. The past civilizations were the ones that brought humanity into a technological revolution. I just liked to imagine there was a better world at some point in time. "They only wanted to do what was good for us," I said.

"Are you that naïve? Come on, kid." Ruggy said. "The writers of the history books always make themselves look as good as they can, even if they are on the losing side. I am sure that the Harvesters paint a pretty glorified image of their past, justifying why they do what they do. Good is relative."

"If you don't trust the history books, what do you trust?" I asked.

"Well," Ruggy said, "I don't trust much. I do know not to trust one stupid book. That's been the issue with humanity for centuries. We put our trust in a single book. Now, we're living the greatest downfall from a repetition of history."

My pace slowed as we reached a massive semi-complete structure. It was about one-third of a sculpted head. A bearded man with a sharp nose and long hair, although it was difficult to tell from the missing pieces, rested sideways.

Amazing, I thought while looking up to the mountain in the near distance. A pile of rubble surrounded the wrecked sculpture's base. An educated guess would be the head had tumbled down the mountainside during an explosion. That was my best guess. I really had no idea.

GODS ON REPEAT

I picked up my pace, realizing Ruggy had continued without me. Once I caught up, I said, "It isn't all from one book, though. There's bureaucracy, corruption, and human greed to take into account."

"True, but they shroud it in justification from their holy books."

"Yeah, it is tragic. We kept repeating the past."

"It's ridiculous. We used to believe in super beings, gods, in the sky that judged our lives. The last 'holy book' was science, and it was just as bad as the rest."

"And the scientific revolution wasn't much different from religion," I said, looking at Ruggy's leathery face.

"Why's that?" he asked.

"Because the Harvesters turned themselves into gods in the sky, judging us."

Ruggy chuckled. "How poetic."

I couldn't tell if he was being his typical unenthusiastic self, or if he was actually impressed with what I said. It was hard to know with Ruggy; he always had the same attitude towards anything.

The two of us continued down the uneven path, hopping over large clumps of city remains and the few plants that had grown over the past world. Looking at it all made a part of me want just to go back to the cruiser and give up. Gathering scraps was tedious, and The Lost was depressive to look at. It wasn't like I had much choice, though. Scrapping was all I was good at. I didn't have any other skills that could help humanity survive. There were no educational systems for me to go to. People that possessed knowledge from the past carefully chose who they shared that info with. We had to operate this way. With no time for everyone to learn everything, we learned one skill fast and stuck to it.

The Harvesters were technologically advanced, mentally superior, and physically herculean. We couldn't wait around for people to make wishes about what they wanted to do. The higher commands would run us through rigorous tests, analyze what we performed best at, and that would be what we'd do until the day we died. It was that simple.

"Here's food for thought," Ruggy said as he reached the top of a steep rock. "Playing off of what you said, about the Harvesters being living gods and such . . . " He extended his hand for me.

"Yeah?" I asked, taking his hand to pull me up.

"You ever fathom that humanity has just repeated itself?"

"What do you mean?" I asked, panting and looking down at my health-cuff. The screen lit up with a flick of my wrist. It stated we were just over fifty kilometres from our cruiser. I thought that was a lot, but seeing that Ruggy hadn't even broken a sweat made me feel like a goof. I'd have to get on a tighter exercise routine when we got back to base.

"The Harvesters," Ruggy said. "They were us at one point. Gods are only projections of what we wish to be. They had the means to become that, and become that they did. Perhaps humanity has gone through similar routes in the past, and religious books are just history books about them."

"You mean like what the Babblers are doing?" I raised my eyebrow with a smirk. The idea was humorous. "You know Babblers are just desperate to find meaning in all this by speaking about it like some prophecy."

"Exactly my point. The Babblers are no different than any prophet. I take it you never got familiar any of the archive's religious texts?"

"No, can't say that I have," I said. "I'm a Scrapper. I rarely have time to read."

"Yeah, but you're also in your twenties. Ah, don't worry about it. I was a baboon at that age, too, chasing all the fucks I could get."

My nostrils flared. Who did Ruggy think he was, summing me up as some young, horny, uneducated kid? He had a way of belittling people.

But unfortunately, I had to work with him. Scrappers stuck together once chosen—Scrapper's code.

"Anyway . . . ," Ruggy said after my prolonged rage-silence. "Perhaps the past religions like Christianity, Hellenism, Hinduism, you name it, all had holy men who saw things for what they were." Ruggy brought out his hand. "I'm not saying this is the kind of stuff that I believe in, but just playing off your idea."

I smirked. "Really? You know a damn lot more than I do about religion. You sure you're not becoming a Babbler?"

"Zip it. Just throwing the idea out there that maybe this isn't the first time humanity has surpassed itself and went for the stars, leaving the rest of us down here."

"It's a wild theory." I wasn't sure what else to say. Ruggy knew a lot more about humanity's past than I did, and it wasn't worth challenging him. As he put it so delicately, I was just a young, horny kid. His statement had me wondering, though—was humanity just repeating itself? Did the past civilizations turn humans into gods, like the Harvesters? It was a crazy idea, and no one truly knew the truth. History was distorted. The details of how they went for the cosmos and left us here was a convoluted—and confusing—rabbit hole that wasn't worth going down. Trust me. I'd tried. Every 'fact' about how humanity's split began contradicted itself.

RETRIEVAL

I followed behind Ruggy as we continued down the mapped-out path projected on the goggle-screens. Of course, the goggles could only estimate where we went. It wasn't like we had any satellites to work with. Satellites would be a giant flag to attract Harvesters. The chips' processors were attached to our health-cuffs. They did some weird science-algorithm-tech thing that was beyond my understanding. All I knew was that the map talked to the cuff, and they could estimate my steps with the city's map's size.

"Looks like we're almost there," Ruggy said.

"So, the operator found some jackpot from their AI algorithms or what? I still don't get why we had to come out this far," I said.

"I don't know, Angie. That isn't my department, nor yours. They tell us where to go, and we get the scraps. That's all."

"Right," I said, while tightening my grip on my rifle. We had never gone this far out into The Lost before. The fact that we'd left our cruiser so far behind made me uncomfortable. If a Harvester were to show up, we would be on our own. We couldn't outrun them—that would be pointless. We had no transportation—we were sitting ducks on foot.

Ruggy brought his rifle up as we turned the corner. The smell of burning metal picked up. This was abnormal. Burning smells meant someone had been here recently. Nothing should be burning in The Lost. Those fires and explosions happened long before our time. I used my eyelids to navigate through the goggles' interface. The screen projected a keyboard and message thread between Ruggy and I. My eyelids twitched in swift movements, stringing together alphabetic characters into words.

DO YOU SMELL THAT? I typed out in the chat.

YEAH, KEEP YOUR GUARD UP, Ruggy typed back as he descended a rocky, narrow path.

I felt the sweat build up in my pits and on my palms. Whatever this was, it wasn't part of our standard protocol. The operators typically had us find piles of rubble to dig through and snag metal. This was something different. We continued down the path, creeping slowly to avoid loose rocks. The last thing we needed was to make noise. Ruggy reached the end of the steep decline to where the path opened up. Smoke rose from the open, charcoaled ground. Even with the goggles' enhanced vision, neither Ruggy nor I could make out what was in front of us.

I raised my rifle as I reached Ruggy's side, stopping right in front of the opening.

My eyelids moved, typing, *I CAN'T SEE ANYTHING.*

NOR CAN I, Ruggy wrote.

YOU SURE THIS IS THE RIGHT PLACE? I asked.

YEAH, CHECK THE MAP YOURSELF.

The map was pretty accurate when it synched with the health-cuffs. Plus, there was only rubble all around us. There was nothing of interest here other than this mysterious smoke and burning smell.

WHAT DO WE DO? I asked.

WE'RE SCRAPPERS. WE SCRAP WHATEVER IT IS.

Ruggy stepped forward. He didn't look back, expecting me to follow. I had to. Ruggy was right—We were Scrappers. With that in mind, I took a deep breath and marched alongside Ruggy into the smoke. As we got closer, the smell heightened and gave me a strange stinging sensation. It overpowered my senses, and I couldn't smell anything else. Shit, I wanted a mask at this point. Scrappers always got the leftover supplies and never the ones we needed. At least we had the goggles. They kept our eyes clear as we moved through the unknown. I stayed slightly behind Ruggy, making sure nothing came from his sides or behind us. We entered the thick of the haze, not able to see beyond a few feet. As we stepped further in, the smoke morphed to an orange-red hue.

BURNING, Ruggy typed.

IT'S A CRASH? I responded.

A roar erupted from the brighter flames farther ahead. We raised our rifles as a humanoid silhouette rose from the flaming ground, deformed from the light. Large limbs reached up for the sky, too large to be human. The roar morphed into a howling groan—a sound of agony.

HARVESTER, Ruggy typed.

YOU SURE? I replied.

POSITIVE. WHAT ELSE CRASH-LANDS ON EARTH?

HARVESTERS NEVER CRASH-LAND.

MAYBE. BUT THERE'S NOTHING ELSE IN SPACE.

WHAT ABOUT THAT THEORY YOU JUST CAME UP WITH? PAST CIVILIZATIONS GOING FOR THE STARS?

SHUT IT, KID. DO AS I SAY.

WHAT?

SHOOT FIRST, ASK QUESTIONS LATER.

I exhaled. A part of me was annoyed. There were so many questions that we hadn't answered. We were making choices that were beyond our rank. Whatever we were witnessing was not a Scrapper's role. Harvester or not, this was something we needed to report. There was also the fact we could end up killed. Scrappers were about stealth and retrieval, not engaging in combat.

WE SHOULD CALL IT IN, I typed.

WE CAN'T, REMEMBER? Ruggy replied. *WE'RE ON A LOCAL CHANNEL. HELPS WITH STEALTH.*

LET'S GET BACK TO THE CRUISER, THEN. THE OPERATORS WILL WANT TO KNOW ABOUT THIS.

WALK 50K? THIS THING WILL BE GONE BY THEN. WE SHOOT IT, CALL IT IN.

I wasn't sure what else to say to Ruggy. We wouldn't be able to make it back to the cruiser, report the finding, and expect to find whatever it was we'd found to be here still. Action was needed. Besides, Ruggy had his mind made up regardless of any protocol. He wanted to find out what this was. I had no other choice. I couldn't leave him behind—Scrapper's code.

DUAL FREAKS

Flames crackled. Our boots pushed the loose gravel aside with each step. My heart pounded as sweat beaded on my face. I kept my eyes on my partner, Ruggy, who moved closer to the flickering orange heat, the only light in the night. The goggles tried to balance out the contrast of light and dark, but were of little use. One thing was clear in our view: the silhouette of that muscular arm reaching for the skies.

The small UI chat message window at the bottom corner of the goggles lit up as Ruggy typed out a new message.

LET'S CIRCLE AROUND. WE'RE HEADING STRAIGHT FOR IT, he typed.

My eyelids twitched, navigating the chat program's keyboard, typing.

GOT IT, I replied.

The two of us circled the target as a haunting groan came from the silhouette's location. The arm moved down to the ground. The being was trying to push itself up. It was wounded—how injured, we didn't know. Ruggy and I had to be cautious. This thing was looking more and more like a Harvester.

As bold as Ruggy was for investigating the fire, I was not. I wanted to get the hell out of here as quickly as we could. The lack of sight, the unusual stinging smell, and this massive being were enough to send me heading for the cruiser. But Ruggy needed me. Scrappers stuck together; there was no other option. Scrapper's code always came first.

Another sound screeched through the fire. This one was more distant. Violent. Ruggy and I turned to the origin, trying to spot anything. Large torn scraps of metal pierced the ground—the remnants of some sort of spacecraft.

THERE'S TWO, Ruggy typed out.

THAT DIDN'T SOUND THE SAME, I replied.

NO SHIT. STAY ON GUARD.

Rustling came from the original silhouette as it attempted to stand upright, limping. A second screech erupted—the target reached for an object on the ground, a large spear.

SEE? HARVESTER, Ruggy typed.

The spear was a clear indicator of a Harvester; all humans knew it. They used those damned electrically charged weapons to numb us. Harvesters needed us in good shape, ideally. But that didn't mean they weren't afraid of brutal force.

WHAT'S THE PLAN? I asked.

The Harvester leaned heavily onto its spear, holding the rod tightly. Okay, it was critically wounded.

KILL IT, Ruggy typed.

A howling shriek boomed before I could type anything—a new bulky humanoid burst from the flames, naked. Caws, spikes—all were colliding with the Harvester. The two humanoids tumbled onto the ground towards us, skidding to a stop. We leaped back as they came into view, rifles aimed.

PAREIDOLIA

The entangled, burnt lump of bloody limbs wrestled, each being trying to get on top of the other. I froze, staring at the Harvester, who landed with its back to the ground. The helmet was half-complete. Hardened foam caked around the damaged edges, revealing the face of the Harvester. It had blond patches of hair, most of which had scorched off the scalp. It scowled, blue eyes staring vigorously at its opponent. The Harvester's large arms shook violently, holding onto the primitive being's wrists. The second humanoid, slightly shorter, drooled with sharp jaws open. Spikes pointed upright all along the back and outer limbs. The clawed feet hooked into the thighs of the Harvester, puncturing the flesh. Reddish-green blood poured out of the wounds.

SHOOT, Ruggy ordered.

I didn't reply. I could only stare at the Harvester's eyes as it wrestled with the naked beast. Harvesters were taller than us. More perfect, you could say—more muscular, and relentless. Yet, they were once us.

An ear-shattering *clack* erupted from Ruggy's rifle. *CLACK CLACK CLACK*. He kept firing as the automatic weapon projected the bullets into the Harvester and beast. The Harvester yelped in pain, a human cry. The creature howled like a dog. It ripped its claws free from the Harvester and landed on all fours, dashing away from the scene, blood drizzling on the ground behind it.

I lifted my rifle and pulled the trigger, firing as the creature disappeared from the crash site, vanishing into The Lost.

Shit, I thought.

Ruggy shouted, "Eat it, gene freak!" as he continued to fire at the Harvester. The bullets pinged off of the remaining armour. The exposed skin was defenceless, letting the bullets pierce into the flesh. Blood splattered all around. Its eyes squinted in agony as red and green liquid oozed out of its mouth.

I turned my weapon to the Harvester and paused. No human had been this close to a Harvester before, especially in such a defenceless state. A part of me wanted to try and help the Harvester. Reason with it. Show the being that we weren't that different after all. We could create a paradigm shift between the two species. No. It had been tried before. It was a foolish idea.

NO TRACES

"He's going to spray!" Ruggy shouted.

Ruggy's words shot me out of my internal dilemma. The Harvester managed to reach for his inner bicep, fingers pressing a touch screen that lit up red.

"Go!" Ruggy said, snagging my arm.

A loud beep came from the Harvester's torn-up suit as small black holes opened all over the armour. Translucent liquid sprayed out of the suit in all directions and over the Harvester with sizzling sounds. The acid liquid came into contact with the Harvester and the ground, fizzing loudly.

We barely made it out of the vicinity. The liquid had wholly covered the Harvester, causing a chemical reaction, transforming it to foam and expanding in size. The Harvester clenched its teeth in pain as the foam ate away its armour and flesh. The foam's colour shifted into a light green as the rest of the Harvester's form was shrouded in the foam substance.

"Dammit!" Ruggy said.

I looked over at him to see that some of the liquid had gotten onto his shoulder. He tried to brush it off as it frothed.

"I think it ate through my coat. It's compressing," he said.

The foam had stopped expanding, turning a slight red—proof that it had eaten some of his flesh. "It's toughening," I said, looking at it.

"Don't get too close, kid," Ruggy said, stepping back. "Shit, it stings."

"We gotta get back to the cruiser and take care of it."

"It's not that bad. It hardened. It doesn't matter if we slice it off now or later," Ruggy said, his gaze locking onto the Harvester's consumed form.

The froth engulfed the being. Snapping sounds rose—bones being crushed by the hardened fizz that had begun to compress. Only a blob remained, in a rough humanoid pose. The surrounding ground had speckles of the foam in a light grey. Every droplet of fizz continued to compress inward, crushing the rocks—and Harvester—underneath.

"Anti-sapiens piece of shit," Ruggy said while walking towards it. "They always manage to pull off that stunt just when we get them."

"I've never seen that before. I mean, I've seen videos of it in training," I replied while walking up to Ruggy.

"Not the same, is it?"

"Not at all. We really can't cut the foam open?"

"No point. The acid eats away the surface, and the foam crushes everything else. Plus, this shit is harder than diamond once it shrinks," Ruggy said, kicking the foam on the ground. "If we could ever get our hands on even a fraction of their tech, it could change everything."

"Or understand their biology better," I replied. "They look so human."

Ruggy sighed. "Don't let their appearance fool you next time. When I say fire, fire, understand?"

"Yeah, sorry. It just threw me off. I've never seen one without their suit."

"Most don't, because they pull off that stupid self-destruct system. Remember, just because they look like a perfect us doesn't mean they are us. Their minds are all fucked up with a superiority complex and gene editing."

"Right," I said, turning to look at the fire and nearby torn metal.

"What do you think happened here?" I asked.

Ruggy shrugged. "The Harvester crashed. The question is, what the hell was it doing with that other thing?"

"I don't know. It ran away before I could do anything about it," I replied.

Ruggy walked away from the foam-caked Harvester and towards the ship's remains. "It was fast. Now it's wandering The Lost. That's something we gotta report."

"We should go back," I said.

"Not yet. Let's scope out the rest of this mess. The operator sent us here. Let's see what was going on," Ruggy said, approaching the flames.

I followed Ruggy, taking one last look at the deceased Harvester. The fizz had compressed to a solid state, roughly outlining the shape of the giant humanoid, like some sort of dried-acid statue. Never before had I been so close to a Harvester. Most people that were didn't survive. The Harvesters were too fast, too strong, and too cunning. If that thing hadn't been wounded and attacked, we would be dead. That was a guarantee. In an odd turn of events, that hostile beast was our saviour.

REVIEW

Ruggy and I walked cautiously through the rubble of the Harvester's spacecraft. There were remnants of cables and hardware on the ground, too burnt to try and sample. We continued deeper into the mess. Most of the ship had been wrecked in the crash. Plus, Harvesters had a pretty clean method of destroying their technology, like they do with themselves. Anything valuable on board, or that was part of their ship, was disintegrated.

SOME GOOD METAL HERE, Ruggy typed out.

YEAH, I'LL GET THE ROVER, I replied while navigating through the goggles' interface. My eyelids made slight movements to get to the rover's retrieval command. The interface confirmed the rover's signal.

It'd be here in no time to carry the scraps. It was always wise for Scrappers to wait till they found something of value before calling the rover. Rovers were expensive, and the one good piece of tech Scrappers got. They saved Scrappers' asses from having to haul heavy scraps. The last thing they needed was for a Harvester to destroy it.

WE MIGHT NEED THE WHOLE CRUISER AT THIS POINT, Ruggy typed out while walking around a large curved exterior section of the craft. He carefully avoided nearby flames and sharp pieces of metal that stuck out of the ground.

YEAH. LET'S JUST SEE WHAT ELSE IS HERE AND THEN WE CAN CALL THIS IN, I replied.

We stopped several times, looking to see if there was anything useful on the ground. Most of it was just strips, the type of things we'd usually gather. Regardless of the danger, we both knew that this was going to be a good scrapping session. The operator would be pleased.

CHECK THIS OUT, Ruggy typed.

I hurried up to my partner to see a human-sized glass-like pod shattered on the ground. It was probably not glass, but some Harvester equivalent. The broken pod was half-melted away and a third missing. Tubes were at the base of the cylinder shape.

"Think that beast came out of here?" I asked.

"Maybe," Ruggy said in a low tone. "Look," he added.

Several smaller pods were beside the large one. These were a little cracked but intact. Inside the pods were flesh-sacks floating in a transparent substance. The sacks were a light pink colour, but semi-transparent. Inside, small baby-like beings floated. Their eyes were closed, sleeping peacefully, undisturbed by the chaos that had just occurred.

"What are these?" I asked, leaning down.

Ruggy extended his arm out, stopping me from tilting any further. "Stay up," he ordered.

One of the small creatures wiggled, moving its tiny, undeveloped hands around in the sack. An umbilical cord was attached to the belly and connected to the top of the sack.

"These are infants," I said, standing upright.

"No, they're not, Angie," Ruggy said, pointing his rifle at the baby.

"Are you dense?" I asked. "I know what a damn baby looks like."

"Yeah, but this was a Harvester's craft," Ruggy replied.

I shook my head. "Harvesters capture people. They take us to mess with genetics. This is a damn baby!"

"They also grow their people in incubators."

"So even if it is a Harvester baby, it's a life," I argued.

"A Harvester life. Or maybe that beast we saw," Ruggy replied. "Either way, it isn't one of us."

"Ruggy, are you listening to yourself? You want to shoot these infants?"

Ruggy let go of his rifle and threw a swift hand across my face, striking me, probably turning my cheek pink. My eyes widened, feeling my flesh hum from the aftermath.

"Angie! Wake up. These are not humans!" Ruggy shouted. "They're genetic freaks. They forced their DNA away from us. They look similar, but so did the great apes, and look at how we treated them when they were around."

I swallowed a thick lump of saliva. Ruggy was trying to be a good person, but I knew he was getting frustrated. That slap was 'nice Ruggy.' 'Mean Ruggy' would have decked my ass and just done what he wanted. He was only trying to educate me.

"I know it's tough to grasp," Ruggy said. "We're living in a fucked-up world where the lines of being human are blurred. This is why we stick to the code. It's us against them. Harvesters broke all morals centuries ago when they edited their first DNA strand. Even if we saved these offspring and tried to raise them, they don't grow like us, and they don't think like us. They'll question themselves, and that is a can of worms we don't need. Now raise your damn rifle." Ruggy lifted his weapon, pointing at one of the pods.

I stared down at the second pod, looking right into the small being's soft face. It wiggled around gently in the sack, stopping until it was facing me. Its eyes flicked open. White. Nothing but a white ball inside of the eye socket. Inhuman.

We fired at the pods. The bullets shattered through the glass, ripping through the embryo sacks and shredding into the small beings. The translucent liquid poured out of the broken glass, followed by streams of reddish-green fluids.

HEADING HOME

The idea of wiping off this gunk was the one thing that kept me going. We had to get back to the cruiser if I wanted a cloth to get all the sweat and blood off me. It turned out those embryo sacks splattered good. The mix of sweat from the intense heat of the spacecraft crash added to the disgusting factor. I couldn't wait to get out of this mess and back to the cruiser.

We were Scrappers, though. It was our job to get whatever goods there were from the location the operator gave us. It was that simple. What we did today, I had a hard time grasping. We killed children. Harvester or not, they were living, conscious beings. The idea of sparing Harvesters was an unpopular opinion. I knew it. That was why I didn't say it often. In the moment, I guess I lost control of myself. Ruggy got me to focus, to remember the training, and we annihilated the infants.

After our rover arrived, we started doing what we did best—scrap. The Harvester's spacecraft had plenty of raw materials to gather. The damn gene-freaks were smart with their tech. Most of it had self-destruct functions built-in. It was unlikely we'd be collecting anything of value other than the metal.

A couple of hours of scrapping proved it true—only raw materials. Another job done. We loaded the rover and returned to the cruiser. I always found the excess humming of the machine's motor from the cargo weight soothing, since it reinforced that we were on our way home. The beast we shot left blood and footprints in the ash. It had retreated deeper into The Lost. A confusing mix of fear and curiosity

took hold of me. I wanted to know what it was, despite knowing the dangers. Maybe that was how the Harvesters eventually edited their DNA: curiosity of the unknown and fear of moral lines breaking forever. Either way, that beast wasn't our mission. We'd report the finding and get back to base. More than anything, I wanted to get out of this wasteland. The old world was unsettling. Every time we entered The Lost, I found it hard to believe that there used to be another civilization before this mess.

EN ROUTE

We marched back to the cruiser with the rover behind us, the six wheels adjusting with the shocks against the uneven surface. The cruiser was barely in view; it was probably another half hour's walk away. I held my rifle tightly, looking at all the nearby rubble. That beast was still out there. I couldn't help but wonder if it would come back. We had no idea what or where it was. The Harvesters dabbled in modifying all sorts of genetics. It could be another human for all we knew.

"We've got to get some intel as to why the operator took us out here," Ruggy said.

"Yeah. It seems odd they'd send a scrapper team out here," I replied. "A military unit might have been more useful."

"One would think. Quite frankly, I am not surprised."

"Why is that?"

"We're disposable. The military is not. They knew it was a Harvester crash site, and they wanted to get to it before the Harvesters did."

"Right, for the metal."

"And we did." Ruggy looked up to the grey-and-black sky. "Thankfully, no more showed up."

The Harvesters were usually quick to come and retrieve their deceased. Lucky for us, we got there first. In truth, we knew why the operator had sent us here. Still, it would be good to hear it from the source. Until then, we did our job and made sure we stayed alive. No one else had our backs.

Ruggy and I reached the cruiser. With a few subtle eye movements, I used my goggles' interface to open the cruiser's back hatch. The rover automatically rolled in with the scraps of metal. We went in after, letting the hatch door close with a satisfying hiss from the hydraulics. We were out of here. I took off my goggles and blinked a couple of times. My eyes burned anytime I used those damn interfaces. It didn't matter how frequently I had the goggles on; I never got used to the light beaming right in my face.

"Angie," Ruggy said, taking his goggles off, "mind starting the cruiser? I've got to take a shit."

"Yeah," I said. *Classy Ruggy*, I thought.

RELIEF

We split from the hangar bay. I made a quick stop at the storage closet to snag that small towel I'd longed for before entering the cockpit. Wiping my face of the blood and sweat was so fulfilling. I sat down in the driver's seat and flicked the machine on, feeling a wave of relief as I continued to remove that grunge from my skin. Harvester baby fluid—disgusting.

The cruiser roared to life as I gripped the steering wheel with my gloves. Now we could go home. I pressed the acceleration pedal while turning the wheel, moving the large vehicle around. The dashboard directly below the windshield lit up with a locally saved map. It was the familiar system that the goggles used that had gotten us to the crash site. The system said we were about halfway through the night. Thankfully for us, the dark offered some shielding from the Harvesters' spacecraft. Sure, they had night vision like we did, but when it came to survival, every little bit helped.

Ruggy stepped into the cockpit and sat in the shotgun seat. He pulled out a small box from his pants pocket and flicked it open, revealing numerous small white sticks.

"Are those . . . ?" I asked, glancing at him.

"Yeah, smokes. Want one?"

"Give it," I said, extending my hand.

Ruggy passed me one as he flicked a lighter, lighting my smoke first. I took a puff of the cigarette and let out a small cough . . . man, it had been a while. The taste of nicotine soothed my nerves. I needed that and a good bottle of whiskey to wash away the day.

"Where'd you get these?" I asked while puffing on the smoke.

"I know some folks at the base," Ruggy said, putting his feet up on the dashboard.

"Tobacco is hard to come by," I said, eyes on the road.

"I know, trust me. You did well today, kid. You earned it."

"Thanks." I brushed my hair aside, exposing my ear. "That wasn't easy."

"I know," Ruggy said. "That's why I said you did well."

"What do you think the operator will have to say about this?"

"Not much. They never do. Operators just run it up the pipeline, and it will be delegated to the 'right' department. That's how these things work."

"Truthfully, I am a little pissed that they had us go all the way out here."

"Get over it. It will happen again. We're replaceable."

I tightened my one hand on the steering wheel. Ruggy's bluntness annoyed me. He didn't seem to mind that we were just numbers when it came to the higher-ups. But we had more value than that. I knew we did. If it weren't for us, humanity wouldn't have any raw materials to work with.

THE CALL

"Speaking of," Ruggy said, flinging his feet off the dashboard. "Let's call this in." He reached for the touch screen in the middle of the dashboard and navigated through the system's interface. The speakers rang, then clicked.

"This is operator 43-S3. Unit S-89, do you reply?" came the operator's distorted voice.

"Hey, operator," Ruggy said.

"S-89, have you reached the assigned location?" the operator asked.

"Done and scrapped. We're on our way back."

Several seconds of silence passed. "What did you call for then?"

"About that scrap. Did you know it was a Harvester crash site?"

More silence.

"You had us rush out here in the middle of the night—" Ruggy persisted.

"We'll want a full report on your findings when you return to base," the operator said.

"Yeah, I get that. That's protocol. But I think we should chat with someone about what we saw."

Silence.

"Hello?" Ruggy asked.

The cruiser made several beeping noises. A red dot appeared on the dashboard's map. That was never a good sign. Someone else was in the area. The question was, who? From the details on the map, the cruiser's sensors detected the motion was above ground. Aerial. Another spacecraft.

"Operator 43-S3, are there any ships in the area?" I asked.

"Don't bother, kid," Ruggy said. "If those were our ships, we'd know." Ruggy pressed the touch screen, cutting the communication with the operator. He flicked some additional switches that shut off the exterior lights. I brought the cruiser to a halt and turned off the engine; this was protocol. Unidentified spacecrafts meant only one thing: Harvesters. We couldn't have this cruiser radiating transmission signals and lights. I watched the map fade out, the red dot getting closer, as the cruiser turned off, leaving us in the dark with nowhere to go.

"This thing doesn't use any global positioning," I said. "How did it find us?"

"No, the maps are local," Ruggy said, eyeing the sky. He puffed on his smoke. "Looks like the Harvesters came for their crashed ship after all."

I inhaled the cigarette while looking out the windshield: dirt, ruins, and a dark sky. There was no sign of anything. The cloudy night sky was working against us. We remained silent, both watching in anticipation. The Harvesters had to be near. The cruiser's sensors were pretty accurate, and we had poorly timed calling the operator. Chances were that they detected the frequency of the transmission.

VISITORS

&&There," Ruggy said. A humming sound rose as lights appeared in the sky, piercing through the clouds, projecting onto the ground below. The beam moved through the ruined landscape, moving onto various cracks and sheltered areas.

"They're looking for something," I said.

"Yeah, us," Ruggy said.

A smaller blue light came down from the blaring light. A craft came out of the clouds and descended to the ground on the other side of a hill. It was probably a good hundred paces away. The dark made it tough to see the details of the craft. There were only bright lights.

"We can't stay here," Ruggy said.

"We can't turn the engine on," I argued. "They'll see us."

Ruggy nodded. "That leaves us with one option."

"No," I said, already knowing.

"We've got to abandon the cruiser."

My heart sunk. We were floating corpses at this point. Without the cruiser, we also had no way of getting home. We'd be stuck in The Lost.

"Grab the survival packs. Don't waste any time," Ruggy said, extinguishing his smoke. He got up from his seat and hurried out of the cockpit.

I stared at the distant lights, seeing smaller purple glows trickling out of the landed craft: Harvesters holding glowing pulse cannons. They were on foot. There was no way we'd be able to fight them. Running was our only hope. I took one last inhale from my smoke, possibly my last ever, and dropped it to the floor, stepping on the drag. It was time to act.

Ruggy and I gathered all the supplies we could into emergency backpacks and met up in the hangar bay. We swung the packs over our shoulders, strapped on the goggles, got our rifles in hand, and buckled our ammunition belts—showtime.

"We can come back," Ruggy said.

"Presuming the Harvesters don't blow the cruiser up."

A loud thump came from on top of the vehicle. It was directly above us. We froze. A moment passed. Another thump. Then a roar. Something was on the roof outside.

VISITOR

"That ain't no Harvester," Ruggy said, lifting his rifle.

"That thing, from the crash site," I said.

Scratching and pounding picked up. The tearing of metal reverberated throughout the cruiser. The beast was attempting to break in. Just what we needed.

"We can sneak out the side," Ruggy said, leaving the hangar bay.

I followed him, keeping my rifle low. The tearing of metal amplified as a loud clang erupted. A howling roar echoed in the hangar bay, followed by a thud. The beast landed inside. Ruggy and I picked up our pace, closing the hall door in the process, hopefully buying us some time. We reached the side exit near the cockpit. Ruggy began to punch in the emergency pin to open the door. With the cruiser entirely off, we had no way of communicating with it from our goggles interfaces. Everything was manual.

Thumping erupted from the hall. It was closing in. I looked back;

there, behind the small circular window of the hall door, the muscular beast from the crash site stood on its hind legs, looking like a swollen, muscular humanoid. The black-and-red spikes on its back erected as the drooling mouth opened, exposing the sharp teeth. It let out a roar, slamming its clawed hand into the glass. It shattered, pushing the door forward with it.

"Ruggy!" I shouted.

Ruggy finished punching the pin into the door's lock, and the door lifted. We rushed out of the cruiser as Ruggy turned around, punching the button the lock the door, letting it swing back down as stomping came from inside. *It* had broken through the hall. The side door locked shut as the beast's feet appeared, its body slamming into the side of the cruiser, roaring. The whole vehicle wobbled. I'd never seen anything shake a cruiser. I couldn't fathom the strength of that beast.

"Damn manual override," Ruggy said. He glanced around while placing his goggles over his head. I did the same, letting the night vision come to life. We could now see the purple lights off in the distance. The Harvesters were on their way.

BRINGING THE FIGHT

*W*E DON'T HAVE A LOT OF TIME, Ruggy communicated through the goggles' chat window. *THAT THING IS GOING TO BREAK OUT. COME ON.*

I used subtle eye movement to type back, *WHERE?*

Thumping and scratching came from inside the cruiser. The beast was shredding through the metal. Ruggy and I jogged towards the Harvester lights.

RUGGY, THIS IS SUICIDE! I typed.

Ruggy turned to face me. *HARVESTERS ARE ON TO US. THEY'LL CATCH UP. THEY'RE FASTER THAN US.*

WE CAN'T FIGHT THEM. YOU KNOW THAT.

OUR BEST BET IS TO LURE THAT THING TO THEM. WE'LL GIVE

THEM A TASTE OF THEIR OWN MEDICINE. THAT THING WILL FUCK THEM UP.

I swallowed heavily. Ruggy was right. The man knew how to improvise. He'd gotten himself out of difficult situations before. Seeing the dilemma we were in, I had no choice but to follow him. This was for our survival. We'd bring the fight to the Harvesters. Give that failed experiment back to them.

CLASH

Fear nearly demoralized me, as I struggled to grasp that this scenario was real. I wasn't trained for this, and neither was Ruggy! He didn't care, though. The hothead wanted to bring the brawl to the Harvesters. I knew he was right—wrangling the beast was our best bet. What other options did we have? Those damn gene-freaks were marching for us. Chances were they knew our location way before we knew theirs. That was what they did. They were faster, more advanced, and less compassionate. They were the bigger fish.

THWUMP! A desperate pounding came from our cruiser, and the whole vehicle wobbled. The beast was soon to break free. Ruggy's crazy plan better work. We couldn't outrun them. We couldn't hide from them. The only advantage we had was that abomination.

ANGIE, THIS WAY, came Ruggy's message.

I stayed close to my partner, hiding behind a boulder. Our night vision from the goggles let us see clearly in the shadowed rocks that shielded us from both threats. Razor-sharp claws peeled the cruiser door open. The beast sprung out into The Lost, charging into the open space on all fours, like some enraged great ape. The Harvesters held their electro-spears, letting them hum with power. The gunmetal chrome suits shined against the light of their weapons. High-frequency clicking noises erupted from the outfits. These were the Harvesters I was used to. That Harvester at the crash site had been a rarity. They were never vulnerable. They were only killers.

GET READY TO FIRE AT THE BASTARDS, Ruggy typed. *THAT BEAST IS CLOSING IN FAST.*

I watched the Harvesters as Ruggy eyed the beast. We were on our own—game time. Sweat poured down my face as I watched the four Harvesters march up the hill. The clicking began to ring in my ear. Their suits' frequencies were always just too high for us humans to handle. They were too close. There was nowhere for us to turn, either. We were backed into a corner. The only way out was to dash at the opportune moment. This plan needed to work.

The beast bellowed, leaping into the air, claws extended. The Harvesters were a good two dozen paces away from us. They raised their spears in defensive stances, ready for the soaring abomination. One Harvester typed something into its wrist, causing the suit to open several holes around its wrist and up the forearm. Pitch-black tentacles slithered out of the holes and up towards the beast. They reached the creature in a blink of an eye, coiling in midair. The beast hacked at the tentacles, slicing some of them apart. A couple of them wrapped around its limbs. Another grabbed the neck, immobilizing the beast in mid-air.

SHIT, LET'S GO! Ruggy typed, sprinting from the hideout.

NEW PLAN

There was no time to ponder. I joined Ruggy, rushing from the spot back up to the cruiser. Glancing back, I saw the Harvesters were stabbing the beast, still in mid-air, with their electro-spears. Each penetration sent a charge pulsating through the creature's body. It groaned in agony and fell limp. The clicking sounds increased in speed.

I THINK THEY'RE ON TO US, I typed out.

Ruggy didn't reply. We ran. Now, I couldn't look back. I didn't want to lose track of Ruggy. Thumping picked up behind us as the clicking continued. They couldn't be far behind. We could only run deeper into

The Lost, ducking underneath a metal bar. I mimicked every jump, turn, and crouch Ruggy made to avoid obstacles. Our best bet was to use the terrain to shake these bastards loose. We skidded on a decline, reaching a cavern near the bottom. Or maybe it was a building. It was clearly human-made at one point in time, based on the concrete and metal frame.

We hurried through the hallway. Large rocks had fallen over, causing the ceiling to cave in. Moss and boulders covered the interior of the cavern. The small entrance would give the Harvesters a hell of a time getting in. Ruggy made a sharp turn left and all clicking dissipated. The humid cavern evolved into an old building as we ventured deeper, the plant life lessening. Parts of the floor were destroyed, showing deeper levels below. We carefully avoided falling, stepping around into the next room.

WAIT, Ruggy typed, holding out his hand. There was a window in the next room.

I SAW ANOTHER WAY, I typed out.

GO.

I took the lead, guiding us back to a split in the hallway. Each step we made kicked up dust, disrupting our view. I tried not to breathe in too intensely. The air was stale, and particles fell softly to the ground. We probably kicked those up as we jogged in. I did my best not to cough. We couldn't make any sound, for the Harvesters couldn't be far behind. We followed an incline. Small holes throughout the building let light in.

WE DON'T WANT TO GO UP, Ruggy typed. *WINDOWS.*

WHAT THEN? I asked.

WE SHOULD GO DOWN, Ruggy typed.

THAT'S THE BUILDING'S FOUNDATION. WE'D BE TRAPPED.

MAYBE. MAYBE NOT. THERE ARE TUNNELS ALL OVER THE LOST.

A loud crash came from behind us. Then the kicking of rocks. Fast rattling sounds. The Harvesters.

WE DON'T HAVE A CHOICE, I typed.

NEXT DROP WE'RE TAKING.

There was no time to argue. We had to keep moving as the thumping rose. It was distant, but it grew louder. I hopped over metal wires, rocks, and other rubble. We passed a corridor to a well-preserved hallway. Never had I run this fast before. I panted; my legs felt like delicate twigs, ready to snap at any moment. Our steps echoed. The air was thick, making me lightheaded, and yet I couldn't stop, for there were no breaks. The light-holes were less frequent as we travelled deeper, a clear sign we were making progress downward.

ONCE THE SAME

Crashes erupted from behind us. The corridor crumbled as a herculean, gunmetal being charged towards us. The Harvester kept its head low to avoid the ceiling as it stormed forward.

SPLIT, Ruggy typed as he dashed into a side room. *I GOT LEFT*.

I took the next right turn I could, leading straight to a large pile of rubble blocking the path.

"No, no, no," I whined. I spun around a couple of times. The ceiling had no gaps to hop up to. The clicking and footsteps amplified. The rubble in front had a small opening below. I could make it. I had to.

I chucked my gun underneath, letting it skid to the other side—my turn. I took a step back and dashed for the gap, falling onto my side and sliding on the dirty tiles. I stopped about halfway through and pushed with my legs for the remainder of the way.

A large hand slammed down as I lifted my foot, missing by a fraction. I got to my feet, snagging my rifle as a hand reached through the gap, attempting to grab anything it encountered. After several pats, the hand slid back. Through the smaller cracks in the rubble, I watched the Harvester stand upright, slightly hunching, in its full seamless suit. Small circuitry, or neurons, in a liquid substance, was just below a translucent layer of the suit, pulsating. The gunmetal texture was just below this outer later. The head stared at me through one of the higher openings. The unsettling part about the Harvester was that there were no eyes. No breathing holes. Only the shiny seamless suit with its complex outer membrane.

I twitched my eye, shutting off the night vision of the goggles to get a naked look at what humanity had become. The moment held as the Harvester stared at me in the poorly lit hall. The clicking stopped.

"Why?" I asked. I wasn't even sure what made me speak. It was kind of a stupid thing to say. This was a Harvester, a gene-freak of another world. They'd left us to die on this rotting planet. They'd decided that they were better than us and would let humanity rot.

MAYBE NOT

The Harvester's head tilted. Breathing calmly, it punched the rubble, causing dust to fall. The sound startled me, but I remained still. If I ever made it out of this, it would be one hell of a story to tell back at base. Now, I was even closer to a Harvester than at the crash site—all on the same scrapping mission. The key was I had to get out of here to brag about it.

A humming came from the suit as small holes appeared on the being's face.

"No," I mumbled, taking a step back.

Black leathery tentacles wiggled their way out of the holes, heading for me. Great. I roared, pulling the trigger on my rifle and firing at the approaching appendages, stepping backward. The gun clacked. Shells hit the ground. Bullets pinged off the Harvester's face. It didn't flinch. The tentacles closed in. I directed my aim. Some bullets shredded through the black things, causing them to fall to the ground, oozing translucent liquid.

They didn't stop as their torn halves wormed forward. This was pointless—It was time to run. I spun around, sprinting down the hall. The Harvester slammed its fist against the rubble several times, sending shards flying. High-pitched clicking erupted like a sputtering engine.

RUGGY, WHERE ARE YOU? I typed.

I took a left turn in a T-intersection and hurried lower into the building. All light vanished. The deeper I went, the more the Harvester's sounds faded. Perhaps the large being couldn't make it through the rubble—a streak of luck. I could only pray to anything listening that this was the end of it. I navigated through my goggles' interface to turn on the night vision.

ANGIE, came Ruggy's text. *WHERE ARE YOU? DON'T SHARE YOUR LOCATION, JUST TELL ME.*

I KNOW THAT. I'M NOT A ROOKIE, I typed back. *I'M FINE. I THINK. WHAT ABOUT YOU?*

I GOT AWAY. I HEARD IT GO AFTER YOU. THEN THE FIRES. WHAT HAPPENED?

IT TRIED TO GET ME, BUT I SNUCK THROUGH SOME DEBRIS. THE FATASS COULDN'T FIT.

YOU LUCKY GIRL, Ruggy typed.

NO SHIT. WHAT'S THE PLAN? YOU IN A SAFE SPOT? I respond.

THERE'S NO WINDOWS HERE. I WENT DEEPER, BELOW GROUND. IT'S COLD, BUT SILENT.

GOOD, I typed, feeling relief as I approached a small turnoff. Maybe it had been a closet at some point in time. Either way, now it was as good a hideout as any.

YOU? Ruggy typed.

IT'S DARK; I HONESTLY DON'T KNOW. I THINK I DITCHED IT, THOUGH, I typed, sliding down to the ground.

ALL RIGHT. WE'LL WAIT IT OUT. KEEP STATUS UPDATES. ANYTHING WEIRD, YOU SHARE, OKAY?

CONFIRMED, I replied.

WE GOT THIS, KID :-), Ruggy typed.

I lowered my weapon with a sigh. We were both safe. Separated, but we'd get out of here. Harvesters had been known to give up on a hunt before. They had better things to do with their time than wait around for a couple of humans.

ONE LAST ATTEMPT

A light touch grazed on my calf, causing me to jump. I spun to face the wall, rifle pointed. Nothing. The sensation moved upward, pricking. I reacted, dropping my gun in a spasm. I twisted my leg. There, on my calf, a black remnant of the tentacle inched its way up me. I squealed, covering my mouth. No sound was my friend. Several deep breaths calmed me down as I watched the thing crawl up my leg. A sharp rock was on the floor. That'd do.

I leaned down gradually, keeping my eye on the wiggler. My hand reached for the rock, carefully avoiding sudden movement. I snagged the sharp stone and lifted it at the thing, ready to sideswipe. One deep breath in, and I swung. The rock slapped the wiggler, knocking it off my leg. It fell onto the floor and squirmed. I landed on my knees as I pushed the stone onto the tentacle, crushing it. That wasn't enough. I raised the rock and continued to smash the wiggler until it was a flat disk, squirting transparent liquid everywhere. Some chunks of it rose from the mess, trying to move.

"Die!" I said through my teeth, slamming the rock down several more times, ending the final blow with a twist. I paused, waiting for it to make another move. It didn't. I had won. Finally, the hunt was over. Now Ruggy and I would wait this out. We'd get out of here.

THE WAIT

Time became an abstract concept. I wasn't sure if I stayed in the abandoned wreckage for hours or days. I preferred it that way. It would be easy enough to turn on the time stamp in the chat thread Ruggy and I had open. But I didn't want to. Watching those numbers go by every moment would be discouraging. We knew that the Harvesters would give up on the hunt eventually. The challenge was knowing when. It wasn't like they were on a stopwatch. The two of us could stay in the dark for days if we wanted. Or we could attempt to return to The Lost, risking our lives, for the Harvesters could be waiting right outside. I was comfortable waiting longer. What was the rush? No one would miss two Scrappers back at base.

The harsh reality was that Ruggy and I weren't anyone special and we would never be. Scrappers were disposable, which was hard to believe, considering the diminishing human population. The higher-ups didn't care. We served a purpose in this new world by gathering the remnants of the old for those deemed better than us.

As the hours—or days—passed, I kept thinking back to the operator that brought us here, operator 43-S3. I'd never met him. Ruggy said he did once, and the guy was a typical computer geek—fast-talking with poor posture. We needed folks like him, though. I just didn't get why he would send us out to a death trap. Operator 43-S3 had known that he was leading us to a Harvester's crash site. Maybe he was taking orders from someone above. Perhaps he thought we were disposable and only wanted the goods from the crash site so he could be rewarded for his discovery. Who knew? We'd get some answers when we got back to base, eventually.

THINK IT IS SAFE THHO GO NOW? I typed with swift eye movements, controlling my goggles' interface. My eye twitched unintentionally, making the typo. The stress and exhaustion were catching up with me.

NAH, Ruggy replied. *WE'D BEST WAIT ANOTHER DAY JUST TO BE SURE.*

A DAY? HOW LONG HAVE WE BEEN IN HERE? I instantly regretted asking the question, knowing that an answer would tell me exactly how long we'd been sitting in the dark.

A COUPLE OF DAYS, Ruggy typed. *I HAVE ENOUGH CAPSULES TO LAST A WEEK. YOU?*

SAME. THE SURVIVAL KIT WAS FULL WHEN I GRABBED IT.

A couple of days. My mind could barely wrap around the fact that I had been sitting in the same spot for that long. The night vision from the goggles made the dark more bearable—barely. Plus, it was warmer down here than on the surface. I kept staring at the Harvester's crushed tentacle. I knew it was destroyed, but I couldn't help wondering if it would pop back up and attack me. Or perhaps it was like a beacon signal for the Harvesters, and they would come for me. It was nonsense. I knew that wasn't going to happen. If it were true, the Harvesters would have come for me by now. Either way, it hadn't helped me get any sleep.

IF WE'RE GOING TO STAY HERE ANOTHER DAY, HOW ABOUT WE MEET UP? I typed.

WE'VE BEEN THROUGH THIS. THE FEWER MOVEMENTS, THE BETTER.

IF THEY CAN SCAN THE LANDSCAPE, CAN'T THEY DETECT HEAT ANYWAY? THIS IS POINTLESS.

WE DON'T KNOW WHAT TYPE OF TECH THE HARVESTERS HAVE, Ruggy typed. *WE CAN ONLY MAKE EDUCATED GUESSES. THE WHOLE POINT IS TO SURVIVE THIS ORDEAL.*

I WANT TO GIVE THAT OPERATOR A PIECE OF MY MIND, I replied.

TRUST ME, SO DO I, Ruggy typed. *THAT RAT KNEW WHAT HE WAS DOING WHEN HE SENT US TO THE HARVESTER'S CRASH SITE. I WANT TO KNOW WHAT WAS IN IT FOR HIM.*

Ruggy and I exchanged some messages back and forth a few times. Other than that, we didn't have much to say to one another. We'd scrapped long enough that we knew each other well—no point in small talk. Most of my time was spent evaluating the digital map in my goggles' interface to try and guess where I was and where he was. The maps were from the old world. We didn't have any satellites to map out The Lost, so I could only guess where I was. Based on the map, it had been some skyscraper at one point in time, collapsed during humanity's split.

EXPLORATION

I was careful not to overuse my goggles' battery life. I couldn't spend days just browsing around the maps and local documents. These things were high tech for humans but lacked the otherworldly wonders that the Harvesters had. So, I eventually did get up from my location and wandered the halls. Ruggy didn't need to know. If he wanted us to wait another day, I needed to get a better sense of my environment. His reasoning about the scanning tech that the Harvesters had was stupid, anyway.

The night vision goggles let me navigate through the crooked, uneven hallways. No light was visible, making it safe to say I was underground. Some of the halls had intact doorways, so I could enter. I walked into a room, avoiding the walls and rocks. The last thing I needed was to make some noise and alert a Harvester, or break something and have the ceiling collapse.

The room was mostly the same as the hallway. It did have some snapped planks of wood, some garbage, and something that was once clothing—I think. Anything we found in The Lost was usually a wreck due to past fires, falling rocks, or deterioration, rendering it useless.

I left the room. There was nothing of value there. The hallways led farther into the unknown, but I didn't want to go too far from my location. All I wanted was to get a better sense of my environment. Everywhere here was as dead as the closet.

MEETING POINT

The wait finally ended when Ruggy texted, *OKAY, LET'S GET THE HELL OUT OF HERE.* Relief. We'd finally be getting out of this dungeon.

WHERE SHOULD WE MEET? I asked.

YOU REMEMBER WHERE WE SPLIT? SEE IF WE CAN MEET UP THERE, Ruggy typed.

IF WE DON'T MEET THERE?

WE'LL FIND EACH OTHER ON THE SURFACE.

Ruggy's order sealed the deal. We could return to The Lost. A second thought entered my mind—what if the Harvesters never left? They had probes. They could be waiting for us to tire out and leave our hideouts. We had no way of knowing. I knew Ruggy must have finally gotten sick of sitting around like me. It was time to face our fate.

I retraced the steps that led me to the dark hideout I'd stayed in all those days. The mouldy, musty smell was beyond irritating. Retracing my path wasn't difficult. The collapsed rubble that separated me and the Harvester was precisely where I remembered it being. This time, there was no Harvester. I slid my gun through the slit and then moved under to the other side. I eyed the opposite side of the hallway, eyes glued to the opposing room—the one Ruggy had entered. He was nowhere to be seen.

RUGGY, I'M BACK, I typed.

I COULDN'T FIND HOW I GOT HERE, Ruggy replied. *I THINK I'M GETTING CLOSE TO THE SURFACE, THOUGH.*

COORDS? I asked.

-22.951470, -43.212165

That was something useful. We'd meet up back on the surface. With the new plan in mind, I backtracked to whence Ruggy and I first entered the cavern. It was easy enough; I was not sure how Ruggy was having a difficult time. But it didn't matter. We'd get out of here, get to the cruiser, and give that operator a piece of our mind back at base.

The closer I got to the cavern entrance, the brighter the light grew. The old-world architecture was replaced with rocks, plants, and rubble—the aftermath of conflict. A part of me wanted to explore further in the cavern and discover artifacts down there, but what for? Our history was mostly archived in digital storage. Anything else took up space, and I didn't need to haul that around.

I found the cavern entrance and hiked out into The Lost. Despite the clouded atmosphere, some light made it through to the planet's surface. It was daytime. I shut off the night vision of my goggles and scanned the terrain. There were no signs of the Harvester ground troops and no sign of their ship.

IT'S ALL CLEAR HERE, RUGGY, I typed while walking towards the coordinates he provided.

GOOD, SEEMS CLEAR HERE TOO, Ruggy replied. *I'M ALMOST AT RENDEZVOUS.*

CATTLE

We had beat the Harvesters at their own game. Sure, we may have wrecked our cruiser in the process from our encounter with that beast, but we'd survived. No one survives the Harvesters.

WE HAVE SOME BRAGGING RIGHTS HERE WHEN WE GET BACK TO BASE, I typed.

The coordinates Ruggy supplied weren't far. Reaching them took no time at all. The area was an open patch of rubble. Nearby rocks and collapsed towers were a good several dozen paces away. This had to be some sort of park, based on the goggles' old-world map.

RUGGY? I typed, looking around the area. The wind blew past me, lifting dust into my face. No one. There didn't seem to be any cavern entrances nearby, either.

RUGGY, DID YOU MESS UP THE COORDINATES? I'M OUT IN THE OPEN.

No reply. Something wasn't right. My instincts told me to get the hell out, yet Ruggy ordered me to come here.

RUGGY, I'M MOVING, I typed.

STAY, Ruggy typed.

WHERE ARE YOU? I replied.

Still alarmed, I took my first step back as a humanoid morphed into the space. The massive being's form rippled from thin air and into full view. The gunmetal armour shined in the daylight as high-pitched clicking began to project from the being.

"Shit! Ruggy!" I called out, pulling my rifle's trigger. The gun clacked, firing bullets at the Harvester walking towards me.

STAY, ALLY, Ruggy typed.

RUGGY, WHERE ARE YO— I stopped typing. *Ally?* I thought, firing at the approaching Harvester. Clarity of the mind made my stomach invert, realizing that I hadn't been talking to Ruggy at all. Maybe at one point I had been. I didn't know. The Harvesters had hacked our communication port. It was supposed to be a closed-off network. But clearly it wasn't.

The bullets pinged off the Harvester's suit as it marched. The clicking sound changed tempo in a wave motion, moving faster and slower. I continued to back up in the open space. Glancing back, I saw I could make a run for it. I had to try. Guns were pointless. I sprinted from my battle stance, dashing as fast as I could.

Footsteps thudded. The Harvester picked up its pace. *CL-I-I-I-I-CK. CL-I-I-ICK. CLICK. CLICK. CLICK. CL-I-I-I-ICK.*

RUGGY, ANSWER ME, I typed. I wasn't sure if he'd get the message. The Harvesters were always one step ahead of us. I had to try. There was no other way of communicating with him.

ALLY, COME HERE, the Harvester typed.

"Ruggy!" I cried out as a large hand snagged my arm, spinning me around.

I pulled the trigger of my rifle, trying to do anything to save my skin. The bullets pinged off the armour. The Harvester swatted the weapon clean from my hand, knocking it to the ground. It snatched my neck as a spear rose from a small opening in the Harvester's palm. The weapon expanded into its full form as it sparked to life, humming. An electro-spear.

The Harvester plunged the weapon into my gut, causing my whole body to tense up. The shock erupted through my chest and into every limb of my body. The pulsation hit my head and travelled through the goggles, frying them. The interface was gone. My head spun. I had lost all control. I could see . . . no. My vision was blurry. I could hear . . . a little. I felt . . . nothing. Numbness.

My captor chucked me to the ground as two more Harvesters rippled into view from thin air. The high-frequency clicking multiplied as the beings stared at me. I tried to fight the electrical current that numbed my body. I had to. No one else was going to get me out of this. I couldn't.

The muscles didn't respond to the stress of the situation. The release of control provided an odd sense of calmness as my captor dumped my body into a large steel crate. Holes horizontally lined the container walls. These were air holes to let me breathe. I could hear groans other than my own. The smell of sweat and dirt filled the space. Other humans were in the cage with me. We were cattle, harvested.

10

An animal in a cage. Numbed. Confinement forces one to witness. The observer is only able to watch and never interact. A power that separates one from suffering also separates them from joy. Neutrality. Calm. The state of an observer can only last if they do not invest in the flesh. You know this, for the grim fate of the Scrapper locked in darkness makes an easy transition for you to leave the observer state. As her reality fades, yours become real until control of your body returns. You are you once more, in the Midway with the strange ghoul who guides you in discovering your lost past.

"Welcome back," Malpherities says. His doubled voice echoes in the cavern, the sound complemented by the black droplets falling from the stalactites and into the golden bowl.

You rub your head and pat your gut. The electro-spear had felt so real. You briefly forget that it happened to Angie and not you. "What happened? I was . . . " you say. "I'm having trouble disconnecting from the observations. It was like it was me."

"That happens when you're a witness to another's life for too long. Their senses, thoughts, and experiences can intertwine into your own. Did you notice anything familiar?"

"I think this was like one of the earlier observations. Cattle . . . Harvesters . . . there's a real conflict with humankind in the future."

"*Future* is an interesting choice of words," Malpherities says. "But yes. Things were, or become, quite dark."

"Hey, yeah!" you say with excitement. "I said *future*. Now we're getting somewhere."

"Let's send you back a bit," Malpherities says, dipping his claw into the bowl. "We'll see if we can find the exact moment in time when you existed. Not in the nineties and not centuries beyond that; perhaps somewhere in between." He leans over you and taps his claw as you embrace the next observation.

BEHIND YOU

PARANOIA

I used to enjoy life. Outside has so many wonders to see. The world is much larger than most people give it credit for. Sure, the Internet has drastically made things smaller by connecting people around the globe. The Earth itself, however, is astronomical in size. Anyway, exploring outside is something all of us do as kids. I know I did. Not so much now. My mom and dad wouldn't let me go too far from the house. They always said the streets were dangerous. As a small child, I didn't understand why. It looked like a pretty safe neighbourhood from what I saw inside.

Now I understand why my mom would get mad at me if I gazed outside for too long. Or if I wandered too far away from my parents without supervision. Mom said there were ugly people in the world. She said there were horrors out there. I believe her now. There's a certain level of bliss that you have in your youth. The innocence overlooks the terrible ones watching in the shadows, in the cracks, or peeking around the corner. What was that saying again? Oh yes, the devil is in the details.

Over the years, Mom and Dad began to grow tired. Maybe they let their guard down, or perhaps they decided that there was no point in fighting the inevitable—the impending doom. *They* are always watching. You might not know exactly where they are, but I guarantee they aren't far behind you. You know that feeling of someone watching, but you're alone? It's them. Whether you're at home, or on the sidewalk, or in the grocery store, it doesn't matter—they are there, always. It's that tingling feeling on the back of your neck or when your hearing thumps just a little harder for a brief moment. Your body is picking up the most subtle of details. The extrasensory perception, I believe. Then, when you turn to look, you see nothing. I've dubbed them the Lightless Ones. We'll get to the definition in a moment.

Most of us just write these experiences off as being paranoid, or that we're just tired. That's easy to do. Just say it's your delusions that are confusing you. We're all a little crazy, some more than others. I sometimes wonder if I am the craziest of them all. The Lightless Ones started watching me from a young age, I know that much. I don't exactly know what they want, even to this day, a couple of decades on. I'm not the only one aware of them. Conspiracy theorists, crack monkeys, delusional fools, pick your title—they know about the Lightless Ones. They are willing to admit there is something more to that feeling, that sensation of something being near. The Lightless Ones are behind you. I know it. Now you know it.

FIRST SIGHTING

My experiences with the Lightless Ones all started when I was in my senior year of high school. I took the same path as I always did after school across the football field to the bus stop. In that field, I saw a man walking on the outside of the fence of the school property out of the corner of my eye. For all I knew, it could've been a strand of my long hair that got in my face. The day was windy. Yet the blotch seemed to walk with me. As I got closer to the edge of the school property, he was still there. I could easily distinguish limbs in a walking motion. This man was as black as my hair—hence the name 'Lightless Ones.' I stopped and looked directly at him, but he vanished. It was as if the man had never been there. I spun around a couple of times, trying to see where he went. I couldn't find him. Weird. At the time, I concluded that my head was playing tricks on me.

The wind-hair theory only lasted a week. More subtle signs started showing up. In the classroom, I could see someone watching from the small window on the closed door that led into the hallway. Just like in the field, I could see them from the corner of my eye. When I looked, the person was gone. Apparently, I was 'daydreaming,' as my math teacher put it. He said I should focus more on my grades. I truly tried. The Lightless Ones kept distracting me. I don't think their goal was to have me fail high school, because I eventually graduated. I didn't have any remarkable scores, though. At least I finished.

GOODBYE, FAMILY

Dad was the first to die. A heart attack. None of the neighbours seemed to care while my mom wailed in pain from the discovery of her husband dead on the kitchen floor—poor Mom. We had a funeral. A few relatives came by, but that was it. A lot of people began to distance themselves from us as I got older. I didn't have a lot of friends in high school, either. There was Scratchy Jim and Hot Jane. I did have a thing for Hot Jane. I don't think she knew since she was too busy ogling over the pretty boys. My acne-infused face probably wasn't much of a turn-on. Scratchy Jim and Hot Jane tried to keep me distracted from the death of my father. It worked for a while until my mom took her own life. I'll always remember the silhouette of her hanging from the ceiling in the garage. That silhouette, a human shape, all black, just like the Lightless Ones . . . always at the corner of my eye.

Mom left a suicide note. It talked about them, the Lightless Ones— the silhouettes. The whole letter was about five-and-a-half pages long.

Most of her words sounded like ramblings, probably because of the empty bottle of Jameson's on the floor beside her hanging body. I still have that last note to me. She mentioned that she saw *them* all the time. It was why she wanted to keep me safe indoors. That explained the homeschooling for most of my life. My dad convinced her to let me go to high school. He believed it was good for me to interact with other kids. Mom was too scared, and now I know why. In the note, she mentioned that the Lightless Ones had spooked my father, causing the heart attack. My mom was tired of fighting them and gave up. She apologized greatly in the note and said how much she loved me. Yeah . . . she loved me so much that she left me to deal with *them* on my own.

My parents' deaths were only a couple of months apart. Mom's was at about the year mark after my graduation. I inherited the house and all of their possessions. Technically, I was an adult now, so I was on my own. I had considered postsecondary education but was too depressed after their passing. I continued working at the grocery store down the road, taking the same route there five days a week through the neighbourhood, passing the local bar and an apartment complex.

Mom and Dad were gone. I had a home. High school was over. That was when I started to see the Lightless Ones more frequently—that tingling sensation. I swear my ears twitched anytime I heard a rattling sound. I can't make my ears move; they did that on their own. I would frantically spin around, trying to see where the noise was coming from. People would watch me, thinking I was crazy. At first, I felt ashamed, until I realized that not all of them were normies watching a delusional freak spaz out. These others, they were familiars of the Lightless Ones. I knew it, because they wouldn't stop looking at me. No normal person does that. Either way, all eyes were on me, especially when I was shouting at the Lightless Ones.

GOODBYE, FRIENDS

I tried to tell Scratchy Jim and Hot Jane. Scratchy Jim was a little more open to hearing my story. He'd say he was there for me in that distinctive raspy voice of his. Hot Jane wasn't so accommodating. She had a stud for her boyfriend and was accepted into university the next province over. The day I confessed to seeing the Lightless Ones was the last time I physically saw Hot Jane. I miss those freckles. She moved with her boyfriend and started her new life. She had no reason to keep Scratchy Jim or me around. Despite the Internet making the world feel small, Hot Jane had vanished entirely. The world is a big place. You can still disappear. It makes me wonder if she felt sorry for me in high school—if she was ever really my friend. Scratchy Jim stayed around, at least for a little while. He was one of those guys that liked to experiment with drugs of all kinds. It started with snorting prescription pills, smoking weed, doing speed, and eventually heading down smack road. That was when he began to dissociate himself. He would hang around those heroin dens. I tried to visit him, but he wasn't exactly there. During my last visit with him, I spotted a Lightless One in the den and freaked out—sorry, Scratchy Jim.

With Hot Jane gone, and Scratchy Jim chasing the golden dragon, I didn't have a lot of other people to talk to. I still don't. My coworkers at the grocery store were either old people or had lives of their own. A lot of the other kids from high school had now graduated from postsecondary or moved away. They wouldn't want to hang out with someone like me.

My walks to and from work became more stressful. The Lightless Ones weren't just at the corner of my eye anymore. I could see them walking right past me. They showed up more often late at night. On my way home from work, I'd think it was a person in the dark until I got close enough to realize that light didn't illuminate their forms. They were pitch black. I'd hurry to the other side of the street, eventually passing them. It worked a couple of times, and I began to wonder if they were simply ghosts or something co-existing in our world.

The theory seemed plausible for a few days. Then, for the first time, a Lightless One turned and began following me. It was fast. They'd hit things, like street signs, sending loud crashes or bangs echoing in the street. I would run down the middle of the road, keeping as visible as possible. The Lightless Ones didn't care. They would chase me until I made it back home and locked the doors. They waited outside. I kept the lights off so they wouldn't know where I was. Home seems to be the only place they don't invade. They can only watch. It's like home has some forcefield or sacred ground or something keeping them out. I've scoured the house for clues that Mom might have left, only to find nothing.

FORCED SECLUSION

I started keeping the curtains closed all the time, more frequently in the mornings. The Lightless Ones are easy to spot during the day due to the high contrast of their black forms and the sunlit environment. I can maneuver around them. Sometimes they are sneaky and appear around corners and trees, or in windows. Seeing them in windows confirmed my theory about the familiars, for the Lightless Ones would be beside them. These people were on the street, too. They'd act like they were looking at their phone or a newspaper, but I could see their eyes. They were watching, taking notes, and seeing what I was going to do next. Some of the familiars would follow me to work and act like they were buying something. That wasn't going to work on me. My mom warned me about them. The familiars wanted to take me to the Lightless Ones and convert me into a familiar. I realized the Lightless Ones must be invading our world, slowly enslaving us to do their mysterious bidding.

My manager saw my performance at work declining. I shouted at some of the customers—familiars—and they filed complaints against me. Sneaky bastards. My manager moved me to the night shift, so I could stock the shelves and have less interaction with customers. At least there was the premium pay for nighttime work. The dark was dangerous. The Lightless Ones camouflage into it, so I started carrying a knife with me. I had no idea if the Lightless Ones were capable of experiencing physical pain. But in the worst-case scenario, I could at least attack one of their familiars.

I started getting fewer shifts at work. I don't think my manager likes me. Every walk home, I would firmly grasp my pocketknife tucked inside my hoodie. My heart raced. I'd sweat a lot. The Lightless Ones and their familiars would walk around me, circling like vultures. I would shout at them, telling them to stay away from me. I'd threaten them with the knife, flailing it in the air. It worked. Except for one day, when, on my walk home, they were more aggressive. From every corner, their black heads peeked out. The familiars watched from their windows, their cars, and then at the bus stops. *They* were behind me. I ran as fast as I could down the middle of the road, staying in the light.

I swear that some of the familiars tried to run me over in their cars. I couldn't help but wonder how long they have been watching. If the Lightless Ones had been stalking my mom, and she managed to avoid them until her death, had they stalked my grandmother too? Or my grandfather? I had no idea. I only knew I had to run. Eventually, I made it home, struggling to get my keys out of my pocket. My free hand still swung the knife in the air, keeping them back. I dropped the keys once, snagged them from the ground, and got the right one in to unlock the door. With my hand shaking, I managed to twist and push the door open, then step inside. I could feel one of *them* grab hold of my back. It stung.

I slammed the door shut and locked it. Panting heavily, I collapsed onto the floor as tears began to run down my face. I dropped the keys and the knife. The Lightless Ones were everywhere. The back of my neck had two scratch marks. I know they were real.

BEST COURSE OF ACTION

That was when I decided I couldn't work anymore. I stopped showing up for my shifts. My boss must've been concerned because the police eventually appeared at my doorstep. I wondered if they were familiars, too, but they seem to be okay. They interviewed me, asking if I was on anything. I wasn't on drugs. I'm not that kind of person, really, I'm stable and have a good sense of judgment. That was how I noticed the Lightless Ones in the first place. They would drive anyone crazy. The police determined there was nothing wrong with me and decided to leave me alone. Now, I can stay safe. I cover every window with curtains and have taped the glass over with tinfoil to prevent the Lightless Ones from seeing inside. I think the tinfoil might deflect their mind-controlling. It's a theory I have about how they convert people into familiars.

I rarely go outside. Anytime I peel back a small sliver of tinfoil to peek at the outside world, I see them. I try to take photographs, but they always come out blurry. They must have some sort of electromagnetic field that distorts technology, or they aren't detectable by light. Photography is light-based, after all. It makes you wonder— are they aliens? Other dimensional beings? Or am I merely suffering from paranoid delusions? I have no answers. I try to connect with others on the Internet—the world-shrinking device—to see if anyone else has seen the Lightless Ones. There are similar stories. Some of these people also believe in Bigfoot and the Flat Earth. I follow this one girl who streams videos, calling herself The Oracle. She doesn't see the Lightless Ones, but her voice is soothing, and she has pretty drawings. She's crazy, too—talking about a galactic absorption—but who else am I going to turn to? It's not like anyone else locally sees the Lightless Ones. At least I can vent to people on message boards. That is one good thing about the ever-shrinking world device: it connects those who are trapped. The Lightless Ones choose who they show themselves to. They select specific people to be their familiars, and they sure as hell aren't going to convert me. I'll fight this to the bitter end, just like Mom did.

This is where I find myself today. Alone. I document as much of it as I can online. I wonder if the Lightless Ones are getting smarter, or if my judgment is getting worse. Either way, I have had a difficult time determining who is a familiar and who is not. I stay away from the outside world as much as I can, only leaving the house to get groceries.

The Lightless Ones have introduced better forms of camouflage. I've seen half-human and half-otherworldly, like some kind of chimera: a hybrid that is part flesh and part blackness. They are evolving. I question how much longer I can fend them off. As the months go by, I am beginning to understand why Mom ended her own life. I can't see anyone. I can't experience fresh air. Nor have I ever felt the touch of a woman. Death may be the only route of escape. I don't want to be absorbed as a familiar. They're clawing at the door, scraping away at the wood. I can escape forever. That's what I hope for as I sit on my bathroom floor, writing this note with one sweaty hand and holding my knife in the other. Thanks for the help, Mom. I'll see you soon.

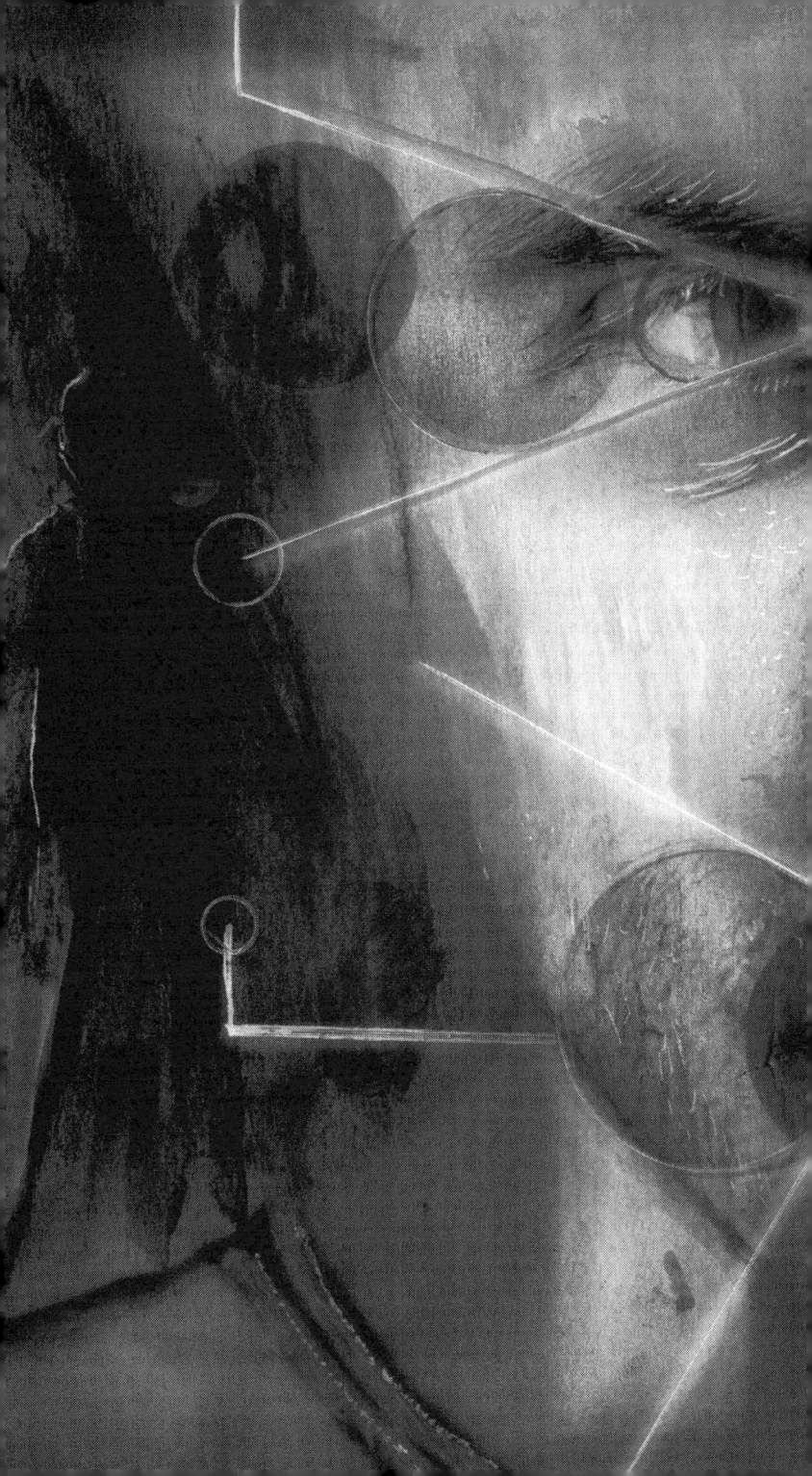

11

Unsettling is the only word you can think of. This marks the third time Malpherities has shown you a soul who was contemplating suicide. The experiences are getting all mangled, and you wonder—did you kill yourself? It's possible, but you're confident you didn't. You had a life, people who cared about you, right? Maybe not. Your memory isn't as trustworthy anymore as you continue to observe others' lives. Which memories are yours and which ones are not?

The ghoul shows little compassion and prepares the black liquid from the golden bowl. You're exhausted, uncertain, and only want to feel fulfilled. Will remembering even bring you contentment? You're dead, after all. Still, trying to remember something sounds more appealing than joining that spiralling vortex of souls above the cavern, and this plateau doesn't go anywhere. So, you widen your eye and, once more, prepare yourself to be an observer of another. Here you go.

RUNNER

The blue windbreaker zips up. Shin-protection socks are pulled on; shoes, tied; toque, on; and Bluetooth earbuds, in. The smartphone syncs to the earbuds, with the music app set to the workout playlist. Everything Dan needs to start his run is in place. As with every day, his head is groggy at six a.m. It doesn't help that he had a late worknight the day before. His lifestyle's hours don't bug him because he enjoys getting up at this time to embrace the brisk morning. It is technically spring, but there are no signs of the snow melting anytime soon— typical of Alberta.

"Let's do this," he mutters, getting up from his seated position. A late-night-early-start day doesn't motivate him to go for a run, but he knows he'd regret not doing it. The clarity of mind, the physical fitness, and the sense of refreshment post-run are not outweighed by the cold. Dan exits his condo, locking the front door, heading down the flights of stairs and out the lobby. He takes in a deep breath through the nose, feeling the crisp air enter his warm system. He presses the play button on the earbuds, bringing the electronic bass to life.

All right, he thinks, recognizing the beat—a favourite track of his to get energized for a workout.

Jams are on. Motivation is growing. Time to burn calories! Dan bursts from his walking speed, exiting the front of the condo towards the river. He glances down both sides of the street before dashing onto the road, covered in fresh snow. This early in the day, there is barely any traffic, like real-life *Frogger* on easy mode. He breathes steadily, moving on the familiar path he takes every morning, down a set of stairs. After the staircase, the path continues alongside the river. From here, he can see downtown just south of the river. It is always a beautiful sight this early on. Dan keeps a steady pace, eyes looking down at the fresh snow. There are a few bike tire imprints but no shoe imprints, which is a big ego boost for Dan. He thrives on knowing he was the only one dedicated enough to focus on his run consistently throughout the year this early in the day. Summertime is when all the posers come out and run.

Just over three kilometres into his run, or three songs later, the peaceful snow suddenly is marred by footprints and pawprints. Both start from the forest to his right and continue on the path. The footprints are behind the pawprints until a splash of red sprinkles the snow.

What? Dan slows his pace. The pawprints are more condensed here, and the blood is more prominent. Farther ahead, the blood smears the snow in a broad stroke spanning several meters before disappearing back into the forest. Dan stops in his tracks, panting as he presses the pause button for his music. He's slightly annoyed that his run is being interrupted. Reason prompts him to ask—what is he looking at?

Dan unzips his windbreaker so he can reach for his smartphone tucked in the inner pocket. This is too weird not to report to the city. He takes off one glove to swipe his phone, unlocks it, and dials nine-one-one. As the phone rings, he checks to see the path is empty behind him. He is entirely alone.

"Hello, this is nine-one-one. What is your emergency?" says the operator.

"Hey, yeah, I'd like to report a slaughtered animal," Dan says.

"Slaughtered?" the operator asks.

"That's right." Dan turns to examine the trail of blood. "I was just on my morning jog down by the Bow River and saw some fresh blood, some animal tracks, and shoe tracks."

"Is anyone else there?" the operator asks.

"No, just me. Think I will be heading back, though."

"All right. For future reference, call three-one-one for disposal of animals," the operator says.

"Yeah, I know that, but there's a lot of blood. I'm just trying to do what is right here." Dan exhales. *Is she stupid?* he thinks.

"We appreciate your concern. Where exactly is this?"

"I had just crossed onto—" Dan's sentence cuts short as a snapping twig catches his attention.

"Sir?" the operator asks.

Where the blood ends, a tall, broad-shouldered being, presumably male from the size, bursts from the shrubs with a blood-dripping machete in hand. The hood of a nice, slick, premium ski jacket is pulled over the ski-mask-covered face.

"Oh shit! St. George's Island!" Dan shouts, dashing back down the trail. His legs stumble slightly before he regains his balance. The limbs are weak from the sudden stop-and-go in his regular run. The few hours of sleep he managed aren't helping his body to recover quickly, either. Dan clenches the phone with one hand and his glove with the other. He feels his muscles burn from the burst of speed. He takes one glance back to see the man is closing in on him. Is this man a runner too? He has that nice ski jacket—admirable—but the man also has a bloody machete. Come on, Dan!

"God no, God no," Dan exhales. How is his pursuer running that fast? This can't be happening. This *can't* be.

The muffled sound of the emergency operator comes from the phone. In the moment of panic, Dan forgot about the operator on the line. He brings the smartphone to his ear, saying, "Help! Send help! A man with a machete is chasing me."

"We have a unit on their way. You said by St. George's Island?"

"Yes! I'm crossing the bridge, west, towards traffic."

"Stay on the line. We're not far off."

Dan makes a swift turn left onto the bridge, crossing the river. His steps are wobbly from his rapidly tiring legs. Heavier steps echo from behind, the stomping footsteps of the man with the blade. He has to be getting closer.

Don't look back, don't look back, Dan thinks. His lungs burn and his legs are jelly, despite the burst of adrenaline. He reaches the end of the bridge at a fork in the road and collides with a passing bicyclist. The impact sends him flying to the side of the pavement; he loses his grip on the smartphone and skids in the snow. The bike tumbles, launching the rider off of the seat and shoulder-first onto the concrete.

"Shit!" Dan rolls onto his back and tries to get up. His feet slide on the ice that's hidden below the snow. He looks to the bridge, only to see no one, then at the fork in the road, which is empty. He turns to his left—no one; right, nothing. He looks back to the island, then the bridge—nobody. The machete-wielding man is nowhere.

"Christ," mutters the bicyclist while taking off her helmet.

"Did you see the man behind me? He had a—"

"Share the damn road!" the bicyclist snaps.

Dan wipes his face, looking around one more time to see if he missed the machete-wielding man. No. He is gone for sure. Dan can't help but smile to himself with relief. He'd gotten away, proving to be the better runner; Dan, the man, the best in the city. He'd always known exercise was good for your health, but who knew the results would be so sudden.

12

Another dud. It's exhilarating and relieving that the man survived, but it wasn't you. You feel like giving up.

"Nothing," you say.

"Go again," Malpherities urges.

You look to the cave entrance, seeing nothing but blackness out there. Deeper in the cavern has the dimension bowls Malpherities mentioned, which are not helpful either. The thought of leaving the cave enters your mind, but there isn't much else to see here. The Midway is some strange state of existing, which raises many questions: How long can you stay here for? Do you get hungry? And what else is here? Maybe you could wander around and see what other mysteries this place holds.

An elongated hiss echoes from the cavern entrance, coming from above. What was that? Your heart skips a beat, hair tingling as the sound mutates into a growl.

"I SENSE A MORTAL." The voice is thick with reverb, quite similar to your ghoulish companion.

"Who is that?" you ask.

"Great." Malpherities sighs.

"Who else is here?" you ask.

A shadow appears from the cavern entrance. It has claws, and tentacle-like hair. Before you can see any more, claws snag your head, lightly cutting the skin, and raise your skull to a falling droplet. You fail to blink in time, and it lands in your eye, stinging. The black observer liquid has entered your system, and you leave your form to become a witness of something new.

SECRETS OF THE UNIVERSE

I was never much of a conspiracy fan. That's probably why this is a difficult thing for me to share. I've been called straight-laced, level-headed, and a head-on-my-shoulders type of a person. My good friend Tristan is into aliens, government cover-ups, and interdimensional vampires. Not me.

Maybe Tristan's rambles prepared me for comprehending what I saw. He would tell me all about the documentaries he watched on the Internet and show me "proof" videos of actual alien spiritual encounters. It's all bogus. The quality of those videos makes it evident that they were set up. Anyone can go to a supermarket and buy a rubber mask to look like an alien. Tristan would get pissed off anytime I discredited his beliefs. Then we'd smoke a joint after class, and everything would be good again. After graduation, everyone kind of went their own way. That's typical. Tristan left town, too, just like I did. Not everyone leaves, though. There's that one kid who worked at the grocery store. He locked himself in his house, thinking that some dimensional beings were chasing him. I don't think he will ever leave his hometown. Strange guy. He always did have the hots for Jane. I knew that if I wanted to make something of myself, I had to go to college, get some sort of certificate, and start working. See? Level-headed.

Okay, so, not to bore you with my past, but that's just to let you know that I don't spend all day playing with crystals and listening to the late-night history channel (don't get me started on that). I work at a small pub during the evening while going to school for architectural design. School is where things changed. An instructor of mine is a bit of a spaz. One evening, he was giving me some after-class lessons on the drafting software we use, and I got to know his inner workings. Roger McCulloch is his name. The building had a half-a-second outage, just long enough to surge the power on the computer, and we had to restart the machine. He muttered that *they* were interfering with it.

Of course, I had to ask, "Who are *they*?"

Man, let me tell you, that was a mistake. Roger unloaded his theories onto me. He told me that *they* controlled civilization. The celestial beings, directly connected to our government, work in uniform to suppress the conscious state of humankind. They don't do this in one giant bang like we see in the movies, apparently. According to Roger, the cosmic ones have been creating a trickle effect of information, brainwashing us for hundreds, if not thousands, of years. The subtle changes are more difficult to notice. Their methods have included promoting false idols through religious teachings, creating government policies, deploying clever marketing tactics through the media, and installing servants camouflaged as our world leaders. There are even secret embedded codes intricately ingrained into surfaces that transmit messages of obedience, projecting into our subconscious and rewiring our very thoughts.

Roger's eyes were wild as spit flew from his mouth with each word he spoke. I'd never seen my instructor like this before. He grabbed me by the shoulder and held it firmly. A part of me wanted to swat his arm away, but I was frozen with disbelief. Roger had always been a bit eccentric in class, but this was too much, even for him.

He leaned closer to me and said, "This is valuable knowledge. You have to keep it to yourself and only share it with those who need to know."

For some reason, I thought it was wise to keep humouring him—

maybe in the spirit of Tristan. Man, I miss him. I replied, "Why are you telling me this?"

Roger's posture relaxed. "You think differently, kid. I can see it in the questions you ask in class and the designs you hand in. You're different."

"And what am I supposed to do with this . . . knowledge?" I smiled, asking the question. I couldn't believe I was playing along with this nonsense, just like old times with my friend.

"You don't believe me," Roger said, taking his hand back. "I don't blame you . . ." Then he went on another tangent, claiming that I was brainwashed from birth and couldn't possibly know. It wasn't my fault, nor my parents'. He said these celestial beings are ancient and far more sophisticated than us mere humans; that they are using us as some sort of test animals. Their end goal remains a mystery, but once you start to see the subtle clues, the thin fabric of reality begins to fall all around you. The construct of our society is only bound by a thin membrane, like a cloak of illusion, trying to keep us contained.

At that point, I just wanted to go home. Clearly, I wasn't going to get any more learning about the drafting software done. I was better off searching for answers online than listening to Roger McCulloch.

"That still doesn't answer my question," I said. In the back of my head, I kept smacking myself for humouring Roger, when I knew I could have just ended it there.

"To step out of the box," Roger said with a smile, "shift yourself from being one of the sheep and see the world for what it is."

"And how do I do that?" I asked.

"Just look at the signs," Roger said. "The astral beings' encryptions are there, the window into realism engraved on the back of them. Everywhere. Cameras. Cell phones. Newspapers. Everything we've made has the engraving."

"On the back of signs, like street signs?"

"That's a good place to start."

After that, Roger returned to the role of instructor and me as the student. I was surprised that was where it ended. I had dealt with conspiracy nuts and knew that once they started, they usually couldn't stop talking. Roger did. It was relieving. Maybe it had to do with old age or professionalism, and I caught him on an off-day. Either way, the evening continued as usual, and I went home.

The next day was when things changed. For some reason, I couldn't stop thinking about what Roger said. I was waiting for the bus, having a smoke. I was the only one out and about this early in the morning. The transit schedule made getting to school a complete mess, but I was determined to learn. Sometimes the bus got here too early, and other times it got here late. Today was one of the late days. My mind started to toy with Roger's words about encryptions as I stared at the bus-stop sign. The words *"just look at the signs"* were on repeat in my brain. I did look at that sign.

Finishing the smoke, I went around to the back of the sign and stretched up, trying to see anything. Nope, just the slab of metal. Maybe a part of me wanted to believe because of how certain Roger sounded, and how confident Tristan always was. I kept staring. There had to be something. That's what I thought, and I guess I was right. I spotted something at the corner edge of the sign. It looked like a scratch, or maybe it was the light reflecting on the surface that emphasized the texture of the metal. No . . . this scratch was different. It was intentional.

This part of my story is where all the reinforcement I made earlier about being level-headed is going to go out the door. I put my backpack down and hopped onto the pole, climbing up to get a closer look. Bus-stop signs aren't very tall, but I wanted to get really, *really* close. I was about an inch from the nick and saw far more than I could have ever expected. The scratch was maybe a fingernail's width and had intricate designs with countless small white lines. As I stared at it, the scratch began to mutate, with parts of it phasing out of reality like someone took an eraser to it. Portions of the scratch faded, and new, strange glyphs I had never seen before appeared from the centre, moving outward. Lines, and shapes in complex patterns, and I think circuit boards. I don't know. The closer I looked, the more they floated outward. I didn't blink, staring into the scratch.

The core of the space continued to expand, and I could see more patterns, then an array of colourful particles. The depth of the core continued onward, with more wiring, colours, and shapes going on forever. My naked eye couldn't see anymore; I would need a magnifying glass to see how many embedded designs there were in that small space.

The scratch was certainly strange, and I hopped off the pole, knowing I couldn't see any more. Roger had been right about that. There was something on the backs of the signs, after all.

I snagged my backpack and spotted a person—no, it wasn't quite a person—standing about fifteen feet from me. Well, it was hovering, not standing. It didn't wear clothes, nor did it have skin. Not even the light from the sky reflected on it like other objects in the area. This entity was coexisting in our space without being bound by the physical laws that make us. That makes me sound like a crackpot, hey? Seriously, it was all black and had millions of tiny little particles moving up and down its form, all held together, like some sort of moving dark static TV.

The loud sound of a vehicle exhaust erupted, making me jump. Looking over, I saw the bus stopped in front of me. The being was gone. I rubbed my eyes. None of it added up.

The bus ride to school was also abnormal. My phone didn't seem to react to my fingers. I tried to check the social media apps, check the news, even check my email, and nothing. There was only a strange overlay of the same alien glyphs that I'd seen in that scratch on the bus sign, expanding outward from the screen as new shapes appeared. I'm still not sure if I became consciously aware of the subtle imagery that was all around our reality, or if that scratch activated something in my brain. Maybe I accidentally took some psychedelics. Not that I ever have, but I couldn't think of any solid reasoning for what I was seeing.

I didn't want to freak out and cause a scene, and these visuals weren't getting worse nor hurting me. But I needed answers. Roger. Man, that bus ride felt like an eternity, watching those shapes fly around the screen of my phone. I even saw them on the ads on the bus, moving along the banner frames. Eventually, my phone started to respond to my touch, so I tried recording these observations with my phone, but none of the obscurities showed up in the recordings, of course. Tristan would not believe this.

Finally, the bus ride came to an end, and I got off at the regular stop. Two men in black suits were waiting there. They had shades on, slicked-back hair, and briefcases. Strange. I kept walking once I got off the bus, assuming that they were going to board. Instead, they began to follow me. It started to freak me out, and I took a different route to school. The two men kept following. I entered the lobby of the tower where my school was, took the elevator to the floor below the school, and then used the stairs to get to the correct level. I hoped my little manoeuvre would shake them from me. It worked.

Once I got into class, I sat down, breathing heavily, feeling sweat all along my back. I had classic jimmy-leg for the whole session, watching Roger instruct the class. I checked my phone. It was still strange. Occasionally I would look over to the classroom door to see if the men in black were there. They seemed to be gone. No strange floating particle-people, either. My heart raced. I needed insight.

The class eventually ended, and I managed to corner Roger before he left for lunch. This time, my eyes were wide and I was spitting saliva, grabbing hold of his shoulder. I rambled on about the scratch on the back of the bus-stop sign and seeing the ever-inward designs of the alien language. I checked to make sure we were alone, then told him about the floating form and the men in black, and asked him if he'd ever seen any of this.

Roger smiled at me.

"What?" I asked.

"You did look."

"What did that bus sign do to me?"

"You saw the truth," Roger said. "You got a glimpse into the secrets of the universe. Now that your consciousness is expanded, you can see parts of the world for what it is."

"And what is that?"

"A fabricated construct, created by those who wish to contain us, limiting our true potential."

"What true potential? And the government is working with them? Are those men in black going to come back?"

Roger shook his head slowly. "More mysteries of life. I wish I could answer these questions for you, but I too only got a glimpse into the secrets."

"Can I go back to the bus stop? It will tell me more, right?"

"Don't do it," Roger said sternly. "You got away lucky."

"What do you mean?" I asked, letting go of Roger's shoulder.

"Too much knowledge catches their attention. You saw the lightless astral being. You saw the G-men. That was a warning. Imagine if you found out more, what they would do with you? If you recall, I said these are sophisticated beings that have been doing this for centuries."

"Then why would they have their secret out in the open like that?"

"I couldn't tell you. Maybe it is part of their experiment. Maybe it is a flaw in the technology. All I know is that once I got a glimpse into the true reality, *they* wanted me to stay away. I did."

"Now, you just hold on to this information?"

Roger shrugged. "At least I'm not living in a lie and am aware of them. I can only share with those that are willing to think differently. I know you presumed me to be a bit of a nutcase. I would, too. Imagine if I tried to tell the world. What would they think? I'd lose my job."

Roger was right. Tristan was right. Whatever these beings were planning to do with humanity had been long in initiation before I was even born. We may never know what their purpose is. The glimpse that I got from the encoded message on the back of that bus-stop sign was all I could think about. Eventually, the strange alien alphabet overlay that I saw on everything dissipated. I guess it had something to do with my consciousness narrowing again. I don't know. The men in black never came back. The strange celestial being did not return. I never looked at the bus-stop sign again. I told Tristan. He laughed at me. I guess he stopped smoking weed while in college and cleaned himself up. Now I'm the crazy one. I wonder if that kid locked in his house back in my hometown would know anything about it.

They knew instantly once I got a glimpse into the secrets of the universe. My human brain can't even comprehend what they are trying to do. Still, I am tempted to go back to that bus stop sign—or any sign—and see more about what makes up the real universe. The mystery gnaws at the back of my mind, wanting to know what else is out there. I'd like to know more about their agenda, what exists beyond this fabrication, and why we are even here to begin with. There are so many questions for humanity. Then, the façade sinks back in. I need to pay bills, finish school, and not be put into the nuthouse. So, I keep my head down, avoid rocking the boat, and stay level-headed.

13

The observing had shown you yet another incident that has no relation to your best guess of the past. This whole process is proving to be a waste of time, and yet you have nowhere to go and nothing but time. You blink. It appears you're you once more, rubbing your jawline where the ghoul had gripped. The skin is irritated. Malpherities is staring at you, arms folded, hovering a head above. The cavern is completely empty; it's just the two of you.

"What was that about?" you ask.

"You're slow," Malpherities says.

"No, there was someone else here. They said they sensed a mortal," you say.

"Oh, I took care of them. Don't worry about it," Malpherities says.

"But who was it?"

"Remember, I'm part of a hivemind? There are other ghouls who come to the Midway."

"What did they want?" you ask.

"They're not so keen on visitors."

"Are they coming back?" you ask.

"No, we're good now. Come, let's do another observation."

"If you had told me, I would have taken the droplet. No need to force me."

"Time is short, and you're letting your emotions get the better of you. I need to know why you are here," Malpherities says.

"I'd like to know, too," you say. "That hurt."

"My apologies; I forgot how soft you humans are," Malpherities says.

"Don't do that again," you say.

"I won't if you stop dragging yourself."

"This is tiring; I'm living many lives. It's a lot to take in. Is there anything else in the Midway that might help?" you ask.

"Not much for you. Besides, finding out who you are is more important."

"Can't those other ghouls help us?" you ask.

"Let's just say they like to participate in the act of death to feed . . . unlike me."

You get his gist. They'd kill you if they saw you. It's probably best to just agree with the ghoul and carry on. You're not too keen on dying again, with Death's Vortex right above, waiting for you.

"What then?" you ask.

"Well, once we know who you are, we can get you out of here. You don't belong here."

"Knowing who I am will get me out?" you ask.

"If your past offers any sort of clue, then yes. Now, did anything seem familiar?" Malpherities asks.

"Sort of. It was a city. The person wasn't me; I know that much. There were buses. Smartphones, I know those."

"Good, we're narrowing down your time. Although you could know those items through a history book, or perhaps your mind is getting muddled with the previous observations. Either way, it seems to me you aren't from humanity's split of Harvesters. You may be around the nineties or possibly before then, during the time and place that I hold dear."

"When is that?" you ask.

"Zingalg, the lost continent. It was around for many years before its collapse."

"And why do you like it?"

"It was home to where a mortal girl once lived," Malpherities says.

"Who was she?" you ask.

"Oh, once a friend. She taught me much about friendship and willpower, but that is not of importance. Everyone fades with time and into memory. Even memories fade, too." Malpherities' voice shakes as he reaches for the bowl.

It appears the ghoul does have feelings for others—at least one other person, anyway. Still, you're not sure if you can fully trust Malpherities. His agenda is clearly a higher priority to him than your well-being. You both have the common interest of knowing the mysteries of your past and why you're here. So far, space ships, evil teddy bears, devils, killers, celestial beings, and street-sign scratches haven't given you any real insight, only small clues. If anything, it has shown you how wild the universe is, and there's no telling where the ghoul will send you next. His claw hovers near the bowl.

You shake your head. "No, I'll do this one."

"How bold," Malpherities says, bringing his claw away from the bowl. "Remember my fair warning? You could end up anywhere."

"Yeah, I know." Now you're second-guessing yourself. The ghoul has sent you to witness some genuinely obscure scenarios. If those experiences were controlled, where could you send yourself? Perhaps it isn't such a good idea.

"I'm losing patience. I will snag your head again," Malpherities says.

"I don't know where I'll end up," you say, walking up to the bowl. Looking inside, you see that the black liquid is perfectly still. A droplet falls from the stalactite above, colliding with the liquid. The droplet ripples briefly, and then the liquid remains undisturbed. It's not like water at all.

"No, you do not. It's fairly risky," Malpherities says.

"But if I only use a droplet, I'll come back, right?" you ask.

Malpherities nods.

"You rub your claws when you grab a droplet. Does that control it?"

"Sort of. You can gain visions in the liquid as you move it around, like a window into a new world."

You muster the courage to dip your index finger into the bowl. The liquid is cold; it ripples slightly as you raise the digit back up. With your other fingers, you move the liquid around, trying to see into this window that Malpherities was talking about.

"That would be an interesting one," Malpherities says. "Nope, gone now."

You stop rubbing your fingers, still not seeing anything. "It's just black."

"Huh. It would appear you cannot see the window."

"And you can?"

"Yes. That looks like a simple one."

The smeared liquid on the tip of your finger is still black. "Where is it?"

"Looks to be fairly safe. Like someone reviewing entry logs. There's no telling where, when, or if that is all it is, but it appears safe."

You're uncertain if you should trust him, but he can see the windows. You controlling the liquid is just an illusion since you're listening to the ghoul. At least entry logs sound less straining than some of the past observations. With that thought, you raise your hand closer to your eye, pause for one last moment of uncertainty, and then tap your eyeball with the tip of your finger, dropping the liquid onto your eye. The familiar sting returns. The attempts to control dissipate as your body fades, and you observe a new life.

TRANSMIT

LOG: 1—06—0

Alain McLeod of the *EX—7006*. I couldn't believe the news when we found out that we could reverse-engineer the ships. I was a young buck then, still learning the ins and outs of mechanical work. The higher-ups let me have a hand in deconstructing the crafts. Lucky me. The thrill of heading for the stars was something humanity had hoped would happen for decades. A colonization mission would finally let us escape the grasp of those organ-picking gene-freaks—the damn Harvesters. Of course, we're no fools and know the dangers of trying to leave Earth. Harvesters orbit the planet continually, waiting for us to stand out on the surface. Where else are they going to look to reverse-engineer their DNA? Their 'perfect' alterations backfired, and now they need us to try and save their skin. Serves them right.

I wanted to be on the first ship to leave the planet. The higher-ups needed me back at base. So, the years went by. *EX—7006* worked just fine. Like myself, the whole crew is seasoned in dealing with Harvesters. Unlike space travel, which took us a bit to get our heads around. Sometimes I wonder if humankind is even meant for the stars. Then I remember we're human. We defy nature. We've managed to surpass every environmental challenge, and space would be no different.

We're the seventh expedition to leave the planet. Most of the previous missions involved returning home, allowing us to understand space travel further. We needed to get a sense of how our bodies handle cosmic travel and synthetic gravity. This mission is different because it's a one-way ticket to a new world. There used to be more crafts in the fleet. Unfortunately, with every launch, we attract the Harvesters. The gene-freaks have gunned a lot of our ships down, killing people. Their deaths have not been in vain, for their sacrifices have brought us here. *EX—7006* is leaving the solar system.

This log will be transmitted directly back to Earth. It will serve as a record for what we may discover as we pass into the unknown, despite the growing time delay that these transmissions will take. I'm sure Captain Ross would prefer if I didn't send these, but what is he going to do? He needs me, and we're limited on our resources.

On a personal note, let me tell you, leaving the Earth behind is unlike anything else you will ever see. The grey ball progressively gets smaller and smaller. Eventually, you lose interest. There was a subtle green hue that came from the kitchen window, slightly distorting the glass. I didn't look directly out the window and didn't think there'd be such a strange green glow out here in space. Maybe it's the tint of the glass. Regardless, it was nice to get one last look at everything before we entered hibernation in the stasis pods. The ship is en route; autopilot is a go.

LOG: 1—06—1

Alain McLeod of the *EX—7006*. We have woken from our stasis pods. It appears to be on time, matching the experiments we conducted back on Earth. The nausea is something else. We couldn't train for it. Adapting to the simulated gravity can have strange effects on your psyche. The light-headedness does go away, and we can now see to our duties. We've all worked together to adapt to this new state of being, soaring through the cosmos. Captain Ross ensures that all procedures are followed, and everyone cleans up and is ready to initiate their tasks.

Some of us handled the awakening a little better than others. Poor Annie started to vomit intensely a few hours later. We were in the kitchen. She was gazing at the stars. She didn't blink, nor move, looking a little too long. I asked her if she was okay. Her skin was pasty. All of us had pasty skin, but hers was more so. That was when she vomited, projecting it all over the glass. The doctor had to take her to the med bay. I'm sure she'll recover soon.

Even with my mechanical background, I oversee counting the food rations. It's a bland and straightforward task, which is welcome. Maintaining the ship's thrusters can be a tedious job. Plus, we should track what we have for supplies. Chances are we won't be going back to sleep. There's only so much power on the ship, and we need to savour the energy as we enter this new solar system. The pilot and crew are already scanning through the digital maps to see where the planets are in orbit around the red dwarf sun. We're staying on course.

A lot of smart minds back home have theorized the possible risks of travelling in space. There is plenty of talk about the psychological struggles that can occur when you're floating around a metal tin can through a giant vacuum. We're resilient. Hopeful, one could say, that we will find a new planet we can inhabit away from the gene-freaks. Most of us do not talk about the actual mission since it has been quite clear for decades why we're leaving Earth. We have more important questions: What else might we find? And how harsh will the weather be? I admire everyone on the ship. The crew are capable people that are willing to sacrifice themselves for the sake of humanity. We will escape the Harvesters' grasp.

Captain Ross has been keeping a formal log of what has been occurring since we managed to launch from the tiny grey-and-brown dot. For me, this log is more about the realism of our trip. Let me tell you, sharing a toilet amongst the crew members can be a bit much at times. The same goes for hygiene powder. It works—mostly—but I can't help but wonder what happens if we run out, or if we don't land on a planet. Or how Annie is recovering. That was a lot of vomit, feeding my worries. Maybe that's the psychological struggles of space travel. I'm sure the other crew members share the same thoughts; there's no point in talking about it. We must work together.

LOG: 1—06—2

Alain McLeod of the *EX—7006*. I believe about a week has gone by since we woke up in the stasis pods. The crew is getting a bit anxious to know when we are going to land. Captain Ross has assured us that everything is going according to the projected schedule. I was never a pilot, nor an astronomer, and couldn't give any professional insight. One thing I did know, though, is if something is on a scheduled route, there isn't much to control. I don't know. Perhaps I'm overthinking it.

Annie hasn't gotten better. The doctor assures us that it's just a bit of space sickness—something like getting seasick. Seems odd. Not my department, though. I just ensure this hunk of gene-freak metal keeps humming smoothly. I clued in that the windows aren't green-hued. It was coming from outside in the one kitchen window. I talked to Zoe, the astronomer; she says she's unfamiliar with the phenomenon. Then again, she proudly has a bit of disorientation from being in a new solar system and seeing space from a new angle.

I haven't looked out the window, but everyone says it is surreal. The green light has no focal point. It merely glows radiantly. I couldn't tell you why I haven't looked. I just haven't. We try not to spread rumours around, as seeing something abnormal like this glowing green space only raises suspicion. Zoe says she is going to do some research and let us know what she discovers. Captain Ross ordered that we don't over-talk the spectacle and hypothesize that it's something it's not. It's not harming us or the ship.

We can't help it. We're only human. Hell, I remember as a kid all the rumours that were floating around about Harvesters. 'Space demons' is what we called them. Of course, that is all bogus. They are just a prime example of where trans-humanism gets you. As a kid, your imagination runs wild, and I don't think that vanishes in adulthood. We just suppress it and accept reality as it is and express it through inventions, like gene editing. What if all of reality is taken away? That's a big question. We're not on Earth anymore and are soaring at immense speeds through space. The reality that we once knew is no more. Thinking this way sparks your imagination, for better or worse.

LOG: 1—06 –3

This is Alain McLeod of the *EX—7006*. Zoe vomited, just like Annie. I saw her in the engine room, and she begged me not to tell anyone. I wasn't sure why I agreed, but I said okay. She's cute. I'm human. Oddly enough, that same day was when Captain Ross brought everyone into the meeting hall to discuss urgent matters.

The doctor was with him, explaining that if any of us feel nauseous, to report to him immediately. He said a virus may have been on board during the ship's launch and has mutated. That's the running theory. I don't know; that's the doc's job. Captain Ross told the crew members to be completely transparent and share anything abnormal that they may witness amongst crew members. It doesn't sit well with me. I know it is for the best of humanity. So, I asked Captain and the doc where Annie was. They said she was in the med bay. I found that odd and asked if they were hiding anything. Boy, let me tell you, that did not go over well.

After that speech, the whole crew was on edge. Zoe found me in one of the storage units where I was counting supplies. She looked sick. Her skin was moist, like she was sweating. She said there was something wrong with her. I told her that we needed to tell the doctor. It was for the safety of the whole crew. She said she understood and knew what happened to Annie.

Before I had a chance to ask, Tom and Lydia, Captain Ross's top-ranked, came into the storage unit and seized Zoe. She shouted, "It's in the damn hue!" as the two began to drag her away. She vomited again, and blood spewed onto the floor. I stood back, watching in disbelief. Zoe's skeletal frame began to turn to mush, convulsing. She leaked red goo from her orifices. Her skeleton melted. She was only held together by her skin. Tom and Lydia let her go, and she fell to the floor like a folding slab of meat. Seeing a human being without the skeleton is . . . difficult to describe, and I don't think I want to. I wonder if that is in Captain Ross's official log. How did Zoe figure out that this was the hue and the doc didn't, nor did Captain Ross? I'm starting not to trust the captain. Zoe is gone. She said it was the hue. How? Does it distort us on a molecular level? Is it . . . cursed? Shit. I don't know; not my department. I liked Zoe.

LOG: 1—06—4

Alain McLeod, *EX—7006*. Despite Captain Ross's best efforts to keep command, the crew continues to talk about what happened to Zoe. I don't bother, even though my mind is burning with questions. The doc had to have known. I don't say anything, though. What's the point? All it does is start rumours. Holding on to the past doesn't help, either. Some of the crew members mentioned that the green space hasn't left. No matter how far we travel, it seems to stay there, right by the kitchen window. I stopped going there and just started grabbing food from the storage unit. I'm usually not one for superstition, but this hue had me creeped out.

We passed several planets in the solar system. There had to be over a dozen. Zachary, the environmental expert, was telling me that we were headed for a sizeable Earth-like planet. He worked closely with Zoe in deciphering where exactly we were going before our ship left Earth. Apparently, the planet is suitable for us humans.

Shortly after Zoe's demise, the crew demanded answers from Captain Ross and the doctor. The captain summoned everyone to the meeting room and finally came clean. He told us that Annie had died shortly after she vomited, and her symptoms matched Zoe's. This caused an uproar. Most of the crew members felt betrayed by Captain Ross and the doctor. They were not honest with everyone. I don't blame the crew. Keeping secrets was no way for us to survive space travel.

Captain Ross ordered that the crew continue to operate as usual. I spoke up, asking what Zoe meant that it is in the damn hue. Another crew member asked about the kitchen. The doc said to stay clear from it until the window is shielded. Just then, Zachary began to vomit. Everyone backed away, watching in horror. The man regurgitated his innards, like meat-paste through a tube.

Several other crew members began projecting blood. Gore was everywhere. I managed to avoid most of it, except for the splatters on my overalls. The doctor, too, began to vomit. Captain Ross, myself, and Lydia were the only ones who remained unaffected. Maybe they didn't look at the green hue, either. We could only watch helplessly as our comrades fell before us. It didn't take long for them all to stop vomiting, collapsing on the floor as boneless sacks of meat.

Lydia entered a full-on panic attack, asking what we were going to do. Captain Ross ordered her to remain calm as we attempted to come up with a plan. There were no more secrets now. We all had to work together. The captain mentioned that the doctor first thought the illness had something to do with the stasis pods. Today, after the doc began to feel some symptoms himself and died, he contacted Captain Ross and told him to shut all the windows immediately. The sickness came from the green hue. But it had all happened so fast, and he was unable to act in time. I regret saying it, but Captain Ross is not suitable for command. The argument got pretty heated, and a couple of fists were involved, too. Lydia calmed down, I got my frustrations out, and Captain Ross was finally transparent with us.

LOG: 1—06—5

This is Alain McLeod of the *EX—7006*. I'm not sure how long these logs will take to transmit to Earth. Hopefully they arrive sooner than later. Everyone back home needs to know what happened. Humanity will no doubt build new crafts and send more people beyond our solar systems, away from the Harvesters. They need to know about the dangers that lurk in the unknown. We've shielded all the windows from the green light and can only presume that it is still there. Whatever it is has been clinging to the ship since we left our solar system. It's hostile. Maybe we flew straight through it while in the stasis pods, like some space seaweed. Whatever *it* is.

We're still on course for the large Earth-like planet and are all overworked. Three of us managing a ship the size of the *EX—7006* is draining. We will make it to this new world. We will inhabit it and continue the colonization plan. This is what we are trained for—to scout out the new planet and bring more ships. I will send a log once we have reached the atmosphere. The three of us can only hope that the green hue doesn't follow the landing pods. We won't know until we try. We're daring the unknown, as humans do.

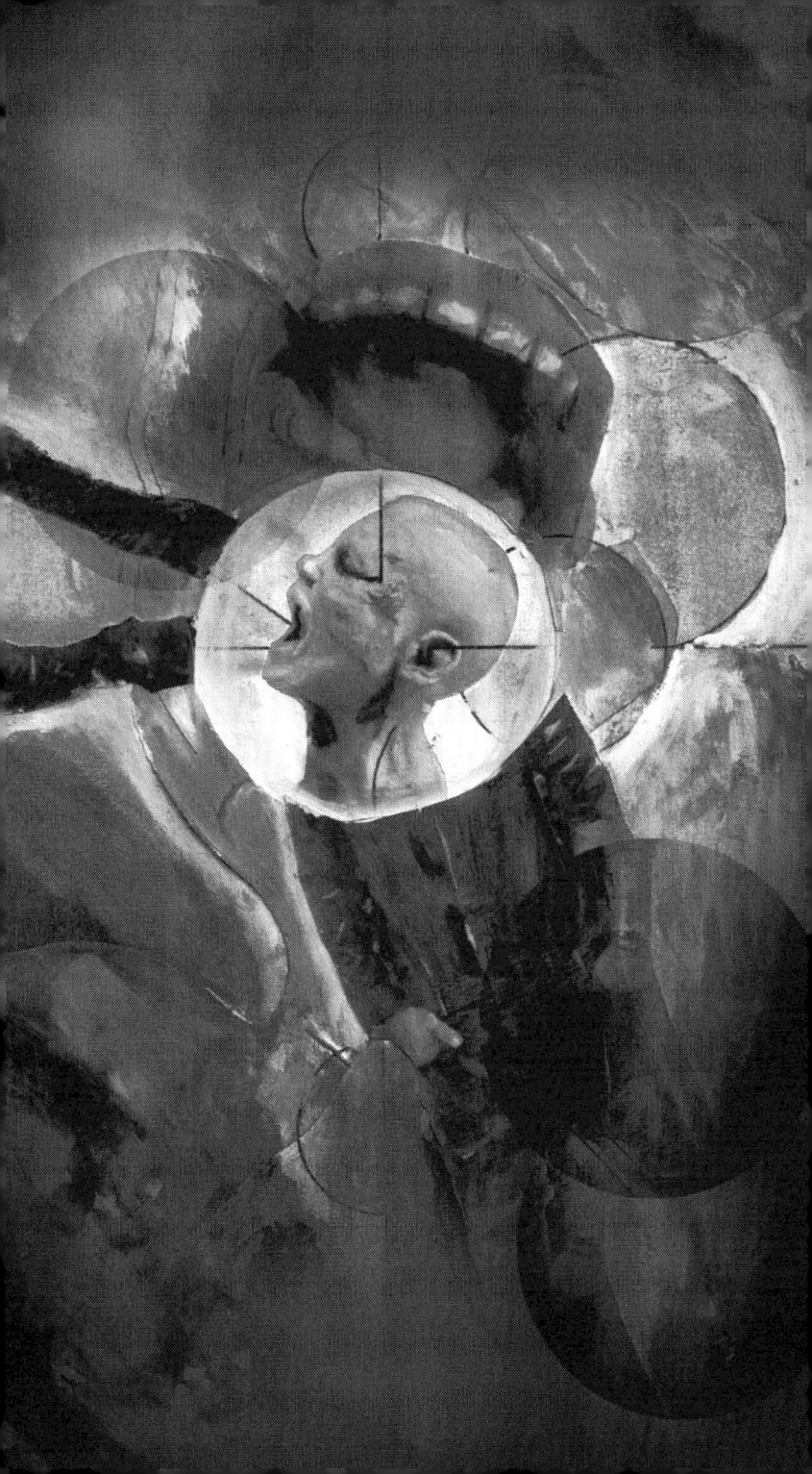

14

S enses return. You feel grim, yet unscathed mentally, unlike some of the previous observations. You take a deep breath, knowing that the witnessing is over. Malpherities is watching, as always, like some kind of spectral cat. You look down at your hands—the black liquid has evaporated. Even rubbing your hands together, it doesn't feel like there is any residue.

"And?" Malpherities asks.

"Nothing. Relatively safe, like you said. Just some spaceship log. I have a feeling I wasn't that far into the future." You dip your finger into the bowl again, grabbing another small droplet, moving the liquid around in your hands. "Tell me when something looks good."

"Of course," Malpherities says, leaning closer, looking down at the liquid. "There."

"What is it?" you ask, raising it.

"Looks like an elderly person dying, with their family in . . . maybe a nursing home."

"Really? That's not too bad," you say, lifting your index finger to your eye, staring at the black liquid. The movement causes it to shift.

"Wait," Malpherities says as you tap your eye with it. "You moved the window."

"What?" you ask as the liquid falls. It lands in your eye, and you blink, trying to get it out—the familiar sting returns.

"Too late . . . ," Malpherities says.

"Where am I go—?" Before you finish your sentence, you transcend from your body, becoming an observer in a faraway land, at a distant time. It's cold, so cold . . .

THE LAST OF KA'DUBARH

RECALL

Family means everything. The belief has been in the hearts of my people for centuries. Our blood is what binds us together. Unity makes us strong. The ancestral tree has grown steadily for generations, keeping us robust and pure. Each new generation carries on the legacy of the last, where we support one another, care for each other, and fight for one another even if it means the most significant sacrifice of all: our own lives.

Our views are why I find myself on the frozen plains of Ka'dubarh, crawling over dozens of frozen corpses. Some of them I recognize; hell, I even had them over for wine and pig back home. Now, their lifeless, cold faces are empty shells. Their souls have moved on to the afterlife. That leaves me here, alone, as the last.

My feet are numb, possibly from the blood loss, or maybe it's the icy wind biting away at my flesh. I don't know. What is for certain is I can no longer feel my lower limbs, nor walk on them. I'm crawling on my arms to push forward. The vast chasm leading out of Ka'dubarh is the one path that protects my people's homeland from the outsiders in Zingalg. If I can just keep pushing on, I can crawl down the mountain and back to the warmer wilderness—back to my family.

I grunt. My arm gives out, and my face collides with the ice-covered chest of a corpse. Pushing myself up, I am eye-to-eye with a bark-like grey face. Curled tusks and an elongated nose come from the skull. The eyes are closed. Green-tinted icicles hang from the tip of the horns and the rims of the nostrils and mouth—blood. This is no friend. This is the corpse of one of my enemies—damn trolls. If they weren't consumed by greed, maybe we could have found some sort of common ground. We aren't that different, after all. It is only the name of our faith that separates us.

A groan rises directly under me as the chest begins to move, by the gods.

IT LIVES!

I push myself off the troll as it slowly lifts its limbs. The yellow eyes open as the ice cracks. The body rises. My enemy is alive and well.

"*Goo'cha abuo,*" the troll mutters in a deep tone, adjusting its leather helmet.

"Goddammit," I whisper, patting my belt for my knife. Wait, where is it? I can't find it.

The troll rolls onto its side, looking up at me. Its bark-like skin crunches into a scowl, adding depth to the skin's texture. It lets out a nasty hiss. "Human!"

I extend my one hand, palm outward. "The battle is over. We can go our separate ways, back home," I say. Maybe I can reason with it. Perhaps we can come to some form of an agreement and leave this blood-filled snowscape.

The troll attempts to get up but collapses with a yelp. Its leg has an arrow through it, proving it to be as crippled as I am.

"No battle over," the troll says. "Your people shun us, and you will die for the dishonour."

"This can be settled another day," I say. "Go home, and I will do the same."

"We fight, human."

"We have fought! Look around you! Our comrades and friends lay slain. The battle is over."

"No." The troll reaches around its belt and pulls out a large, jagged black dagger. "For my fallen brethren!"

I'd thought the cold was overbearing. Now, I wish it were all I had. My hopes of survival are dwindling as I watch the troll crawl towards me with the knife in its mouth. I push myself to the side and scurry away with what little strength I have. The troll is directly in my path— the path leading back to the village. I need to get around it. I *must* get around it and get back to my family to see my wife's face once more.

"Humans will pay!" the troll shouts, drool running down its chin and freezing midway from the cold wind.

"Back!" I shout, feeling the troll's hand slap against my boot—a failed attempt to grab me. I pick up my pace, crawling faster, feeling my arms shake. The troll has longer limbs and can easily catch up. Time isn't on my side.

THE CHASE

The troll's grunts and my panting breaths echo against the sides of the rocky chasm as we crawl over our poor fallen comrades. If only we had settled our differences in another way, I wouldn't be looking down at some of my dear deceased friends as I flee for my life, hoping not to join them. My eyes are keen on the curved path ahead, and I'm focused on trying to move around the troll. My lungs burn. My body begs for me to stop moving, wanting me to end it all right now, stop trying, stop fighting, and join the dead. I can't give up. My wife and my son wait for me back home. I didn't come to Ka'dubarh with my comrades to die. I came to defend my family and return to them alive.

A piercing sound comes from behind, and a sharp pain spikes from my ankle. I let out a grunt, realizing the troll got me. The leg is so frozen that I barely noticed the pain until the blade had sunk deeper into my limb. I turn around, kicking the troll in the face. I don't feel the impact on my numb foot against the enemy's nose; only my thigh responds to my command. The blow makes a crunching noise. The troll hisses, letting go of the dagger embedded in my flesh.

"Give me strength, brethren," I say, clenching my teeth. Even with the weapon in my ankle, I continue to crawl. The sound of the troll's movement picks up in the crunching snow. It's on the chase again.

"Your people hate our kind, kill our kind. I will gut you!" the troll shouts.

Now, I realize I can't out-crawl this troll. It has far more energy than I do. They are more resilient and have more stamina than humans. It isn't willing to be reasoned with—no surprise. I have no choice but to fight.

"You," I grunt, rolling onto my back, arching to reach for the stabbed leg, "invaded our land." I coil my hand around the large dagger. "Ka'dubarh is the sacred entrance!" I shout, yanking the weapon from my ankle. Some blood pours out of the wound and onto the snow, quickly freezing.

The troll roars, clutching both of my legs. "Ka'dubarh hides our holy temple."

"Then why do you shed blood on the holy?" I growl, pushing myself upward, thrusting the dagger at the troll's arms. It lets go of my limbs and rolls away, and the dagger stabs ice. I fall forward, crawling towards the troll. Oh, how the tables have turned.

"Our ancient temple belongs to us!" the troll says, moving on top of the corpse of one of its allies. It pats the body, searching for some sort of weapon. A toothy grin fills the troll's face as it pulls a smaller dagger out from the corpse's belt. "We will claim back our land," the troll says, hurrying towards me.

END OF ALL

Here we go. A sharp, biting wind blows past us; my hair covers my face. This is it, the final battle of Ka'dubarh. I pray that my people will give me the strength to avenge my fallen allies, for I fear I cannot do this alone.

The troll roars, forcing itself onto its knees, giving it the upper hand. It makes the first attack, slashing the knife down. I roll out of the way and plunge the blade into its outer thigh. The dagger pierces its skin, causing it to roar. The troll backhands my face, and I land on the snow, clutching the dagger tightly. Thick forest-green blood oozes from the troll's new wound.

"You will die, human!" The troll thrusts the knife down at me; the blade pierces my gut. I cry in pain, mustering the strength to stab my foe. The blade impacts the troll's chest, piercing the lungs. It pulls the dagger out of me and slashes the weapon down again as I lunge up once more. Our weakening bodies make our attacks clumsy; we are victims to each other's weapons, puncturing our torsos repeatedly. Red and green liquid sprays over each of us, our blood mingling, sprinkling the snow.

The troll howls in pain as its strength dwindles. It nearly falls on top of me, using its one free hand to keep upright, still poking at me with the knife. The pain is too great, and I feel the blood in my mouth. I have to believe it's only in my mind. I can overcome this, for the adrenaline is coursing through my veins. The spirit of my fallen people surges through my body, giving me the strength I need to defeat this foe. I have to. I must honour them!

Letting out a roar, I rush the blade up, piercing the troll's heart. My enemy gags, dropping the knife as it collapses onto me. The tusks scrape against my cheek, slicing the skin open as saliva drizzles down onto my face. The vile stench of mould and rotten meat reeks from the body—the typical troll smell. I never thought the stench would be the last smell I ever experienced. I suppose it doesn't matter. After all, I had defeated the enemy; my people gave me the courage and strength to make one last critical blow.

I lay in the snow as blood runs out of every new and old hole in my body. My warming flesh and the glowing sun overpower my mind, causing all of Ka'dubarh to turn white. My overstimulated senses relax. My breathing slows down. The vile stench of the troll dwindles and is replaced with a soft, sweet aroma. A familiar one . . . is it? Yes. My wife.

My vision fades, and only the white light remains . . . I am warm now, and feel no pain. My family is near, and they're safe. We defeated the trolls at Ka'dubarh, protecting our village. My family can live peacefully now, and I will reunite with them in the next life.

15

The cold bite of death. A warm light. The welcoming of home. These experiences are familiar—ones that you, too, went through upon dying. Could this man be you? Did you live the life of a warrior, dying on the battlefield? Perhaps. The soothing sensation of family and warmth dissipates as the observing state leaves you, and you are you once again.

You pat your body, feeling to make sure everything is intact while moving your legs up and down. They work. You're not frozen. "That was *not* an elderly person dying peacefully," you say, annoyed that the ghoul hadn't told the truth.

"You shifted the liquid the moment before it touched your eye. You need to be careful," Malpherities says. "It's a sensitive element, no different than your soft skin."

"Right," you say. Then you shift to the memory the experience sparked. "Some of it was familiar. I felt so cold when dying before experiencing euphoria."

"Is that so? Cold is a common experience when dying, but not for everyone. We know you didn't die in an explosion or were burned at the stake, then; that is quite hot."

"Yeah! All right, we're on to something. Can we go back there?" you say.

"We can do our best. I caught a glimpse of the window before it touched your eye. The mountains, the ice, the dead."

"There was a . . . troll?" you say.

"Yes, Zingalg," Malpherities says, dipping his claw into the bowl. He stirs the liquid around, eyes focused on the blackness. "Mount Kuzuchi. Let's see if I can get you close to where you were. Trolls, ice, and mountains. There's a lot of death on Mount Kuzuchi—and one catastrophic event that may be relevant. Perhaps I know where you were, and can come close to who you are."

"What about me knowing smartphones?" you ask. "Zingalg didn't seem to be around when that tech existed."

"No," Malpherities says. "But you've seen smartphones in a few observations. You may be confused. Humour me this one time. Then we'll find more of a smartphone era."

"Okay." You open your eyes, looking up, ready for the next droplet. "Let's do this."

Malpherities rises above you, tapping his claw and letting the droplet fall onto your eye. Into the land of Zingalg you go.

CRUSADERS

PART I: DEVOTION

Loyalty—making the conscious choice to embody this trait is a highly respected feat. Devotion is what drives families, tribes, unions, and nations to work together. This act is the power of humanity, seen through the darkest and most difficult times, such as the Drac Age. The unshakable trust ensures that no one will have to face the horrors of the draconem ever again. Humanity guarantees it. The Knight's Union enforces it.

Brown scaly legs stomped one by one. Rusty metal shackles dangled between the ankles of chained-up reptilian humanoids. They marched in a large pack like cattle, some hissing, others groaning. The scraps of linen clothing they wore were torn and stained with blood; their skin was marred by bruises and cuts. Others were shy and too afraid to even look up at the path ahead, where they were being directed towards a larger group of reptilians huddled together.

A one-eyed man, mounted on a black steed, shouted, "Keep them moving!" The sun reflected off his silver-and-steel plated armour as he rode around the outer rim of the reptiles. "These vazelead scum will pay for their loyalties to the Drac Lord Karazickle."

One of the reptilians—or vazeleads—hissed at the man. The black feathers on his skull stood straight up.

The man spat on the vazelead before strolling off. "Drac-serving scum," he muttered. "Vixor!" he called out, directing his horse towards a long-haired man on horseback.

"Yes, Captain Franthar," the man identified as Vixor said. He looked up at his captain, eyeing the red fabric that draped down from his steel shoulder pads. The sign of a captain. A symbol of loyalty to his duty. *One day,* Vixor thought. *One day I will lead my own squadron in the Knight's Union.* The all-too-appealing idea of being the leader of a band of knights was something he strived to achieve. Something that one could only obtain through devotion, persistence, and a key demonstration of ability. Vixor knew he could do it.

"Vixor," the captain said again, now only a meter away from him. He halted his horse, causing it to snort.

The words shot Vixor back to reality. "Yes?"

"You showed admirable effort today, raiding this tribe of vazeleads." Captain Franthar extended his hand to the burning huts nearby. "I wanted to inform you that you are showing an excellent set of skills. Key skills that can result in advancements."

"Thank you, sir," Vixor said. He kept his head low, his black hair dangling in front of his face. That was what he wanted to hear. Those few words were more rewarding to him than graduating from the academy or even completing their task of rallying the reptilians. He knew he was one step closer to climbing the ranks.

"I could use some warriors to serve next in command. We'll keep talking. Now," Captain Franthar started, "I know you and your brother are both striving to show your worth. You're both Purehearts, and you'd make your father proud." He extended his index finger at Vixor. "Don't make family turn you soft. Lorthuum may be more skilled, but your fire and dedication are far superior. I'd hate to see that extinguish."

"Thank you." Vixor wasn't sure what else to say. The captain didn't often give pep talks. He was strong, cold, and commanding. Vixor's eyes wandered over to the other side of the pack of vazeleads in the centre of the village. Several knights were there on horseback, keeping the central group of reptilians compact and close together. One lone knight trotted down the road back towards the group. He had his helmet off, revealing his sweat-drenched face and dirty-blond hair that draped over his eyes. Vixor knew that man. That man had constantly been by his side ever since childhood—his brother, Lorthuum.

"Keep this between us," Captain Franthar said.

"Of course," Vixor said, looking up at his captain. *Not sure what else I would do with this information,* he thought.

"Good. Continue rallying these fiends," Captain Franthar said. "Heeyah!" he shouted, spurring his steed to storm off.

Vixor lashed on the leather straps attached to his mount and trotted around the vazeleads. The reptilians merged into the larger group, all staying close together. Some of the beings kept their heads low, and some stood in front of the weaker ones, hissing and keeping their eyes on the knights, tails perked high. Some snarled, exposing their teeth, while some held up their claws, despite being chained up.

Monsters, Vixor thought.

"Brother!" Vixor called out, riding to the opposite end of the vazelead group. "Well done today! We're closer to eradicating these Drac Lord-worshiping fiends!"

Lorthuum looked at his brother with a cold face. He didn't express joy or sadness. He nodded, saying, "Aye. You are correct, brother. Another tribe down, many more to go."

"Where were you wandering off alone?" Vixor asked. "We've triumphed. Celebrate!"

"We're not done yet. I was simply making sure the outskirts of the tribe were cleared." His voice was lower, almost as if he was discouraged.

Vixor brought his horse close to his brother's so he could pat him on the arm for comfort. "Are you feeling the burden of how many tribes we have left to gather?"

"I suppose you could say that. We're exiling an entire race of people. It is a lot to digest."

"People?" Vixor laughed. "These dimwitted creatures aren't worth being called *people*. Hell, the only advancements they have shown occurred when humans enslaved them during the Drac Age."

"That was a century before our time, brother. You can't always trust the stories you hear."

"Well, they're difficult not to believe when some people have lived in that era and speak of the tales," Vixor said, looking over to a pale red-headed woman on a white horse. She watched from atop a small hill as the knights rallied the stragglers that attempted to escape. Despite being covered in dirt and blood, her gold-plated armour still radiated with an unnatural warm glow.

Lorthuum extended his hand, saying, "Of course. She is a Paladin of Zeal. Fierel Flamesworth is not of mere men."

"I can't imagine what it must be like to have such power."

"Being blessed by the hand of God?"

"Correct, brother. They even challenge the strength of angels."

Lorthuum sighed. "Brother, these are simply stories. You can't trust each one you hear just because a higher command says so."

"Perhaps. One thing I do know is that these creatures are going straight to the top of Mount Kuzuchi and then dropped into the underworld. A sight I dearly desire to see."

Lorthuum raised an eyebrow. "Come, let's take one last round through the village, make sure we didn't miss anything. I didn't get a chance to review the east side."

The brothers steered their horses away from the village centre and trotted down the road. To each side of them were huts, some burning, others collapsed to rubble. The path was littered with corpses of reptiles and debris, forcing them to tread lightly and avoid the mess on the gravel.

"It seems like such cruel punishment," Lorthuum said while keeping one hand on his sheathed sword. He eyed the huts to his side.

Vixor mirrored Lorthuum's actions, looking into every crack and shadow, trying to spot any hidden vazeleads. "For worshipping the last of the Drac Lords, they're lucky we aren't executing them."

"Permanent banishment from the surface? Do you know what the underworld is like? Death would be a blessing."

"Of course I don't know what the underworld is like. But I have read about it. No one can escape it."

"Exactly. We're basically causing their extinction."

"Good riddance," Vixor sneered. "Quite frankly, brother, it isn't my word to say either. The Council of Just has willed it so."

"That is our reality," Lorthuum said. "Dictated by the heroes that led us out of the Drac Age. Their will cannot be questioned."

"Nor should it be. Their wisdom and expertise are beyond our own."

"We're simply the footmen," Lorthuum replied.

"Not for long. I will get that captain title."

Lorthuum smiled. "I hope you do, brother."

"What of you? Is that not something you wish? We've been through the academy side by side. This is what Father willed us to do before passing to the Heavenly Kingdoms."

"Yes, I do wish for the prestige of a title. Perhaps all the death has started to wear me down, and I need time to reflect."

Vixor wasn't entirely buying Lorthuum's words. He felt an odd sense of sorrow emanating from his brother. Why was he so downhearted? Normally the two of them fed off one another's energy. "Remember what loyalty to the Knight's Union can bring?" Vixor asked. "Praise, honour, riches, and women! I, for one, would like to find myself a lady worthy of standing by my side and call her my wife."

"Aye, an equal is the desirable goal." Lorthuum clutched the one-feathered necklace that wrapped around his neck. The green feather was smaller than those seen on grown vazeleads. It was also too large to belong to a bird.

The action drew Vixor's eyes. "That's a rather small feather," Vixor commented. "Is that what has you in a piss-poor mood?" He reached down to his belt, where he pulled on a rope covered in vazelead claws, each tied tightly to it. Some of the trophies still had the flesh on them, while others were coated in dried blood. "I'd say I've got about eighteen on here. You need to step up your effort." Vixor smirked.

"It appears so." Lorthuum let go of the feather and gripped the handle of reins tighter.

Vixor scratched his head. He wasn't getting anywhere with his brother. For whatever reason, Lorthuum clearly wanted to sulk in his misery. "How about we see if we have any wine left in our supplies, have a small toast to today's—" Before Vixor could finish his sentence, a rustling came from one of the nearby huts up ahead.

The two men brought their steeds to a stop. Vixor drew his sword and eyed the huts. One was on fire; the other was a pile of wreckage.

The rustling erupted again. This time, it was clear the sound came from the collapsed structure.

"Show yourself! We will have mercy, as is the will of the Council of Just," Vixor shouted.

Nothing. Only the sound of the crackling fires and the nearby cries of vazeleads filled the air. A brisk wind picked up, blowing against the knights' sweaty faces.

"Soft-skins!" came a hiss as a scaly humanoid sprung out of the rubble in front of them, its tattered toga blowing in the wind. The reptile soared through the air and collided with Lorthuum, causing him to fall off his mount.

Vixor slashed his blade down at the vazelead. The reptilian dodged the attack by rolling off of Lorthuum and leaping back onto his feet. He bent his legs, leaning forward, tail wiggling rapidly in the air. His elongated, sharp claws returned to his sides.

"Soft-skins! You will pay for what you have done!" the vazelead sneered. The black and white feathers on his scalp stood straight up, making him appear larger than he was.

Lorthuum got to his feet as Vixor dismounted, standing next to his brother. Lorthuum drew his blade and stood in a defensive stance.

"I go left, you go right?" Vixor whispered. "I attack low and you high. He won't stand a chance."

"This is no mere troll, brother," Lorthuum said. "That tail is an opponent all on its own."

The vazelead hissed and rushed towards the knights.

"Too late!" Vixor shouted while charging the vazelead's back.

The reptilian lashed his claws at Lorthuum, forcing him to block the attack. His tail flailed wildly at Vixor, who attempted to deflect the tail with his blade, but the thick scales were too dense for the weapon to have any effect. The tail glided off the metal and coiled around Vixor's wrist.

"Dammit," Vixor muttered under his breath before the vazelead's tail yanked him forward, knocking his sword free from his hand and throwing him face-first into the ground.

Vixor wiped the mud from his eyes and rolled onto his back, looking around for his sword. It was a few paces away from the vazelead. The reptilian lashed a couple of times at Lorthuum and then paused his advancements. He eyed Lorthuum closely before lowering his claws and stepping back. The vazelead looked down at Vixor as his claws pressed onto the handle of the human's sword, dragging it closer to his side.

Vixor pushed himself up. Luckily, he always came prepared and pulled out a dagger he'd had tucked in the back of his belt.

The vazelead's feathers relaxed as he took another step away, pulling Vixor's sword with him. He looked over at his two opponents. Lorthuum stared back at him, lowering his blade.

Snorting, the vazelead dashed away from the knights, his feet raising gravel as he sprinted away from the village, kicking the sword to the side. The trotting of horses picked up from behind Vixor as three steeds came rushing past the brothers. Two of the knights rushed after the vazelead, holding nets and chains. The third steed, a black one, came to a stop, turning around to look at the knights. It was Captain Franthar who mounted it.

"This reptile got the upper hand on you two?" the captain chuckled.

"It appears so," Vixor said, eyeing his brother. *Why did that vazelead stop?* he thought.

"So, you two have met your match?" Captain Franthar asked.

"It got lucky." Vixor smirked.

"Of course. Don't worry, Alloth and Godor will seize the creature," Captain Franthar said before rushing off to catch up with the other two knights.

Lorthuum sheathed his blade and reached down to grab his brother's sword, holding the top of the handle. He brought the handle to his brother, keeping a blank face.

Vixor took it and sheathed his weapon, keeping his gaze on his brother.

PART II: REASON

The raid on the village was completed shortly after the incident with the loose vazelead. The Knight's Union, led by Fierel Flamesworth, took the captured reptilians away from their homes, leading them towards Mount Kuzuchi—the highest peak in the known world. The journey would take days for them to complete.

Think of the glory, Vixor thought on several occasions during their travel. He and Lorthuum rode near the back of the captured vazeleads alongside half a dozen more knights. Fierel led the group of Captain Franthar and six more knights. Their squadron was smaller than some of the others, but their skills made up for the low number of warriors. For Vixor, it was easier for him to shine with less competition.

He watched the reptilians in front of him move step by step. Lashes of a whip occasionally broke out from one of the knights beside him. Anytime a vazelead showed a sign of weakness, the knights ensured that the fiends kept pace.

Their travel continued through the day, leading out of the grassy plains and into rocky mountain territories. The road continued on an incline as it progressively became rockier on one side. The path cut close along the edge of a cliff, making it a sudden drop if anyone got too close. In the far distance was the base of Mount Kuzuchi. Its true height was shrouded in clouds, vanishing into the sky. The clouds kept the sun hidden from view, leaving the group under a gloomy atmosphere. The light gradually diminished as the sun set.

The inclining path levelled out into a circular opening before the road continued. The path was clearly defined by the sharp-angled walls of the mountain. Fierel brought up her hand as she came to a stop. The sign caught the attention of each knight, and they paused in their tracks, along with their captives.

The pale, red-haired paladin turned to face the large group. "We set camp here tonight," she announced. Her voice was strident and pierced through the winds, commanding every knight to begin their duties.

Vixor and Lorthuum joined their comrades and set up camp. They kept the vazeleads off to the far corner against the mountainside, cornering them from any attempt to escape. The knights set up their sleeping bags, several fires, and the captain's tent in the open space in front of the reptiles. By the time the camp was complete, darkness had covered the land. Fierel and Captain Franthar stood near the edge of the cliff, talking softly.

"What do you suppose they are discussing?" The words were spoken by the blonde knight. She sat in front of one of the small fires. The orange glow from the flame projected a soft hue over her smooth face and steel armour.

Vixor knew her well; her name was Ellieth. They had gone to the academy together. The two of them and Lorthuum were the only three of the same graduating class in the squadron. There was a sense of familiarity and safety when raiding with his fellow classmates from so many years ago.

Vixor chewed on a piece of freshly cooked meat and shrugged. "Who knows. Discussing our path, perhaps."

"Fierel is making us move," offered another knight around the fire. Her long hair was braided and parted to the side.

"Aye, Valerie, that I agree with," Vixor said, looking over at Lorthuum, expecting him to speak up. The man only stared into the fire with a glazed-over look in his eyes.

Ellieth said, "We spent all day travelling, raiding, then travelling some more. It's going to exhaust us."

Vixor finished his meat and said, "This is what the academy trained us for. The day we defend humanity was bound to come. This is our glory."

"All I'm saying is she is a bit of a hardass," Ellieth said. "I don't see why we need a paladin to lead the Knight's Union squadron. We're fully capable on our own."

Valerie pointed up to the sky, saying, "Paladins are blessed by the hand of God. Their will is his."

"Plus, the Council of Just puts high faith in them," Vixor said. "Fierel is here to ensure *their* will is made real. Not God's."

"Pessimistic much?" Ellieth smiled, her hazelnut eyes watching him. She'd had a wholesome grin ever since they were young. He admired that she was always able to maintain the kindness of her smile, even in these dark times. Most knights couldn't manage that.

'*An equal is a desirable goal.*' Lorthuum's words echoed in Vixor's mind. He had always been aware of Ellieth's beauty. They also had a lot of similarities. Vixor had always been too busy trying to climb the ranks to do anything about it. Now, with the chaos of banishing the vazeleads, initiating anything with her seemed next to impossible. Perhaps once all of this was complete, he could explore his emotions for her—presuming she felt the same.

Valerie spoke, breaking Vixor from his romantic thoughts. "It is God's will. Paladins are his hand of action. The Council of Just members are our heroes but not our words."

Vixor cleared his throat. "It is the Council of Just who ensure we don't plummet into another Drac Age. They rescued humanity out of that dark time to begin with. Paladins like Fierel take decades to age, meaning all paladins were alive during the Drac Age and have experience with the draconem. We're listening to their will."

Ellieth said, "Quite true. Fierel and the captain are either talking about how they'll drive us to exhaustion or how we'll keep these reptiles in check."

"Simple: we'll keep them fearful," Valerie said assertively, as if she wanted to inflict terror.

"Valerie," Vixor said, "we have done a fine job of that already. These creatures are hostile, like draconem. We have many days of travel ahead of us, and they will resort to violence. So, keep your guard up."

Lorthuum spoke up. "They're not violent. Their diet consists of berries and nuts. They live in small, supportive groups to raise their young. Those aren't the signs of hostility if you ask me."

Vixor shook his head. "They serve Karazickle, Drac Lord of the Night. They have his symbolic moon crescent banners. Trust me, brother—they are not peaceful."

Lorthuum looked away from the fire, staring into the large group of reptiles. The beings mostly remained quiet and huddled close together. "I've never seen one with the symbol," Lorthuum said.

"Saule did," Ellieth said. "And since he's the leader of the Paladins of Zeal, his word is holy."

Lorthuum looked at his three allies. "Have any of you seen Karazickle's symbol on a vazelead?"

The group fell silent, looking at one another to see if any of them could confirm the story.

"That's food for thought," Lorthuum said.

Valerie leaned forward, saying, "Think about their name, Lorthuum. *Vazelead.*"

"It is of draconem origins. I am aware," Lorthuum said.

"Not just that," Valerie said. "It is draconic, meaning 'drac men.'"

"That means very little if you ask me," Lorthuum said. "I am simply asking questions. If you forget, we enslaved the vazelead people during the Drac Age. The Drac Lord Fongoxent freed them and then shortly learned neither draconem nor humans cared for them. What would vazeleads gain from serving Karazickle?" Lorthuum's voice grew louder in his last statement, enough to catch the eye of Fierel and Captain Franthar. They eyed the group of four closely with their cold stares.

I really should have checked if we had any more wine, Vixor thought.

"Better safe than sorry," he said. "Saule has spoken. We will obey." He glanced over at the paladin and the captain to see they had looked back at each other.

"I think we're too cruel in our accusations." Lorthuum got up from his seat and said, "I'm only asking that you keep an open mind." He stepped away from the group, walking further away from the cliff's edge.

"Testy," Ellieth teased.

Valerie snickered as she stabbed a slab of meat with a stick, bringing it to the fire.

"He had better be careful," Ellieth said. "Talk like that will put you on Fierel and Captain Franthar's watch list."

Vixor shook his head. "I'll talk to him," he said, getting up from his seat.

"See if he will volunteer to be part of the first night shift!" Valerie called out.

Vixor hurried over to his brother. "Brother!" Vixor said, grabbing hold of Lorthuum by the arm. "Speak to me. What haunts your mind today?"

Lorthuum turned to face his brother. His brows slanted inward. He was upset.

"You speak such bold words, brother. You mustn't say such things in passionate terms. You'll catch unwanted attention from the captain. Think about what we've worked towards," Vixor said.

"You want to be a captain, Vixor."

"Don't you?" Vixor asked.

"Yes, but not if it means this. Think about it, brother. You are smarter than I."

"Nonsense," Vixor said, although he knew Lorthuum was right. Vixor had always been the strategic child, but he didn't want to gloat in front of his brother.

"It is true," Lorthuum said bluntly. "My skills with the blade are my specialty, but you have a strong mind and a fiery passion. If you don't guide it, you will go down a path of evil. Just like our fellow men do."

"I don't follow," Vixor said.

"Think about what is happening here. Think about what we are becoming. The draconem attempted to enslave all life during the Drac Age and rule the known world. We fought back and won. Now, we are removing any possible threat to us. Don't you see? We're becoming just like the draconem."

"No," Vixor said. "This is entirely different. We are eliminating any potential threat that could *become* like the draconem. Karazickle is the last Drac Lord. The vazeleads are his army."

"I disagree. I think we are being misled. The draconem wanted to destroy anything that could outpower them, and we are mirroring that fear-based behaviour."

Vixor looked over at the group of vazeleads. He locked gazes with one male with black and white feathers. The yellow eyes of the reptile did not blink. *Him,* Vixor thought. *He chose not to attack us.* "I don't see it, brother. Look at them. They're monsters."

"You only grew this way of thinking since Saule, and the Council of Just, told us to think this way. I fear for you, brother. You are not thinking like a free man."

Vixor looked over at him. "Why did that reptile stop attacking you?"

"Sorry?" Lorthuum asked.

"The one, in the front there." Vixor pointed at the vazelead. "The one who watches us keenly."

"I don't know," Lorthuum said. He brushed his hair from his face. "Perhaps he realized he was outnumbered and didn't want to risk his own life."

Vixor nodded. The words his brother spoke weren't truthful. Vixor had been there. He knew what he'd seen: the reptile had acted as if he recognized Lorthuum. But why?

Perhaps my brother needs rest, Vixor thought. "Of course, brother," he said. Vixor wanted to argue with him, but both of them were already heated from their debate. They were also exhausted from the long day of travel, battle, and bloodshed. "Let's get some rest," he suggested.

Lorthuum locked eyes with the black-and-white-feathered vazelead and nodded.

PART III: FAMILY

The night had moved well past dusk. The members of the Knight's Union had settled into their camp, and their prisoners had long been asleep. Most of the knights had removed their armour and lay fast asleep under the stars.

For some of the men, Captain Franthar and Fierel organized a shift-based night watch over their camp. One could never be too sure of any trouble from outside forces or the prisoners themselves. Captain Franthar retreated to his tent after organizing the shifts. Fierel slept outside with the knights and vazeleads. For whatever reason, she always slept amongst the warriors.

A part of Vixor wanted to ask her why she chose to sleep under the sky. He had many questions for her. What were her thoughts on the recent order from the Council of Just? Was the vazelead banishment birthed from a misguided accusation? His brother surely thought so. It was beginning to make Vixor's life difficult. He couldn't quite grasp why Lorthuum was so opposed to their task.

"I don't get it," Vixor mumbled, sitting on his sleeping bag. "Lorthuum has never doubted the direction of the Knight's Union before." He watched the three knights on watch move around the camp. Two were on the opposite end with Lorthuum, who had volunteered to be a part of the first shift.

Ellieth brushed her hair behind her ear, saying, "Perhaps he is feeling his moral compass being brought into question."

Vixor sighed and looked out at the mountain landscape. Some of the clouds were beginning to pass, revealing the stars. The fire had lost its flames, but the embers still provided a soothing warmth.

"Why? They're animals," Vixor said. Their primitive tools and tribes made it difficult for him to see the vazeleads in any other way. "They may speak English like any man and can wield a weapon, but that doesn't give them the same rights as a man."

"I'm not sure what to think of them. The Knight's Union is my life, and I show nothing but loyalty to them," Ellieth said.

"Aye, same here. I wish I could just snap my brother out of it. I fear he may be doing himself more damage than good. What if he takes this too far? What do I do then?" Vixor didn't expect Ellieth to give him all the answers he needed, but he wanted to use her as a sounding board. They'd known each other long enough, and she knew Lorthuum, too. He needed some form of guidance.

"That is a real challenge," Ellieth mumbled.

"What would you do?" Vixor asked.

Ellieth shrugged. "Well, I don't have a sibling in the Knight's Union. If my brother did join, though, I . . . " She paused and stared off into the distance. "I don't know. Family comes first. But the Knight's Union is doing the work of humanity, and God."

"That is the dilemma I am in. I don't want him to piss away his life because he is asking questions. True or false, he shouldn't be challenging Saule or the Council of Just. He should know that from his training."

"Perhaps you need to have another talk with him." Ellieth lay down on her sleeping bag. "Or perhaps his sour mood will pass, and he will swallow whatever misconception of the world he has."

"Perhaps," Vixor said. "I need to walk this off."

"Don't get lost," Ellieth said.

Vixor smirked and got up from his sleeping bag. He snagged his knife and horn, just in case. It was impossible to know what type of dangers may lurk in the night. He strapped the sheath and horn to his belt as he walked away from the camp.

I really must ask about her feelings towards me, he thought. Vixor had known this woman for so long, and there was something between the two of them. He would be a fool not to engage romantically.

Vixor passed two men who were part of the night watch, both holding torches. He nodded at them, walking back to the descending path from whence their group had arrived. There was a small trail leading farther into the wilderness where he was able to get some privacy. He wandered for a short period around the landscape, moving up the mountainside. Vixor had never been on this side of the kingdom before, but he figured it was reasonably safe. Besides, he had a weapon if he needed to defend himself.

The knight began to lose track of time as he walked around, trying to calm his mind from the raid, the travels, and his brother's emotions. With any luck, he would be able to get some shut-eye before the night's end. The path led him to a view overlooking the camp, where he was able to see the night watch, the tent, his sleeping comrades, and the reptiles. The higher view allowed him to see everything in one full scope, taking in everything they had done.

I can't wait for all of this to be over, Vixor thought. Perhaps then, Lorthuum would calm down. Vixor could engage with Ellieth. Life could return to peace.

Hissing erupted from the cluster of vazeleads. One of the reptiles was beginning to throw rocks at the resting knights.

"Hey!" called out one of the night watch. Two men rushed towards the vazelead. "Stop it, or we will have your throat!" The man shined the torch towards the reptile's face, exposing the black and white feathers in the light.

That one. He's trouble, Vixor thought. He contemplated coming down to intervene in the altercation but decided to hold off. This was the night watch's job. His was to try and relax so he could conserve energy for tomorrow.

The vazelead's body began to lash out. Despite having his limbs and tail shackled, the reptile's violent movements were fast and forceful, sending the two knights backing up.

"Do we stab him?" asked the one knight.

"No, that is the last resort. We're humane. Try to hold the fiend down," the other knight said.

The two men attempted to calm the vazelead. It was no use; he was too violent, and the men resorted to kicking and punching to keep the reptile still. The jingling of chains from the opposite side of the vazelead group picked up. Another man, with no torch in hand, was fiddling with the shackles of one of the reptiles. The two on night watch were too distracted by the black-and-white-feathered vazelead to notice the activity.

What? Vixor thought. He leaned closer to the edge, trying to make out who was there.

The man unshackled the vazelead and urged it to move. Both the reptile and the man rushed off away from the camp, leading deeper into the mountains.

"No," muttered Vixor. He couldn't stand back and watch this betrayal happen before his eyes. Vixor hurried around the upper path, leading towards the road that the man and the vazelead had taken. He wasn't entirely sure if the trail would point in the same direction, but it was his best bet to keep up with them.

Dodging large rocks and sudden drops, Vixor skillfully navigated over the rocky path until he could hear stomping footsteps below. He was right on their trail. Vixor slowed his pace as he followed close to them, peeking over the edge to see the man and vazelead running side by side. Now that he was closer, he could see the man had dirty-blond hair—Lorthuum. From the vazelead's thinner figure, it was safe to assume it was female.

What are you doing, brother? Vixor thought. He found a descending path from his higher ground and carefully followed it until he was on the main road. He followed the two escapees from a distance, keeping far enough away that they wouldn't be able to hear him.

The path split off into two directions, one leading deeper into the mountains and the other descending back into the grassy hills below. Lorthuum and the vazelead took the descending road that curved backwards, leading back to the tribe in the direction they'd come from earlier. Lorthuum and the vazelead travelled for a long distance, making Vixor wonder if they were merely going to run throughout the night. At this point, he wouldn't be too surprised. His brother was acting out of character. What other secrets could he have?

Vixor's thoughts were put to rest when he saw the two turn off the path, heading for some rocky hills. They reached a small, dark den poking out at the base of one of the mounds. They leaned down on their knees, peeking inside the little cave for a moment before standing back up.

Vixor continued to creep behind towards Lorthuum and the vazelead until he could hear their conversation.

"And what of Tolodon? My poor brother. We have to get him!" the female vazelead cried.

Lorthuum extended his hands, taking hold of the reptile by the hips. "I will do what I can. He and I fabricated the plan so you could escape, and the three of us could be together."

Brother? Vixor thought. He could barely comprehend what was happening in front of him. His brother, the man he had grown up with and fought alongside, was living a double life—with a reptile. How could Lorthuum see anything remotely attractive in such a creature?

The female coiled her tail around Lorthuum's leg. "I fear for my brother," she said. "He only wants what is best for me. I don't want that to be his ultimate sacrifice, though." Her green feathers puffed up slightly and relaxed as she stared into the man's eyes.

"My dear Taliedon," Lorthuum said, bringing the vazelead closer. "I will try and save him." The two embraced one another with a long hug.

"I don't understand why the Council of Just think we are serving the Drac Lord. By what means are they justifying these claims?" the female—Taliedon—said.

"I do not know," Lorthuum replied. "It troubles me greatly, and I wish I could convince my brother and allies that the Council of Just is wrong. They do not hear my words of reason."

What do I do? Vixor thought. He knew he couldn't let Lorthuum continue with this second life. His brother was betraying the Knight's Union by allowing a vazelead to escape. Vixor also wanted answers from his brother. How long had he been hiding this life? Vixor felt an intense mixture of emotions run through his system. Rage, confusion, and pain—all of them brewed together into some unidentifiable burst of energy that coursed through his body. He needed answers. Lorthuum had to provide them.

Vixor burst from his hiding place, pulling the dagger from his belt. "Brother!" Vixor shouted, pointing the blade towards the two. "What is this?"

Taliedon gasped as Lorthuum stepped in front of her. "Vixor," he said. "Please, lower your blade."

"How can I?" Vixor asked, stopping about a dozen paces away from his brother. "What is this treachery? You betray the Knight's Union, the Council of Just, and the safety of humanity itself. Speak!"

A soft yawn echoed from the small den as a tiny, flesh-toned figure stepped out, rubbing its reptilian eyes. "Mother?" it said.

"Stay back," Taliedon ordered, extending her hand to the small child.

Vixor stared, not blinking, at the unexplainable sight. Behind his brother and the vazelead was a child of the same size and skin tone as a human boy. A tail swayed side to side behind him. Claws extended from his hands and feet, and green feathers ran along the skull where hair should be. Brown scales ran along the back spine. The face was slightly extended outward, like a vazelead's.

"What . . . what is that?" Vixor asked, pointing his blade at the child in horror. "How . . . how is that even possible?" Vixor knew half-breeds could exist amongst more commonly related races, but a vazelead and a human were so different in many aspects of their physical makeup. This seemed impossible. "Is this some form of witchcraft?"

"No, brother," Lorthuum said. "This is my son. We are a family."

"Your son?" Vixor exclaimed. "That is an abomination! What have you done? With this . . . reptile?" Vixor couldn't believe what was in front of him. His entire life that he knew with his brother shattered. "Who are you, Lorthuum? You're blending worlds that should never merge! We are not like these creatures. We're human!"

Lorthuum took a step forward, showing both hands. "I am your brother, no different than before. I know you must be greatly confused about all of this, but I need you to believe me. I have always been by your side. Taliedon and my son are my family."

"No." Vixor took a step back. "No, they are not your family. I am your family!" He pointed the knife at Lorthuum. "You are someone entirely different. Do you have any idea what type of disloyalty this demonstrates to the Knight's Union? You assisted in the escape of a vazelead—one that has birthed some type of monstrosity of our people."

"This is my family, Vixor. Do you not see why I was so enraged about the vazelead banishment? These peaceful people are not serving the Drac Lord Karazickle. Saule and the Council of Just have some other agenda they aren't sharing with us. We're pawns in a bigger game, Vixor. How can you not see that?"

Vixor shook his head. He couldn't even grasp the words that his brother was saying. "How long?" Vixor asked. "How long has this been going on for?"

Taliedon gently stroked her son's head, saying, "We met many seasons ago, before these false accusations were made upon my people."

Vixor's nostrils flared. He felt a pulsation of rage rush through his body. The vazelead had spoken to him. He was talking to his brother. "But the Knight's Union," Vixor said. "Everything you and I have worked towards."

"It is at risk," Lorthuum said. "How was I supposed to know that Saule would blame the vazelead people for being servants of Karazickle? Or that the Council of Just would sentence them to banishment from the surface world? How, Vixor?"

Vixor paused. He knew his brother had a point. But it didn't change the fact that he did not like what he was hearing. Lorthuum truly had a relationship with this vazelead. He had a son with it. "Even before the order of their banishment, Lorthuum, we did not mix with vazeleads," Vixor said. "Their enslavement is why they haven't communicated with us since the Drac Age."

"We have a dark and unfortunate past between our people, all because of the draconem. The vazeleads are not their servants, believe me. They are like us. They want peace."

Vixor pointed at Taliedon and the child. "They're nothing like us. Brother, you mustn't go down this path. Think of our future. Think of your father's name . . . our family's name! Do you want to be known as the traitor?"

"I am not a traitor, Vixor. The Council of Just are the ones betraying humanity. We want to leave here."

"You mentioned another, Tolodon. You don't want to leave here. You want to sabotage the banishment by letting these creatures free."

"Brother, please do not see it that way. That is far from the truth. You must see that what the Council of Just is doing is wrong."

Vixor felt a deep level of conflict. On the one hand, this was Lorthuum, his brother, the man who had stood by his side his whole life. They had protected one another and worked together since childhood. The two of them were supposed to continue their family's name and carry it with pride. On the other hand, Lorthuum was betraying his family's name and the Knight's Union. Everything was upside down. If Vixor did not act now, he would be shaming his father and destroying any chance he had at climbing the ranks of the Knight's Union. Lorthuum was his own man. He had chosen a dark path of no return.

I'm sorry, brother, Vixor thought. He sheathed his dagger and reached around his belt, feeling for the horn that was laced to it. "No, brother. I can't let you betray everything we've worked towards." He unlaced the horn and brought it to his lips, taking a deep breath and blowing into the animal bone. The horn made a loud, deep rumble that reverberated off the rocky landscape, amplifying the sound.

The horn blew for several moments before a solid force slammed into the side of Vixor's head, causing him to drop the horn. He stumbled for a moment as a rock tumbled to the ground, covered in a small splatter of blood.

Vixor looked up at his brother, who remained wide-eyed, one arm in a lowered position. A drizzle of warm liquid ran down Vixor's forehead and cheek. He felt it with his hand, realizing it was blood.

"Go, Taliedon!" Lorthuum shouted as the vazelead grabbed the child. "We don't have much time!" He turned to look at Vixor and shook his head. "I'm sorry, brother. You of all should know family is first. I hope we have the chance to meet again, and under better circumstances."

Vixor tumbled to his knees as his vision blurred, watching as his brother, the vazelead, and their abomination hurried from the scene. He collapsed down onto his shoulder just as his vision turned black.

PART IV: MARTYR

L oyalty is a relatively simple concept in theory. In practice, it can become challenging. How can you remain faithful to a loved one when you are troubled to your moral core? It is not an easy question to answer. The dilemma can destroy your sense of being, regardless of the choice you make. You can either stay true to your beliefs or remain devoted to your loved ones and dissolve everything you believe in.

For Vixor, the situation was a challenge. He felt betrayed by his brother, which hurt him on a deep level. It was as if he was looking at a different man. That was not Lorthuum. Whoever that was who stood before him was not the same person he'd grown up with. Lorthuum had willingly chosen to hide his life from his brother. The pain of this was what had driven him to sound the alarm horn for backup.

"Vixor!" came a muffled voice.

Lorthuum chose to hide his affair, Vixor thought. *He didn't trust me. My own brother.*

"Vixor!" came the muffled voice again, this time clearer. It was feminine but stern.

I blew the alarm. Perhaps that is why he didn't trust me. Can I blame him?

Cold water ran over his face, causing him to sputter.

Lorthuum, betrayer of humanity. An ally of the vazeleads, an ally of Karazickle. Is he? Where is the proof of any of this?

A steel gauntlet slapped against his face, bringing him back into reality. Vixor's eyes shot open as his vision began to clear. He rested against his arms and looked up to see Valerie leaning over him, wearing half of her armour. She held a small leather sack that was covered in beads of water. Beside her stood Captain Franthar, wearing only chainmail over his tunic and trousers. Another man, in some of his Knight's Union armour, stood beside the captain. Both men held torches. Three horses were behind them.

"Vixor!" Valerie said. "Do you know where you are?"

Vixor looked around and saw the small den farther ahead. Closer to him was the rock that Lorthuum had hit him with.

"Vixor," Captain Franthar said. "What happened here?"

Vixor got up and scratched his head, feeling where the rock had hit him. The cold water had moistened the dried blood, and he could wipe it from his face. He brushed his hair back and exhaled with exhaustion.

Valerie stood up. "You sounded your horn," she said. "What did you discover?"

"Let me ask the questions," Captain Franthar demanded.

"Of course, Captain." Valerie stood to the side as Captain Franthar took a step closer to Vixor.

"Vixor, I need you to tell me everything that happened here. Your brother is missing from the camp."

Vixor stared at the captain's blue eyes. The two were the exact same height, yet the man's stance made him far more intimidating than any regular man. "Captain, I sounded my horn to call for backup," Vixor explained.

I called to capture my brother, he thought. The grim reality hit his heart, and he felt a sharp pain run inside his ribcage. It was like being punched, but from within. Vixor cleared his throat before continuing, "There was an escapee."

"Vixor, what happened?" Captain Franthar asked. "I know that blow to the head was not done by you. Who escaped, and where did they go?"

My brother, who attacked me, who betrayed me. "Lorthuum, sir. I followed him after he let a vazelead escape."

"That fool," Captain Franthar sneered. "I had my suspicions of his loyalties."

"I am afraid he is defending the reptilians. He believes they have done no wrong." The words were difficult for Vixor to say. His brother fully believed that the vazeleads had no ties to the Drac Lord Karazickle. Or was he being seduced by that creature he called his lover?

"Your loyalties to the Knight's Union will not go unnoticed, Vixor." Captain Franthar put his hand on Vixor's shoulder and marched to the horses. "We ride. Show us where they went."

Promotion. His mind was still foggy from the rock hitting his head. His thoughts ran between his feelings for his brother, the confusion of Lorthuum's betrayal, and Vixor's own beliefs.

"Your horn," Valerie said, extending her hand to him, holding the horn.

"Thanks," Vixor said, taking it. He strapped it to his belt.

"Ride with me," Valerie said as she leaped onto her horse.

Vixor hopped onto the back of her steed, as Captain Franthar and the additional knight brought their horses around to face them.

"Vixor, point the way," the captain ordered.

Instinctively, Vixor pointed down away from the small den where he saw Lorthuum and his family go before he'd passed out. The motion was without thought, and after he put his hand back around Valerie, he thought about his action.

We're on a manhunt for my own brother, he thought.

"Ride out!" Captain Franthar shouted as he commanded his horse to dash down the hill. Valerie and the supporting knight followed without question. The subtle wind blew in their faces as the horses charged down the slope.

Promotion, Vixor thought. *This will be rewarded.* He couldn't help but think about what would happen once they caught hold of Lorthuum and his family. In the back of his mind, he knew that the vazelead, Taliedon, would be killed upon capture. For the child, its similar fate would surely follow, after a thorough examination of what it was. As for Lorthuum, he could be punished severely—sent to prison and most likely disowned by the Knight's Union.

He made his mind up, Vixor thought.

"What was your brother doing out this late, Vixor?" Valerie asked.

"I don't know," Vixor said. "It is like I don't even know him anymore." Vixor felt ashamed. He didn't want to get into the details with Valerie, especially if they were in the midst of hunting Lorthuum down. The whole situation was unreal to him, and he could barely swallow it himself.

"His behaviour has been off since we started rallying these reptilian fiends," Valerie said.

"Aye," Vixor replied. Now he knew the truth why. Unlike his comrades, Vixor knew that Lorthuum was only defending what he believed to be his family. A family, unlike anything humans or vazeleads had seen before. Taliedon's brother, Tolodon, whom Vixor presumed to be the black-and-white-feathered vazelead, seemed to accept the situation. Even in Vixor's hazy state, he clearly recalled how the reptile identified Lorthuum and lowered his attack during the raid.

Did those reptiles poison my dear brother's mind? Vixor thought. The more time he stayed awake, the clearer his processing ability became. *How could a primitive people learn how to brainwash sophisticated beings like us?* Vixor was not fond of the vazelead people, but now he was becoming skeptical of the accusations against them by the Council of Just. Lorthuum's shocking choices were challenging his beliefs. *Or was it the Council of Just that brainwashed us?*

"You're going to impress Ellieth with that bump on your head," Valerie said. "You ever going to just tell her how you feel?"

Ellieth, Vixor thought. The warm smile of the woman flashed through his mind, followed by his last conversation with her. *'I don't know. Family comes first . . . ,'* she had said to him.

Family, Vixor thought.

"I see them!" shouted the knight beside Captain Franthar. "Further

247

ahead near the next hill."

"Heeyah!" Captain Franthar shouted, causing his horse to snort.

Vixor looked over Valerie's shoulder to see three distant figures moving up a steep hill. One was smaller, held by another. It was difficult to see much more due to the darkness, but it was unmistakably Lorthuum and his family.

Family, Vixor thought again. *Lorthuum, who couldn't trust his own brother enough to reveal his new life with his family.* Vixor felt another surge of pain as he realized why Lorthuum could not tell him about his son and lover. Vixor's loyalty was always to the Knight's Union, not to him. Vixor, the man who was responsible for Lorthuum's and his family's forthcoming demise.

"No!" Vixor shouted.

"What?" Valerie asked, looking back at him.

Vixor slid his arms from Valerie's waist and coiled a fist, slamming it into her face. The blow hit her in the nose, cartilage crushing inward. He snagged her by the neck with both hands, tossing her off the horse, sending her tumbling on the ground

The man pulled out his dagger from his belt, eyeing the two men in front of him. They hadn't even noticed the altercation yet. Captain Franthar was ahead of the knight, who rode to his right, torch in hand. He wore a breastplate, with no helmet or shoulder protection.

He felt the dangling of the rope trophy covered in vazelead claws against his leg. Looking down at it, he felt a sense of disgust. With one slash, he cut both ends of the rope; the trophy fell to the grass.

Better, Vixor thought.

Vixor carefully held on to the steed with one hand as he brought his blade-wielding hand back. He had to make this shot count, for Lorthuum. He launched his hand forward, tossing the blade in a rotating fashion. The dagger flew through the night air, a shimmer coming from the metal as it flew near the torch. It hit directly into the back of the knight's neck, causing him to go numb. The man dropped the light and slid off his steed, tumbling to the ground. The horse strayed off into the darkness, leaving the group.

The loss of light from the second torch caught Captain Franthar's attention, and he glanced back. His eyes widened as he noticed only Vixor and one horse behind him. The captain shifted his steed to the side, slowing it down.

"Vixor! You unpredictable fool!" shouted Captain Franthar. "Where do you think this will take you?" he asked as their horses came parallel to each other.

Vixor patted around the animal's leather saddle, trying to feel for any weapons. Nothing. He had used up his only dagger to remove the other knight, and now he was left with his bare hands against his squadron's captain.

Captain Franthar lunged the torch at Vixor. The flame lightly grazed his arm, lighting it ablaze. Vixor quickly patted the fire down as the captain swung down again with the torch, this time hitting him in the shoulder.

Vixor yelped in pain as ashes and flame burst into the air. There was no way he would be able to continue dodging the attacks this way. He had to act fast. Letting go of his horse, he let out a roar as he swung his legs around to face the captain. Captain Franthar brought his arm back, ready to attack, as Vixor leaped from his horse and onto the captain. The two men collided as the captain brought the torch between them. Vixor's mass compressed the torch against them and knocked them off the captain's steed. Captain Franthar landed back-first on the ground with a heavy thud.

Vixor quickly rolled off and patted his burning hair, face, and clothes. It was bad, he knew; the burn marks would most likely cause scars.

Captain Franthar released the torch, patting himself down to remove the flames.

Vixor roared again as he slammed his foot down at his captain. The man rolled to the side. Vixor's boot came into contact with dirt. Captain Franthar got to his feet, drawing his sword.

"What the hell has gotten into you Pureheart brothers?" Captain Franthar sneered. "This is treason!"

Vixor held out his hands, ready for combat. He knew he stood no chance, but he had to buy his brother time to escape. "You must forgive me, captain, but I cannot let you hunt my brother."

The two men began to circle one another as Captain Franthar made subtle movements towards Vixor.

The captain pointed his blade at Vixor. "You, yourself, said he sides with the vazeleads—followers of the Drac Lord Karazickle! Are you a servant of the draconem? Or of humanity?"

"I serve humanity, captain. But you must see the chaos we are causing. We are banishing an entire people based on speculation!"

"It is the will of the council!" Captain Franthar shouted, rushing forward. He lashed his blade down—a miss. He swung diagonally—a hit.

Vixor let out a yell, feeling his outer thigh split open. Another blow from the captain hit him in the arm, then another on his calf. He collapsed to the ground. His captain was too skilled and armed with a longsword. In the back of his mind, Vixor knew the fight would end in only one way.

Captain Franthar brought the blade to Vixor's throat, forcing him to look up.

"You showed such promise, Vixor," Captain Franthar said. "But you assaulted your fellow knights and now you attack your captain? That is enough for removal from the Knight's Union and imprisonment."

Wait until you discover what I did to the other knight, Vixor thought. Ending the life of a fellow member of the Knight's Union was among the worst crimes a knight could commit. He knew the grim consequence: death.

"I had faith you would rise in my ranks and fight by my side as your father did. I suppose I put too much hope into one man."

"Apologies to be a disappointment, captain," Vixor said. His eyes strayed over to the hillside, where the three figures could be seen reaching the top of the steep incline.

"Have you gone mad, Vixor?" Captain Franthar asked.

Two of the figures continued down to the opposite side of the hill.

One stood up and turned, looking back at them. Vixor could only speculate, but deep down, he knew it was his brother.

Lorthuum, I will miss you, Vixor thought.

"Have you got no loyalty?" Captain Franthar shouted at Vixor.

The figure on the hill turned and disappeared down the other side of the mound. Vixor looked back at his captain.

"I do, sir," he said. "I should have never questioned it." *Family comes first*—Ellieth's words echoed in his mind.

16

Who knew coldness would be so warm? Yet, the further from the cold you are, the less familiar it seems. The strange land of Zingalg isn't home to you at all. The last observing experience and the one before that were from an alien land. The feeling of death was what you latched on to with the man on Ka'dubarh. That aside, there's nothing here for you other than confusion. The theme of family holds true. Loyalty and honour are good traits. You wonder if they were ones you lived up to during your life. Maybe. Hopefully you weren't some dirtball.

"And?" Malpherities says. His doubled voice is the first thing you detect. Your eyesight is next, then the rest of your senses exit the observer state.

"No, I think this is a dead end," you say.

"That's good. I was too optimistic about Zingalg. The land hosted so many critical events in your world's history—powerful ones that can disrupt a soul's natural path post-death, like what happened to you."

"It seemed pretty magical," you say.

"Yes. There was an unholy gift for a brief time known as Mental Damnation. It was a common thing during that era."

"You think that I had that gift?"

"Not now. But it did send mortals into the afterlife while still being alive. Your case is a bit different, and I made an educated guess that you came from Zingalg. You're most likely somewhere in between the days of godly powers and the distant planetary colonization. We're getting closer."

You groan. "That's a long stretch of time. What now?"

"Care to try on your own again? Or shall I just keep dabbing the droplets? I'm far more able."

You sigh. "Okay," you say. "Let's try somewhere else, maybe shortly after that talking goat one? The nineties seemed familiar."

"Good call. It seems like you have a useful mind after all." Malpherities scoops up the black liquid and drops it into your eye, sending you into a new observation.

TYNE CABIN

THE MORNING

I sit patiently in the car, twiddling my thumbs, wondering when I will be able to get up and stretch my legs. I have already spent over two hours on the highway, watching trees, rocks, and the occasional animals go by. It's cold at first, but after a while, you get tired of seeing the same thing. The fact that I get squirrelly easily doesn't help either. Maybe that's why my parents insist on those prescription pills and less time on the Internet—too much stimulation.

I sigh, watching the condensation from my exhale build up on the window, then slowly fade. At least it is something new to look at instead of the same old scenery of tree . . . tree . . . tree. Oh, look a rock! When are we going to stop?

"We're almost there, gang!" Dad says from the front seat.

Mom looks back at me with a warm smile. "You're going to love the lake," she says. "It's beautiful."

"Yeah," I reply with little enthusiasm. I tried, really. As far as I know, we could be driving for another hour, or worse, forever. The gloomy thought is shot dead wrong as Dad decelerates the car, turning off the main highway and onto a range road. The sudden change in the engine's humming catches my attention, and I perk up, looking out the driver's view. We're *in* the trees now. Branches are everywhere. The road is bumpy. This is new.

"We're here?" I ask.

"That's right, champ," Dad says. "In about a half hour, we'll be at that lake. You'll get to see where your old man spent his summers with your great-uncle."

Mom sighs. "Chuck was a sweet man."

"Yeah," Dad says.

Mom gently touches Dad's arm.

Oh, if you haven't pieced it together, Uncle Chuck is dead. I never met him. Supposedly he went missing in the forest. They never found his body, but I heard chat amongst my aunts that he started getting into some non-Christian things, like magic. My family are pretty heavy believers, too. I'm not too sure myself. Either way, Uncle Chuck is gone.

Dad smiles. "He sure showed me how to enjoy life. Back then, we didn't have all those handheld devices."

"Like the one I couldn't bring?" I ask.

"Trust me. You'll thank me when we get there," Dad says.

"I hear it is called a digital detox," Mom says.

I sink back into my seat and try to zone out for the next half hour. What else can I do? The trees got boring again, and I am still annoyed that my folks didn't let me bring my smartphone. I want to keep tabs on my girl, but I suppose a couple of days away doesn't hurt. I'll see Tania in school on Monday.

My thoughts wander over to Tania. Yeah. Thinking about her smell and her laugh are great. What's better is all the sexy stuff, the kinds of details any teenage boy thinks. The brain-wandering takes up the remainder of the drive. At one point, I got a boner and sat cross-legged to hide it. I don't need my parents to see that! Thankfully, it goes away just as we come to a stop. A crystal-clear lake and a beach are right in front of us. To the right is a white-painted wooden cabin. A firepit is to the side of the cabin, surrounded by a series of logs for sitting.

"We're here?" I ask, unbuckling my seatbelt.

"We sure are," Dad says. "That's the Tyne family cabin, probably as old as Gramps himself."

"Same cabin?" I ask.

"Yep. Amazing, isn't it?" Dad says.

Dad puts the car into park, and we all hurry out of the vehicle. My parents are already gathering our luggage from the back trunk. I run to the lake, kicking up dirt and sand to reach the shores. I skid to a stop, taking a deep breath of that fresh air. I don't have my phone, but I sure as hell am enjoying this view. It's the kind of view Tania would like. Ugh.

"Jacob!" Mom calls.

I look back to see my parents are walking to the cabin. My dad is holding a set of keys.

"Coming!" I call out, rushing back to them.

"Here," I say, reaching for one of the suitcases Mom is holding. She lets me take it, and all three of us walk up the front porch. Dad unlocks the door and pushes it open. The hinges creak, exposing the dark interior inside; this place is old. We step into the entryway, inhaling the stale smell of dust. I cough several times. Looking around, I see that the floor, the furniture, and even the walls are covered in white flakes.

"When was the last time this place was used?" I ask.

"It's been a while," Dad says. "Dust travels from the car exhaust on the highway. It's pretty common." He drops his luggage. The weight of the baggage creates a large cloud that envelops the scene.

I cough and lean towards the entrance, avoiding the white dust. "Dad, watch where you drop that! What's with this dust, anyway?" I ask, noticing one large flake that gently landed on my forearm. "What is this?" I ask.

"It's an old cabin," Dad says. "I wouldn't be surprised if it had some termites eating at the wood. Let's enjoy it this summer and see if we can fix it up in the next."

THE EVENING

The three of us clean every surface of the cabin to make it livable. We remove the excessive dust and wood flakes, which takes all afternoon and even some of the evening. We spend our night cooking hotdogs over a campfire and enjoying the stars—you know, the typical cabin thing. My folks tell me about how the other Tyne family members used to come out here, but we haven't talked to them in a while. Dad thinks we pissed them off or something. Who knows.

All three of us are exhausted and don't do much for the remainder of the night. Mom keeps complaining about itchy eyes and a sore throat from the dust. Dad seems pretty beat too.

We conclude it is time to set up our sleeping bags. Mine is on the couch, and my folks bring theirs into the bedroom. The two of them hit the sack shortly after. I'm left awake, trying to fall asleep. All of the momentum from cleaning is keeping me up, not to mention the excessive dust that I've been inhaling keeps making me cough. I examine my arm, noticing the bone-white dust and flakes are causing my skin to dry out. Sawdust will do that, but this seems a bit much. Maybe I'm allergic? I'm always learning something new about my body. I wonder if there is a pill for that too.

I spend most of the night sitting on the front porch, watching the large mass of water. We don't even have booze. My folks are too traditional even to consider letting me have some. I guess I can spend the weekend just staring at the lake, getting introspective or whatever. I feel like I'm too young for that garbage and should be with Tania. But it's only two days. I stand up, deciding it's time to try and get some sleep. The air is so much better out here than in the cabin that I think about sleeping outside. We'll see. It is warmer inside.

A rustling noise comes from the shrubbery near the beach. I spin around to see some bushes bobbing up and down in the aftermath of the sound. I pause, scanning the scene.

A high-pitched snickering rises from the darkness.

"Yeah, good time for some sleep," I say, realizing no one else is around to hear. The last thing I want is for some coyote to bite me. Do they even attack people? I'm no animal expert. With that, I hurry back inside the cabin, lock the door, and slip into the sleeping bag, ready for a good night's sleep.

WAKEY-WAKEY!

Scratching and scraping sounds are like a broken record, looping over and over. I am dreaming of being in the car. Is the vehicle scraping against something? A snickering noise, or maybe screeching, pierces my ears. I shift in my sleeping position. It's one of those half-awake, half-sleeping states where you aren't sure what is real and what is a dream. They're cool sometimes. But times like this are frustrating. I'm groggy and exhausted. The sounds—real or fake—are keeping me half awake.

A gentle object lands on my nose. Then another, like leaves falling. The subtle touches answer the question—it's no dream. A few grunts and another snicker finally seal the deal, and I open my eyes. Directly above me is a naked, crusty-skinned man, scratching his neck vigorously over my face. I scream and scurry backwards. My head bumps into the armrest instantly.

The man looks down as his one leg slides off the backrest of the couch. His eyes are too dark to see under his puffy eyelids. The nose extends way out, ending in a twist, so close it could have brushed against me. His elongated ears bob up and down as he continues to scratch his neck, cackling as he clutches my forearms. "Wakey-wakey, it's Flaky!" he says with a rotting toothy grin.

"Mom! Dad!" I shout, kicking the man in the chest.

He squeals, letting me go to scratch his chest. "Ouch! Yeh took me flakes, ya little prick!" He scurries backward on the couch, leaping onto the hardwood floor, bringing his sagging wrinkly behind into view.

"Dad!" I shout, kicking the sleeping bag fully off.

The man scampers around the couch and to the kitchen. He continues to scratch and groans until he disappears around the corner.

What the fuck? Seriously, what the fuck? I bet Dad wishes I brought my damn phone now to call the cops. Dad . . . Mom! I get to my feet, panting heavily, shouting their names. I rush to the half-shut bedroom door beside the open doorway to the kitchen.

My face itches, forcing me to scratch the skin thoroughly in an attempt to get rid of the flakes. What is this?

"Mom?" I ask, stepping into their bedroom, scratching my forearm. I stop, checking the kitchen to see if I can spot the freak. I can't see him. A draft picks up from the kitchen—the window has to be open. Maybe he's gone.

"Mom, Dad?" I ask while wiping my face. Dammit! It feels like a swarm of mosquitos just stung me. The itch is reaching unbearable levels. I should go to the hospital. First, get Mom and Dad. The room is too dark for me to see anything. I run to the curtains and pull them open, letting the moonlight highlight the sleeping bags on the bed. They're empty. Only a large pile of flakes remains where my parents should have been.

"Mom!" I hurry to the bed and swat it a couple of times to check if they are under the sheets. My hand hit the sleeping bag and the mattress below, causing the flakes to fly into the air. I cough, accidentally inhaling some of the particles. Smart move. I spin around the room, looking in every corner to see if I can spot my parents. They are nowhere. I have a sinking feeling that I am alone.

"Dad!" I shout, rushing out of the bedroom, vigorously scratching my face. The skin peels back in thick layers with each dig of my nails. Blood seeps out with each scratch. This isn't good—it's just so itchy! My body temperature is increasing, too. It's like a fever.

"What'd you do with them?" I shout, running into the kitchen.

I step onto the green-and-white-tiled floor, feeling my left leg collapse. My elbow hits the floor first, then my head, which thuds. I groan, feeling my body flare up in heat. I can't get up. Neither of my legs are responding! My pant legs are thinning; flakes and dust are blowing out from where my limbs should be. I don't feel them, either. It's like they're just gone. Okay, this has to be a dream.

"Help!" I cry. My arms feel frail; my whole body itches uncontrollably while the heat rises to a fiery burn. I should try crawling to save my skin, but I just keep scratching everywhere like some kind of flea-infested dog.

"Itchy and bitchy, aren't we? HE! HE! HE!" a high-pitched voice says from the ceiling.

I stop scratching for half a second, just to look up and see that the naked freak had mounted himself in the far corner of the kitchen ceiling. His claws dig into the walls and his puffy eyes stare at me, as he uses one hand to scratch his crotch. Particles of his skin gently glide onto the kitchen tile. Some blow in the slight breeze from the open window, landing on me.

The man leaps down from his perch, thudding onto the floor. The motion causes my leg-flakes to fly into the air as he raises his arms, embracing the particles. He takes a deep inhale, relishing in his victory. The man catches one of my flying leg-flakes and smiles. "Welcome to the family!"

17

No. That couldn't have happened to you. The sense of numbness of flaking away is not the coldness of death that you know to be true. The timeline seems to be right. Smartphones . . . they're a thing you know. Time to keep looking. You and your ghoulish companion prep another observing trance, sending you into another's life. You're determined now. Whatever else is in the Midway can wait. The phone is your clue.

.

MERCER WAREHOUSE HAUNT

OFFICE OVERTIME

Just one more email. Come on. My fingers hammer that damn keyboard like some kind of machine syncing with the one on the table. We are together. I am the laptop. These are the crazy things I tell myself to power through another mundane late night of working. Most people have left the building. I'm possibly one of the last ones in the office. Well, me and the startup space on the floor above. They often host events after hours for their entrepreneur community. It's pretty cool if you're going down the businessperson route. For me, even in a small studio, I don't have that go-getter attitude that everyone seems to relish in here. Mercer Warehouse is a pretty cool old building with all sorts of shops, studios, and cafes in it. There's even that digital arts college. It's worth checking out if you're into all this startup local stuff. Me? All I want is to clock in, do my job, and get home. The funny thing is I can't stand the big corporate factor, even in my symbiotic state, with the machine on my desk. So, I've found balance in a fair, small studio. Unfortunately, small studios mean overtime all too frequently.

Footsteps echo from the hallway outside the office, breaking my fusion with the laptop. My fingers stop at the word "Mark!" The voice is nasally. Ethan.

"Yeah?" I shout, trying to get back into my rapid keyboard-typing trance. Come on.

Ethan appears from around the corner, his frizzy hair bouncing with each step. Nope, the trance is gone. Free from the machine's grasp, I tune in to the muffled voices upstairs—people mingling. The open concept and exposed beams mean this place has no soundproofing. Yeah, the zen is gone. I type the last bit in my email, sign off, and hit send. One down. Victorious, I lean back in my chair and ask, "What's upstairs like?"

"Not bad, some potential hires," Ethan says.

"I'm sure Todd will love that," I say, pushing my glasses up.

"They're wrapping up the event. Alice and I think we'll go down to Mercer Tavern for some drinks. You in?"

Now that is something I could go for—a beer. This work is draining. I could . . . I shouldn't. I look at my computer screen to see over two dozen unread emails and the main document I was working on earlier before this fucking email swarm arrived at the end of the workday. Why do people do that? Don't send something 'mission-critical ASAP' when everyone is about to leave for the day. It's a dick move. Still, I am a professional. As tempting as it is to get piss-faced with my coworkers after a long day, I know I can't. The fact that our office is in the same building as a pub doesn't help the deep temptations every day.

"Man, I'd love to"—I'm forcing these damn words out—"but I've got a pile of work to do here." I stress-brush my slicked-back hair. The statement is final. I've sealed my fate to slave away at the machine. I am bound to it—a hostile symbiotic relationship.

"Save it for tomorrow!" Ethan says with a toothy grin.

"Can't. Todd will have my head if this briefing isn't written for the dev team." Confirmation sent. I am the laptop.

MERCER TAVERN FUN

Footsteps rise from down the hall, growing louder. Boots. They're coming here. I'm not meant to get anything done. Alice, the brunette intern we hired, steps in. Damn. That's the best way to describe her. I try not to stare at her hips wrapped in that tight skirt, or whenever she wears a low-cut top. Oh yes. No. I have workplace ethics. I am the machine.

"Mark," Alice says. "What are you still doing here?" she asks in a playful tone.

I wave my hands at the laptop. "Here," is all I can say. There's nothing else to mention. It's obvious I'm working late, unlike these two.

Ethan's head pokes from around the corner. He says, "told you. Mark just can't look away from that screen."

Alice smiles at me and shakes her head. "Don't work too late, okay?"

I give her a closed smile. "Yeah." As if the pub wasn't tempting enough. I'm so wrapped up in work that I didn't even realize that Alice stayed for the mixer. I'd love to get her out for a drink and see where that goes. If I had my way, it'd back to my place for some mattress mambo.

A loud thud clangs. All three of us jump.

"Christ," Alice says, placing her hand on her chest.

Don't look at her tits.

Ethan scratches his mustache. "Someone has had one too many drinks."

I shake my head. "That sounded like it was on this floor. Anyone else still here?"

"Apparently," Alice says, waving her hand. Her face and chest have a slight glimmer. She's warm. Don't look at her tits.

"Who knows. This place is full of sounds."

"It makes it extra weird at night. Trust me," I say, unbuttoning the upper portion of my shirt, feeling whatever heatwave Alice was getting. For some reason, the building's furnace decided it was a good idea to blast the floor with warmth. This place is close to one hundred years old. It has its kinks. We know most of them, but when you combine the original brick walls and wooden floors, elevators, and many rooms, this place can be as mysterious as my clock-out time.

"Okay, this is ridiculous," Alice says, still waving her hand.

"Probably one of those ghosts in this building," Ethan says.

"What?" Alice says. "There are no ghosts here." She looks at me for confirmation—those blowjob eyes. Stop it. Machine: does not compute.

I shrug. "I have no idea about the history of this place."

Ethan scratches his head. "I swear it was something about a fire. It used to be a stable, I think."

"A stable?" I snort. "This place doesn't exactly fit the profile."

Ethan shakes his head. "Look, that's all I've been told. People talk about it here all the time."

"I've never heard anyone," I say.

"Me neither," Alice says.

"Small talk, I suppose," Ethan says. "It's way too hot. I'm going down to the pub."

Alice nods. "If you finish up, come find us downstairs," she says.

"Yeah," I say.

Ethan waves goodbye. "Remember to lock up."

"Of course. Hey, have a drink for me!" I call out as the two leave.

Ethan gives me a thumbs-up before disappearing from view, leaving me with my work. Alone, with the machine. I can do this. Time to fire up that brain and stop thinking about Alice's tits. What about that thudding noise? I wonder if it is worth investigating. Probably not. I'm trying to distract myself. I swear working late is just a mental battle with yourself. There are beer and a girl downstairs—the temptations of man. I'm overworked, drained, and it may be resulting in paranoia. Plus, I have to get this shit done. Taking a break isn't optional. Maybe a piss at some point. That is all. I am the machine.

WORKING HORSE

Yes. There we are. The trance. The synchronization of man and machine through the finger to key. Those emails have melted away. This doc for the dev team is like a beautiful symphony. It's elegant, direct, and innovative. The machine and I are one once more, orchestrating music. Thirteen hours on the clock means nothing. What is time, anyway? Productivity is all that matters. Time is just an abstract concept. Those dazzling digital alphabet glyphs popping onto the screen with each key I press are all that matters. I am the conductor. The music fuses into my words . . . when did Alice and Ethan come by?

Stop.

Typing: graceful.

An hour . . . or two hours ago?

No, stay with me.

Tits.

Shit.

It's lost. I honestly can't remember when they came by. It doesn't matter. My human self just overthrew the fusion of machine. I could use that beer. The temptation to join my coworkers is all too potent. No. Piss break. I get up from my seat, hitting the save button—can't lose that treasure. A stretch and a good leak can't hurt anyone. I'm making good progress and deserve a break. Time doesn't matter. No matter how late or early I leave, no one cares, as long as this damn document is done for the morning.

Some heavy walker in high heels is stomping on the floor above. Jesus. I check the time on my smartphone. It's just about midnight. The heat in the building hasn't cooled off either. Peeling my ass from that chair is making me realize the intense temperature. I'm unsure if it's getting hotter or if I'm just paying attention to it for once. Regardless, I have pit-sweats now. That'll get Alice's panties wet.

I walk out of the office and down the hall to the restroom. The other office doors are shut and locked—everyone else is home. I am the last one on this floor, possibly in the building—minus the tavern below, and maybe that trotting mammoth of a woman above. *THUMP!* Wow, another stomp. It reverberates off the empty walls. The sound is more substantial than a high-heel, like a pole hitting the ground. It's close, more levelled than the ceiling. Maybe there is no woman. Plus, the mixer upstairs is long over. It has to be those old pipes.

I sigh, pushing the bizarreness away. I need to piss and get back to work. That document is so close to being finished. I enter the gender-neutral bathroom, lock the door, flick the light on, place the smartphone down, and flip the lid open with my foot. Everyone on this floor shares the two bathrooms we have. Most people are forward-thinking; anyone who isn't, well, tough shit. When you gotta go, you gotta go, like now. I whip out my man for business—nature's kind. Relief. The moment passes. Flushed. Lid dropped.

THUD!

I jump, snagging my pants to keep them up.

THUD! THUD! The bathroom door pounds. The whole thing pushes inward with each sound.

"Cut it out!" I shout. It has to be Ethan pulling some stupid prank.

THUD! THUD! THUD! The temperature drastically increases. Sweat drips down my face. A snort comes from the hall. Then more thudding.

"All right! Give me a moment," I say—those drunks. I buckle my pants up, wash my hands, and swing the door open. The hall is empty. Huh. I flick my wet hands in the air, looking down both ends of the hall. No one.

ONENESS WITH MERCER WAREHOUSE

"Hello?" I say, wiping my forehead of sweat—this heat.

Silence.

"Ethan? Alice?" I say, walking down the hall to the staircase. They have to be pulling some joke. The floors need a key to get in at this hour.

I open the door to the stairwell and look up and down the steps—no one is there. This end of the hall is clear. I close the door and hurry to the other end of the hallway. The temperature is still rising, leaving me a soaking mess.

"Okay, I get it!" I shout, reaching the other end. No one. Every office is locked as it should be. Clearly, I'm working too late. Despite the heat, I *need* to get the work done. Even though I have a laptop, I must make sure those stupid files are on the local server. There is no other option than staying here. I have to remain resilient in this temperature, like a computer working overtime, overheating. I am the machine.

Okay, back to the office. I'm airing out my shirt. Christ, this is inhumane. I enter the room, noticing an intense grey haze rising in the space as I reach my desk. I take a sniff, picking up . . . smoke? Oh, shit—the building is on fire! I left my smartphone on the bathroom counter. With no hesitation, I rush to leave the office to get my cellphone. Before I make it to the office entrance, a large pile of wood collapses in front of it, blocking me inside. Intense heat, piercing flames, and smoke shoot through the cracks of the collapsed timber, forcing me to shield myself with my arm. It's so hot!

A whinnying sound cuts through the crackle of fire, trailed by echoing thumps. The smoke thickens. I can barely see anything—only a few feet in front of me. I cough violently, bringing my shirt up to my face, trying to keep my head low. The noise of heavy trotting rises inside the office. The crashing of desks and computers roars. I can barely see. I look up and see the unfathomable. No . . . how? Through the haze is a silhouette of a massive steed stomping through the office.

No way. It's the lack of oxygen. That's the only logical explanation.

The creature gallops towards me, knocking over my desk and sending my laptop to the ground. Flames burst from the animal's nostrils and eye sockets like some sort of hell creature. The animal neighs as its long mane bounces with each step. I jump to the side, trying to dodge the stomping animal. The attempt is futile, and the animal gallops to and through me like a spectre. It leaves a trail of flame behind its feet. I fall, face first, skidding on the burning wood.

This can't be it. I can't process what is going on as logic melts away. The machine is gone. All that is left are memories. Reminiscences that are not my own. It is as if another entity has pierced into my psyche and is filling my mind with visuals of a century before: horses . . . and fire. Emotions of fear, agony, and distress wash over my body as I condense into a fetal position. The impression of loss and confusion is all I can feel. The fires around me continue to envelop me until there is nothing but brightness; not even the heat can touch me. The whinnying sound of the horse echoes through my mind. Then more thuds.

The poor animal. I understand it now. These visions . . . they're . . . they're from the horse. The stable that Ethan talked about. The animal was burned alive, I think. The creature's agonizing death is running through my mind, seeing the horse's flesh burn off its body. It's crying in pain. The animal's soul must be communicating with me. It's trapped within these walls, channelling into me. The horse . . . a working horse. I am the horse!

An instinctual urge surges through me, and I lift myself onto my knees. I bellow an ear-piercing neigh as the fire begins to consume my form. The horse ghost and I are one.

REALITY CHECK

Mark! A voice echoes in my head.

"Christ, Mark!" the voice shouts once more. This time, it is distinguishable. The sound didn't originate in my head. No. That was my co-worker. He's in the room with me. He's in the fire!

"Ethan!" I use all my strength to spring to my feet. "Get out of here!" I shout, looking to the hallway. The office door is wide open. There is no collapsed wood. Alice is there, wide-eyed. A hand touches my shoulder, and I flinch.

"Mark," Ethan says. "What on earth are you screaming about?" The man is right beside me.

"What?" I ask, glancing around. The fires, the horse, the smoke—all of it is gone.

"Are you okay?" Alice asks.

"I . . . I don't know," I say, wiping my face.

"You were shouting on your knees," Ethan says, laughing.

I didn't answer, still looking around the office. Everything is as it should be. The desks are upright, and the computers are on top, unharmed. How?

"You're drenched in sweat," Alice says. "Maybe you should take the day off tomorrow."

"The heat gotcha," Ethan says. "Lucky we went back up here to check on you."

"Yeah," I say. "It has to be the heat." Did I just shout like a horse? Great. My coworkers just found me neighing like some kind of role-playing furry. I can barely process what just happened. Sure, I could tell my co-workers that the whole floor caught fire, and the wood began to collapse around me. Then a horse ghost appeared on the third floor, channelling its essence through me. No way. That's crazy. Ghosts aren't real. At least that is what I try to tell myself. But if that were true, then what was the vision I had? What was the sensation of oneness I had with that creature? I've never felt such a connection before. No amount of work machine-fusing, or women, or beer could come close to this. I think I had a spiritual awakening through this graceful animal, sharing its experience intently with me.

Maybe I will never have any answers. I can only accept what I saw and felt: the impression of an animal in agony. It chose to share its story with me, of burning alive in the fire at the Mercer Warehouse.

Thank you.

18

Another observing. Another uncertainty. You rub your eyes, feeling exhaustion run over you. The more you do, the more drained your mind, body, and spirit feel. It is scattering your thoughts. How many lives are you supposed to live just to find your own?

"No one died in that one," you say. "Except for a horse."

"Not all of these are death-related, remember?" Malpherities says. "We want something that makes sense to you." He dips his claw back into the liquid. "How was the observing?"

"I think we're getting somewhere with the time. But I still don't know my name or who I was." You walk up to the black bowl, seeing a faint reflection of yourself. At least you know what you look like. "This is starting to seem pointless."

"Possibly, but I want to know why you are here," Malpherities says.

"As you keep saying. I want to know, too, but maybe I'll never know, you know?" you say. "Do you have any guesses why I'm here?"

"A couple, but they're guesswork."

"Like what?"

"Someone got their hands on an ancient book," Malpherities says.

"What book?"

A wicked grin spreads across the ghoul's face. "No one speaks of it anymore. If I told you, I'd have to send you to Death's Vortex so you couldn't go looking for it."

"I won't," you say.

"No such luck," Malpherities says. "Let's just say it has the power to undo all of creation, which fits with disrupting your soul's natural journey. I've seen it happen before in a different life."

"So *someone* did try to interrupt my post-death experience?" you ask.

"Not necessarily. As I said, it's one theory," Malpherities says.

"What is the other?"

"A thaumaturgic event with such a minute chance of happening that is so unlikely, it even resurrects wonder and awe to my very core."

You stare at the ghoul, uncertain what he means.

"I'm quite old, if you haven't guessed. I've seen many things, if not everything. Every now and then, an unexplainable incident occurs that keeps me engaged in your universe."

"Like that girl?" you ask.

"Yes," Malpherities says.

You nod. It seemed pretty safe to say the ghoul was old; for all you knew, he was immortal. At least you have some possible leads as to why you're here. They're theories: some book, or a random unfortunate event. It's better than anything you can come up with.

A small pebble tumbles from the staircase leading into the cavern, followed by a hiss. "MALPHERITIES," a reverbed voice growls. It appears you have a visitor.

"Let's keep going," Malpherities says.

"Is your friend back?" you ask.

"It appears so. Let me handle that while you explore another observation," the ghoul says, grabbing some of the black liquid. "We haven't given up yet. Unless your mind is completely scrambled."

"Not yet," you say. You're tired, but are getting the hang of these other lives. The ghoul taps his claw, dripping the observer droplet onto your eye for a new experience of another soul.

BEST FRIENDS

PRE-DRINK

We got our masks, accessories, and outfits together and moved to the front door. Our group was ready to head out for a night of debauchery and chaos. A couple of my friends stuffed the bottles of vodka and gin into plastic bags, carefully trying not to make them clang. It took us an abnormal ten minutes or so to get our shoes on. It probably didn't help that we were swaying around from the five (?) rounds of shots we'd just done. Pre-drinking can get a little carried away when the three of us get together, which is all part of the fun. October also doubles the drinking mischievousness. Halloween season was our favourite time of the year. What better way to celebrate?

"You think Brandon is going to be there?" said a black-haired girl in a grey alien mask, better known as Emma.

I slipped my boots on and adjusted my plastic skeleton mask, shrugging at her.

"Why does it matter?" asked the second guy, Nick. His blue eyes stared at us from underneath the rubber mask of a man with a crown. He carefully stood up as the polyester material of his king outfit stretched tight against his skin. Working out sure could make you look good. Nick's ass is proof of it. It's impressive, but it also makes fitting into costumes difficult. They're made for the average joe, not one that's been jacked up.

Emma pulled out her vape and turned it on, saying casually, "I was just curious, that's all."

"It's just because she is looking to bone him," I said, grabbing the plastic bag of booze off the ground.

"And what if I was?" Emma asked.

"Go for it," I said. "Just explaining it to Nick because he has had a crush on you for years."

"Dude, shut up. I haven't," Nick said while scratching the back of his neck.

"Oh, Nick." Emma rolled her eyes as I unlocked the front door, stepping out. Emma and Nick followed right behind me. I nudged Emma's arm. "Unlike Nick, I want to chance my luck with an actual girl."

"Sometimes you're so stupid," Emma said. "Where is this place, anyway?"

It was a pretty rude thing for me to say, but I had to give her a hard time and lighten the mood. I couldn't stand the constant tension between Emma and Nick. Why didn't they just plow already and get it over with? We've all been friends since junior high. We're adults now. They can get their freak on if they want. That's what adulthood is. You try new things. Sometimes it works out, and sometimes it doesn't.

MOVING ON

I pulled out my phone and accessed my ride-sharing app, typing in the address. "I hear this party is pretty gnarly."

"Party or club?" Nick asked, holding his ticket.

"Oh," I said. "No, it's a house party."

"Really? A house party that takes tickets?" Nick said.

"It's an exclusive masks-only party. From what I hear, it's one of the crazier ones. It happens every year," I said.

"Keep in mind they haven't partied with us yet," Emma says.

"Cheers to that," I said.

"Why the masks?" Nick asked.

I shrugged. "They like to keep things anonymous, I guess. Glen gave me the invite this year," I said. "Last year, I couldn't even grab a ticket before they sold out."

After calling a car through the ride-share app, I stuffed the phone in my pocket as we took the elevator down to the main floor. The three of us waited out in front of the apartment complex, staying huddled close to each other to avoid the winds. Even though it was still fall, the night temperature dropped intensely. That's Canada's weather for you. Nick pulled out a flask from his back pocket and took a chug of liquor. He passed the container to each of us so we could take a shot of whiskey. That marked the fourth type of hard liquor I'd had this evening.

A black car with a glowing ride-share company logo stuck to the windshield arrived—our ride to the house party. We scooched into the back of the car, with Nick and me on either side of Emma. I handed each of my friends their tickets, and we awaited our arrival. It didn't take long for the driver to navigate us to the opposite end of town. The guy seemed to know the city well, taking side roads to cut through the traffic jams. This man would be tipped graciously for such excellency. He understands the drive-distance-to-intoxication levels. It's a complex ratio of carefully balancing your vehicle speed to keep your passengers on that liquor buzz, and we rode it with no downs.

PARTY TIME

Our ride arrived at an older, quiet neighbourhood of war-time homes, mostly single-levels and bungalows. Old homes means cheap rent, resulting in more party-minded folks. Hell yes.

"Here you are," said the driver.

"Thanks," I said as the three of us exited the car.

Nick spun around, looking at each house as our ride accelerated away. He scratched his head. "Which house is it?"

Emma pointed to the house directly in front of us. "See those lights?"

The house in front of us had a red glow inside. It was the only house that had any lights on. Duh.

"That obvious?" I said, marching up to the home.

The three of us reached the front door, each adjusting our costumes before I pulled open the screen door and knocked on the main solid entrance. A muffled bass rumbled from inside the house. Chances were they didn't hear the knock. I reached for the knob as the door swung open, and a man in a PVC mask and undies stood in front of me. His hairless form was highlighted in the red glow behind him.

"Hey," I said while pulling out my ticket.

The man reached for my ticket, looked at it, and then waved me in. I entered casually, trying to keep a calm appearance. The last thing I wanted to do was enter a party too abruptly. That doesn't win you any cool points. Funny how we get fixated on convincing people we are cool in the most mundane situations. Then again, everyone accepts the strange facade; therefore, in return, it helps you get your grind on.

My mask made it next to impossible to see anything in my peripheral view. I could make out the main foyer, a hall, and the living room to my right. The entry was jammed at every corner with folks in wild costumes and masks. Some of the outfits were as minimal as the door greeter's, and others were far more concealing. Each guest's costume followed some sort of dark, artistic, or bondage theme. The sight made me realize that my friends and I had gotten the wrong idea when it came to a 'masks-only' party.

A hand gently brushed against my back, sending my skin tingling. I looked, expecting to see Emma. No. A girl in a black feathered bra, panties, and masquerade mask released her hand from me as she walked past, entering the hall. Maybe we weren't so out of place as I first thought. My gaze was hooked on the girl's exposed hips and rear moving side to side as she disappeared into the crowded hall.

A shoulder nudged my own. I turned to see Nick and Emma were now beside me.

" . . . is classy A.F.," Nick said. It was difficult to hear him through the pounding bass, but I managed to catch his point. This party rocked.

Emma leaned in to the two of us. "We are so out of place," she said.

"No way," I replied.

"Why?" Emma asked.

"Give me a shot of that whiskey," I said.

Nick reached into his back pocket and handed me the flask. I snagged it and took a chug of the liquor before passing it back to him. "I'll be back—gotta catch a birdie."

COURTSHIP

"What?" Nick said.

I ignored him and hurried through the small hallway, carefully avoiding people so I didn't knock their drinks. My balance was slightly off-centre. That new shot of whiskey—not to mention the one outside the apartment—was mingling with the other liquors swirling around in my body. I needed to keep it together and find those hypnotic hips of the mysterious bird-feathered girl again. No, I'm not into animals or anything. It's just sexy, with a bit of fun, you know?

I spotted bobbing feathers a good couple of metres ahead of me. Bingo. She hadn't gotten too far. The girl moved through the hall, past the kitchen, and down the staircase leading to the basement. Not thinking twice, I followed her down the stairs. The basement had a blue glow to it and a new type of thumping bass music. This tune was faster, thicker, and grimier. All right!

The girl came to a stop near the centre of the unfinished basement den. She danced to the music, waving her arms and shaking to the rhythm. I'm not much of a dancer but seeing a girl I like with moves like that is precisely the type of encouragement that'll make me indulge. I busted out my gnarliest moves and appeared in front of the girl. She didn't seem surprised at all, as if she was expecting me. Okay, she was leading me on. Man, do I enjoy a good courtship dance.

My moves felt smooth as I swung to the tempo, in sync with her. I made sure I stayed close enough to her body to welcome her to me, but not so close that we touched. Teasing was all part of the game. The girl spun around, facing away from me for a portion of the track. She brushed against me with her ass, looking back with a playful smile. Holy . . . shit. She bumped against me a few more times until the DJ shifted the track to a new beat. The girl turned to face me, so close I could feel her heat and smell her girl-sweat-and-hairspray scent. She lifted her hand, revealing a palmful of small pills. Truthfully, I couldn't have even guessed *where* she'd concealed them with the little amount of clothing that she wore.

"Want to have some fun?" she asked.

"I'm down," I said, without processing her words. I should have—what was I thinking, grabbing one of her pills? But it was too late. She took one, too, and we popped them into our mouths.

JOIN IN ON THE FUN

"Paul!" came a female voice.

A girl in a gray alien mask and a king appeared beside us. Right on, my friends had arrived just when I needed them. Now bird-girl would know I wasn't some loser alone at a party. My friends would talk me up.

"Hey!" I said.

Emma punched my shoulder and leaned in to me. "What did you just take?"

"Just enjoying the party. Relax!" I said. Leaning closer to her, I added, "This girl is into me. Let's keep this going."

The bird girl began to dance to the beat, keeping her hand holding the remaining pills extended towards the three of us.

I nodded at them, saying, "I thought you said this crowd hadn't partied until they partied with us."

Emma stared at the pills for a moment before saying, "All right. You got me there." She stepped up to the bird girl, snagged one of the pills, and popped it in her mouth.

"Whoa!" Nick said while taking the last one for himself. "We're doing this, huh?"

"Let's party!' I said while patting Nick on the back.

"Who's your new friend, anyway?" Emma asked.

I turned to face the bird girl. "Oh, this is . . . "

"Victoria. Come dance!" she said, voice buttery-smooth, as she moved back into the crowd.

The three of us didn't question our new companion and joined her. We weren't exactly sure what we'd taken. It could have been anything. MDMA? Acid? Who knew? What we did know was that we were here for fun and had just showcased our dominance in the realm of partying. Not to mention I was on a conquest mission.

Usually, I had a good sense of my party supplies, but when the pill began to kick in, I didn't realize it. The music amplified as the depth of the room drastically widened. My body heat intensified as other forms danced around me. The nearest body was lightly covered in a few feathers, the second was a man of royalty, and the third was a strange alien. More people had to have come down to the lower floor because the four of us were pushed pretty close together, grazing against one another. Yes, there's a rabbit-man. Full-on PVC suits, gag masks, you name it, all dancing so close that bodies brushed against everyone else. The place was packed. It was all okay. I felt a deeper level of connection with them all; it was clearly the drugs.

The blue light from the ceiling brightened. Movements were fast. Colourful echoed versions of people's bodies moved with the music in a slight delay. Skin and clothing felt welcoming. Smells were alluring. Sensations, overpowering. Body temperatures increased as limbs began to melt into one. How many of us were there?

Material slipped away until there was just skin. Only skin, panting, bodies against and inside one another with passionate grasps.

Was I sleeping? The drunken self I was once was now gone. My sense of self and the new collided into this melting pot of sexual sensation. Whatever it was, it was bliss.

AFTERMATH

A bright white light beamed directly over my face as my eyes slowly peeled open. The eyeballs were so dry that the lids scraped against them in dehydration. A throbbing headache pulsated all around my head—a typical hangover. My skin was quite warm and coated in dried sweat, which was abnormal. I felt numb, slightly depressed, and out of energy—very unusual for a night of drinking.

Sitting upright, I felt a small hand glide off my chest and onto my bare thigh. I hadn't even noticed the arm before because it was as warm as me. Looking to the side, I saw a naked girl. Her black hair was spread all over the sheets. A grey alien mask was beside her.

Oh shit! I thought while scooching away, as naked as she was. Did Emma and I just . . . ?

As I backed up, my butt pressed against firmer skin. The sudden touch caused me to jump. I turned around to see a jacked man wearing a rubber mask of a bearded man with a crown. It was unmistakably Nick, and he was also as naked as Emma and I were. No way, this couldn't be real.

"Fuck," I groaned while brushing my hair from my face. The skeleton mask I'd had the night before was gone. That mattered little to me as I began to piece together what the three of us had done, bringing me here.

Glancing around the room, I spotted windows high above, indicating we were still in a basement. This had to be a guest room or something. The door was closed, our clothes were spread all over the floor, and the bird girl was gone. It was only the three of us. Victoria had to have vanished at some point in the night. The three of us probably got way too close together and freaked her out. What the hell were we doing? Those damn pills. I can handle my party supplies, but something about the bird girl's drugs and our pre-drinking mixed with full-on horny tension was clearly not a good combination.

Friends since childhood, trying new things in adulthood. Who knows? Maybe it wasn't all that bad. I'd ask these two once they got up so we could all stare at each other's bare asses in embarrassment. At least they'd finally boned and gotten it over with. I don't think any of us expected a third wheel to join in.

19

The observation fizzles out and you return to your body, rubbing out the black flakes from under your eyes. Malpherities is here with you, and there are no other ghouls around.

"Nope," you say, shaking your head. "That wasn't me. Those were just some hot-and-heavy college kids or something."

"Nothing?" Malpherities says. His tone is quick and impatient.

"Not exactly. Parties are familiar. This one seemed so . . . illegal. Maybe I've gone to some of these?"

"We'll go again." The ghoul disregards your words and dips his claw into the bowl.

"What happened to the other ghoul? Are they coming back?" you ask.

"They might; I can't keep them back forever. Let's just keep at this." His words are fast; he must be growing tired, like you. How long does he wait here while you are observing, anyway? No time to ask. The droplet burns, and in you go again.

RED, THEN WHITE

The sound of fingers tapping a touch screen and the constant humming of an SUV are the only sounds. The vehicle glides down the pitch-black highway underneath the star-filled sky. Thin, elegant fingers with monster-green nails scurry against the lit smartphone. The driver keeps both hands on the wheel, focusing on what little he can see in the darkness. The vehicle's high-beams provide some visuals of the road, but truthfully, if something were to jump out on the side from the ditch, the vehicle couldn't stop in time—not at these speeds.

"I hate nighttime driving," the driver says, stroking his neck with one hand. A flash of lightning briefly lights up the night view. The mountains go on forever.

The passenger stops typing and brushes her blonde hair with her hand. "Mason, I know. We don't have that much longer."

Mason sighs. "I still can't believe your boss didn't give you the day off. We'll be driving most of the night."

"No, really, it will be fine. We only have a few more hours left. We'll be in Jasper in no time."

"They'll be done the welcome party, Chloe."

Chloe continues tapping away on her phone. *TAP TAP TAP.* "I'm just making a post on the event page right now. Besides, we'll have all day tomorrow to catch up with everyone."

"I get that. It's just that these reunions don't happen every year, you know?"

Chloe finishes typing on her smartphone, looking up at the hilly road leading west. Two red lights are visible farther ahead.

"You sure we're still on highway sixteen?" Chloe asks.

Mason nods. "Yeah. It's the main road leading to Jasper. Driving in a straight line is pretty simple when you think about it."

"Just checking. No need to get snarky." Chloe folds her arms.

The SUV is going about five kilometres over the speed limit. This late at night, the highway is crawling with peace officers just waiting for someone to misbehave. Even five over is living on the edge. Plus, it's dark, and it's better to drive cautiously, even if stopping isn't exactly possible.

Mason tightens his grip on the wheel as the radio lights up with fuzzy noises. *"YUK-YUK-YUK-ACH-ACH-UCK."* He relaxes his grip. It seems the dark has him a little more nervous than he anticipated. Something resembling screams shortly follows the strange sounds. Truthfully, it all sounds like noise from the distortion.

"What are you playing?" Chloe asks, reaching for the radio.

"I didn't turn on anything," Mason says. "It's probably picking up a bad signal. Cheap radio."

"It's super annoying," she says.

Chloe presses the power button, shutting off the hideous sound, then returns to her phone. The tension they'd just had ends with a silent treatment. The two remain quiet for what seems like ten minutes when, in actuality, it is only a few. Time has a funny way of elongating minutes on road trips when you're bored or nervous. The red rear lights of the vehicle ahead grow larger.

"That car is going pretty damn slow," Mason says.

Chloe looks up from her phone and squints. "How fast are you going?"

Mason double-checks the speedometer. It is still hovering at 115. "Five over."

"Maybe the night has him more spooked than it does you."

Before Mason can reply, the distance between their car and the red lights of the vehicle ahead diminishes drastically. It's right in front of them.

"Christ!" Mason shouts, heart skipping. He swerves into the opposite lane, missing the parked car by a few meters.

"Holy shit!" Chloe puts her hand on her chest. "What was he doing, stopped right in the lane? He should pull to the side."

"I don't know," Mason says. "Moron."

"Should we call it in? Maybe they're having a heart attack."

"No, they're just stupid. Let's keep driving."

A flash of light bursts from the sky, lighting up the roadway. Lightning, yet no rain or thunder. Mason points to a sign on the right side of the road, lit up in the high-beams. It states "ALBERTA 16" with the numbers inside a shield. Very Albertan.

"See, Chloe? We're still on the right road," Mason says.

Chloe folds her arms. "It just doesn't look familiar this late at night."

"Nothing does at this hour," Mason says, adjusting the wheel as they come upon a slight turn. A second vehicle appears. The red rear lights increase in size. It's worrisome.

"Another one?" Chloe asks.

"I guess?" Mason says, bringing the wheel back, congruent with the straight road.

The radio flickers on with a distorted "*YUK-ACH-ACH-UCK . . . No!*"

Chloe reaches for the radio, shutting it off. "Seriously, Mason, what is wrong with this?"

Mason doesn't reply. He focuses on the lights of the new vehicle, which continually grow larger. The vehicle isn't moving, just like the last one.

"Mason, move over! We're going to hit him," Chloe says.

"I am." Mason squints, seeing that the red lights are perfectly in line with the middle of the road. "He's . . . "

"He's what, Mason?"

"He's in the middle of the road," Mason says, pressing his big toe on the brakes of the vehicle. How strange—two dead vehicles on the highway.

"Move into the shoulder lane and get around him. This is beginning to creep me out."

"Yeah, me too." Mason gradually moves the vehicle off to the right, still pressing on the brakes. The vehicle slows to about fifty kilometres. "See if you can take a look," Mason says, moving halfway onto the shoulder. The vehicle vibrates as the right-side tires drive on the rippled pavement. The new sound accompanying the SUV's humming is unsettling. Everything about this situation is making both Mason and Chloe want to get out. Driving forward is their only option. Chloe sits straight and looks out Mason's window as they drive by the stationary car. Anticipation.

"What do you see?" Mason says, glancing at the car as they drive by. He can't get a good look and returns his gaze to the road, exhaling stress.

"Nothing," she says.

"What?" Mason doesn't believe it.

"No one. The vehicle was empty."

"It can't be. It was probably just too dark."

"No, I am telling you, there was no one in that car."

Mason looks directly into Chloe's hazelnut eyes for just over a second before returning to the road. She keeps her gaze on him. She's serious. Chloe never keeps her eyes on anyone that long unless it is her smartphone. She's certain.

"Can we stop? Just pull over for a moment," Chloe asks.

"Why?" Mason asks.

"Mason! There are two cars dead on the road, one of which I know no one was in. I just need a damn smoke."

Mason stops himself from replying. Wise move, for his first instinct is to tell her that they aren't sure that someone *wasn't* in the vehicle. Someone had to be, right? It doesn't matter. Chloe doesn't enjoy being challenged when she is convinced she is right. He will never hear the end of it.

"Fine," Mason says, the vowels forcing their way out of his throat.

He slows the vehicle down. The vibrations lessen. "Call the cops. Or have a smoke. Whatever it is." He presses the flashers button as they come to a stop, putting the vehicle into park. Mason leans back in the driver's seat and waits.

"Well?" Mason asks. "Let's hurry. I'd like to make it to Jasper and call it a day."

"Just a quick dart, okay?" Chloe says, reaching into her pink purse with one hand.

"Yeah, cool. I'll wait here." He folds his arms, wishing she'd just stop smoking. Mason wants to argue with her about the health hazards, let alone the stench, but there isn't a point. Smoking is the same as any situation with this gal. When she is set on something, it doesn't change.

"Great." Chloe undoes her seatbelt and opens the door with one hand. She flicks the lighter, bringing life to the cigarette as she puffs, halfway out of the vehicle. She always does that. Can't she light the smoke once she is out of the vehicle? Then Mason wouldn't have to buy car fresheners all the time. That smoke trail lingers in the seats. Disgusting. Too late now—Chloe is set in her ways. She closes the door to the SUV and steps out of view. Time to wait.

Mason fiddles with his thumbs, looking out the side-view mirror, then the rear mirror to see if he can spot Chloe, but she's completely out of view. He sighs and looks down at his shoes, then at the clock on the dashboard. It's 11:15 p.m. He needs a distraction, so he doesn't think about Chloe's stupid smoking habit. She's out there, inhaling a mouth full of cancer.

Mason rechecks the clock. 11:19 p.m.

Okay, that's enough. Mason unbuckles his seatbelt, opens the door, and steps out into the cool spring air. He rubs his arms, causing the windbreaker to make that annoying squeaky noise, like a kid's jumpsuit.

"Chloe?" he says, walking around the front of the vehicle. She isn't anywhere in the front. Mason guesses she has to be by the rear passenger side if he couldn't see her from inside.

Mason puts his hands in his pockets and walks around the vehicle to the passenger side. "Chloe?"

"Yeah?" she says.

A beam of light flickers above the vehicle so bright it blinds Mason's eyes momentarily. The vehicle bounces up and down as the whole scene lights up bright like daytime. Then nothing. It vanishes. The vehicle wobbles slightly. Mason steps back.

"Chloe?" he calls out, moving around the vehicle. No sign of Chloe. Where did she go? He glances back to the side of the road, leading into the forest. It's pitch black.

"Chloe!" Mason shouts.

He runs around to the driver's side of the vehicle and finds nothing. The blonde is nowhere to be found. The subtle sound of *"YUK-YUK-YUK-ACH-ACH-UCK"* comes from inside the vehicle. That damn radio. A women's scream roars from the speakers.

"Chloe!" Mason shouts, running to the back of the vehicle, looking into the woods. Did someone grab her? Did she run? The light, what was it? Mason can only wonder. That stupid radio won't shut off, either. His mind is running a million questions through his head. Was she pissed off at him? He has no resolution.

A burst of light flashes. This one is different. An immense suction rips him from the ground. The pressure feels like a vacuum hose sucking his entire body, stretching his skin upward, pulling on his clothing, eyelids, and lips. The light vanishes, leaving him in pure darkness, skin reverting to normal. The light flashes again, revealing the road as a small line below, amid acres of forest. He's being pulled up into the sky.

"Chloe!" Mason screams as his skin stretches again. The light gets brighter, blinding him. The air is so cold. The suctioning stops as he lands on a suddenly new chrome flooring. Everything is so bright. Red eyes are everywhere, and the haunting voices from the radio begin to chant, *"YUK-YUK . . . "*

20

Aliens? An abduction? Events you know. You've heard of them. Now, have you ever been abducted? A thought to ponder that isn't bringing any clues. You know the timing is roughly right, but that is all.

"Darkness . . . cold, then warmth," Malpherities mutters, tapping his claw against his jaw.

You shrug. "That's all I have so far. And the timing. The white light seemed familiar, but I don't recall a chrome floor."

"Perhaps you were part of an interesting situation that happened to humanity." Malpherities scoops up more black liquid and rubs it between his claws. "A strange cosmic scenario that puzzled many. Here." He rises above you, taps his claw, and lets the droplet transcend you into an observer. Maybe this one will be the lottery ticket to your memories.

ABE

CONTACT

The Saskatchewan plains are supposed to be a simple place to grow up. My folks have always said, "Saskatchewan was a wonderful place when I was a child. Things sure have changed." I understand why they would say that since they were raised before the Galactic Believers formed. At first, no one thought that the Galactic Believers were a problem. We would hear about them on the radio, the TV, and online. It seemed like a goofy hoax or some sort of New Age spiritual awakening. They followed the one they call The Oracle. Some chick who started a streaming website, preaching her prophesies globally, showing her bizarre drawings of a triangle. To me, religious beliefs are naïve. Not everyone agrees with that. But most people did agree that the Galactic Believers were off their rocker. Everyone loved to make fun of them. As time went by, the jokes started to dwindle as the seriousness of the situation escalated.

I can recall the day when they first showed up. It had to have been about five years ago. Summertime was coming to an end, which meant it got darker much earlier. I was still going to school and working on the farm with my dad and Uncle Fred. Mom was making dinner. I had just wrapped up for the day and finished showering. There was a knock on the door. We never got knocks on the door. My dad and Uncle Fred were still out working—something to do with the tractor not starting. Mom was too busy with prepping dinner, so I did the responsible thing and saw who it was. This was the moment I met the Galactic Believers. It was just past six when I went to answer the door.

There were three men. Each one was well-dressed, all in black, and had a cold, expressionless face. At the time, I didn't know who they were. I had heard about the Galactic Believers on the news but had never seen them face-to-face. My gut told me they were not normal men. Straight-laced and well-dressed people don't come out to the farm very often unless they have bad news to share. I asked them what they wanted, and they simply clutched their leather-bound books tighter.

The one in the middle spoke. "We are visiting each resident outside of the city. Do you have a moment to discuss your future in the planetary absorption to come?"

After he asked the question, I knew they were the Galactic Believers. The three of them wanted to tell me about their extraterrestrial worshiping. The whole concept was a crackpot's dream. I told the men that we didn't want anything to do with what they had to offer. Without giving them the chance to talk, I began to close the door. The man in the middle made one more remark, saying, "Your terms within the Galactica Array must be decided soon."

My mom did not even bother to ask who was at the door. Cooking distracted her. Uncle Fred and Dad came home that evening, and everything proceeded as normal. Several weeks went by before the Galactic Believers arrived again. This time, they visited early in the morning. So early that it was still dark, and the sun was on the edge of the horizon. My dad answered, and I could hear them asking him about his future in the planetary absorption. Dad could not help but laugh because he's a straightforward kind of guy. The New Age beliefs don't mean anything to him. If it wasn't something he could see or touch, it wasn't real to him. The Galactic Believers continued to babble, explaining to him that ABE had selected the Earth and we would be joining a Galactica Array. My dad snickered again and closed the door on them. Life continued as normal.

PERSISTENCE

For the first couple of years, the Galactic Believers did not come back. It wasn't until the third year to the day from the first visit that they started arriving again. The Galactic Believers' visits became more and more frequent. With each knock at the door, they would share new information about the Galactica Array and Earth's part in it. They explained about the All-Being Entity known as ABE, who rules over this planetary merger. My dad began to think these visits were harassment. He would tell them to leave and even threatened to shoot them. Of course, that has no grounds in Canada. The empty threats were of no use. The Galactic Believers continued to visit multiple times a day. We even called the RCMP, who said they were getting similar reports similar from all around the province. On the television, the news stated these visits weren't just provincial or happening across the country. The Galactic Believers were contacting people across the globe. No one knew why there were so many of them. We only knew that their numbers continued to grow as The Oracle babbled nonsense online. Even people I knew were becoming members.

SPACE

Coincidentally enough, as the Galactic Believers' visits became more frequent, NASA made a public announcement about an astronomical object coming towards our galaxy. The size of this object was equal to, if not larger than, the Milky Way. It appeared to come out of nowhere, and was much closer than the Andromeda galaxy, which is predicted to collide with the Milky Way well beyond our lifetime. NASA's sudden announcement was met with criticism. People thought they were incompetent for their lack of foresight. NASA responded that they were working diligently on understanding the nature and speed of this unknown object.

The announcement only stirred up more confusion and fear in everyone. People began to wonder if it was related to the Galactic Believers. Plenty of people expressed their opinions on the news, online, and on the streets. Some trash-talked The Oracle, calling her a terrorist. Doomsday was a collective agreement. The arrival of this new object heading for the Milky Way was enough to convince many people to become Galactic Believers. To these converted, the space object was proof that the Galactic Believers and The Oracle were speaking the truth and wanted to help humanity. I wasn't so convinced. There had been plenty of cases throughout human history where people were sure doomsday was here. It never came. People enjoyed fantasizing about the end of the world. My opinion didn't matter, though. People still became Galactic Believers.

VISIONS

A nyone who becomes a Galactic Believer is sworn to an oath of secrecy to 'the bigger picture.' One of my high school buddies, Ron, even tried to get me to join the organization, or religion, or whatever you want to call it. He told me that the All-Being Entity, ABE, was accepting of everyone. His wisdom and powers are beyond human comprehension. Ron said ABE is willing to talk to you through a mental link in your consciousness. ABE shares visions, feelings, and sensations that cannot be expressed through simple words or through our limited forms. Perhaps bliss is the best way to describe what ABE shares with you. The reason I am saying this is because ABE visited me.

At first, I thought it was merely a dream, the result of stress from having to take care of my folks in their older age and the constant harassment from the Galactic Believers. The dreams continued to happen over and over again. These visions projected me beyond Earth, flying well beyond our solar system. I was taken out of the Milky Way galaxy and to a foreign astral realm where I could see unexplainable swirls of colour. Some of them took the shape of humanoids, watching as I soared through this plane. All of these colours and abstract beings were unified under a large triangular object. The first time I was brought to this foreign space, it shot me back to the real world far too soon to see any more. As the dreams continued, I saw more and more of this celestial realm. I learned that the triangle was not a spaceship, nor a pyramid, but a two-dimensional shape that always stared directly at me. It didn't matter what angle I approached it from. It had no depth. It was the same bright white triangle, always.

ABE

These dreams gave me a sense of warmth, wonder, and fear. I was not in control of the motion. I was simply a passenger experiencing unity with these swirls of colour under the watchful white triangle. During the fifth dream, ABE revealed himself to me. His voice was strident, welcoming, and soothing. In the dream, the voice projected from this triangle. It made me realize that the triangle was ABE. ABE said to me, "Your planet has many wonders. Your people are a young spark in this old galaxy. We welcome you to the Galactica Array, the next evolutionary step in your species."

I was confused and unsure of what to say. This was everything Ron had told me about from his dreams and the initiation process with the Galactic Believers. How could this be? Was there truth to what the Galactic Believers and The Oracle had to say? Was I being drugged? Or was I simply stressed out? I didn't have an answer. I simply stared into the white triangle.

ABE continued. "I am sure you are confused. Do not be. Your consciousness is bound to this three-dimensional plane, and you are not capable of understanding what non-carbon-based life is capable of. There is more to existence than the simple dimensions that your life-cell constricts you in. I can bring you to greater heights. Embrace me. Accept me, for I am the beginning and the end of this dimension."

I wanted to ask ABE what he wanted. Before I could, I woke up to a loud bang. I sprang from my bed in a sweat, trying to figure out where the noise had come from. It was close.

CONFRONTATION

Hurrying out of my bedroom, I saw Uncle Fred and my mother looking through the window where a ring of men, dressed in black and holding torches, stood outside of our home. My dad was at the doorway, holding a shotgun, staring at the men. He shouted, telling them to leave and that we wanted nothing to do with their bullshit beliefs. The men didn't respond. They only stared at our home, torches flickering. I asked Mom if she had called the RCMP, and she said the lines weren't working. I hurried to the television to turn it on, and only static grains showed up. Next was the radio. It worked. Most of it was noise, but a country-wide warning played on repeat. The sound cut out, making it difficult to understand what they were saying. The gist of it was that this was a state of emergency.

One of the Galactic Believers stepped forward in a calm, relaxed manner, his palms open. With a wide smile, he said, "The All-Being Entity is near. The Oracle has guided us." He pointed to the sky, and the other Galactic Believers looked up. My father, myself, my uncle, and Mother also looked to the stars to see a large black triangle, darker than the night itself, directly above us.

The Galactic Believer said, "It is not too late for you to agree to the terms of ABE. He is all-loving. He is all-knowing. Earth will be absorbed into the Galactica Array. We want to take you with us."

My father fired his shotgun in the air again and shouted, "Leave now or I will shoot!"

The Galactic Believer continued, "Those that do not willfully accept ABE into their soul will never join the Galactica Array. There is no room for the disbelievers of ABE and his power. We carbon-based creatures cannot understand the greatness that he has to offer. He is old, wise, and his consciousness spans well beyond the fabric of this three-dimensional space."

Another blaring sound erupted from the shotgun. Smoke rose from the barrel's tip as the Galactic Believer flew from the ground before dropping into the dirt. My mother screamed. My uncle swore and hurried over to my father, who pointed his shotgun directly where the Galactic Believer once stood, smoke still seeping from the gun's chamber. My uncle started to yell at my dad, asking him what the hell he'd done. My mother was crying. I comforted her as the black triangle in the sky continued to grow.

ARRIVAL

Another shot erupted. My uncle shouted, trying to grab the gun as my dad attempted to reload it. The bullet missed the Galactic Believers. They did not move or flinch. They extended their arms outward, torches in hand.

"What the—" my dad said.

My mother and I looked to the front walkway to see what my dad was looking at.

"My God," Uncle Fred said.

The Galactic Believer my father had shot rose from the ground as if an invisible force lifted him. He did not use his limbs. His face was motionless, and no blood oozed from his wound. The eyes had rolled back, leaving only the sclera visible in each eye socket. Once the Galactic Believer was fully vertical, his mouth opened, and a voice projected from within, saying, "The galactic absorption has come."

Instantly, I recognized the voice of ABE, the All-Being Entity. He had arrived. The Galactic Believers had warned us. Earth's absorption into the greater was here.

"Those that are willing to join humanity's next phase will be embraced, accepted, and loved within the Galactica Array. Those that refuse are simply part of the natural process of evolution. This is life's progression on Earth. Removal of the unfit is the continual stage. All life that embraces the Galactica Array, and myself, the All-Being Entity, will see beyond the space-time limitations found within this realm. Those that accept me will be brought to new heights of dimensional exploration. Those that do not will cease to be."

ABSORPTION

My uncle wrestled with my father, who was trying to shoot the Galactic Believer projecting ABE's voice. Before either one could get the upper hand, a white light shot from the black triangle in the sky. The light was so bright, it blinded everything in view for several seconds. Once the light vanished, my mother—who I still held—disintegrated in my arms. Following her, the walls, the furniture, and the entire house dissolved like they were being eaten by acid. My uncle and father were too busy wrestling with the gun to even realize that this dissolving entity absorbed them. They also ceased to exist. The grass, the dirt, and everything around Earth began to dissolve. The Galactic Believers remained. I remained. Not for much longer, for the Galactic Believers and I began to disintegrate. Our particles levitated upwards with millions of other particles—or atoms—from around the world, and merged into the triangle. I did not feel pain or agony; instead, there was a sense of coming home.

ABE had spoken to me through dream form. The All-Being Entity was the way, and I wish my relatives could have seen the same truth I had. Whether they know it or not, they have been absorbed into the Galactica Array. Their atoms live on, as do I, with my consciousness intact, for I now join the other Galactic Believers who are under ABE's eternal watchful eye in the next phase of humanity.

21

ABE . . . Glowing light . . . Welcoming . . . Euphoria? These were feelings you had before, when you were crossing into the Midway.

"Malpherities! I think we're on to something!" you say. "I remember the bright light while dying. This All-Being Entity might be related to my life."

"Is that so?" Malpherities raises one eyebrow. "Let's find out," he says, dipping his claw into the bowl. "But first, while you were gone, I thought about your previous observation. Let's toy with the white light you mentioned. Try this."

You're a little agitated that Malpherities isn't taking your hunch seriously, but decide to listen to him. What's one more observation? You've experienced . . . how many now? This is becoming a standard procedure. The droplet hits your eye, the burning rises, and you leave your body to see if the ghoul's theory holds water.

COMPATIBILITY

DREAMING OF MEMORIES

A golf-ball-sized sphere remains stationary in front of a matte black sheet of paper. The ball is painted in blue, green, and white blotches to represent the ocean, land, and clouds. The black space around is covered in tiny white dots. Earth. The planet that everyone has named home. Calling another world home is a far-fetched idea, with space travel being a dream. The astronomical distance to other Earth-like planets is mind-boggling. Even the idea of light years is tough for many people to grasp in a practical sense. Scientists have many theories about how we can travel the vast distances of the stars, often proposing yet-undeveloped technologies. There is also the possibility that the human race will kill itself off before developing a form of energy for space travel. None of this changes the fact that we are fascinated by the stars.

The man leans down to look at the model of Earth more closely, inspecting the tiny moon attached to the planet by a wire. He eyes each of the major continents of Earth before sighing. He can't help but wonder where it all went wrong. If only humans had learned to work together sooner.

"You examine that every day," says a cold feminine voice, echoing in the bright white-and-chrome room.

The man gets up, facing the woman, who is at a kitchen bar, boiling water on a stovetop.

"Yeah," he says, walking over and leaning against the counter. "We've been down here for so long, I wonder if I will start to forget what the surface is like."

"Is your memory that bad, Mr. Morin?" the lady asks.

"I'm not sure," the man says. "I hope not. It's just a concern of mine."

"Do you think staring at that miniature model of the planet will help?"

"Maybe?"

"No," the lady says, opening a foil packet of oats and pouring the contents into the boiling water. "Humans are resilient; we can rebuild. That is what we did after the great empires had fallen. Take the Egyptians and the Romans, for example."

"I know, I know."

THE BIG PICTURE

The man looks up at the ceiling, over to a closed hatch at the far corner of the room. A ladder is just below it, beside a console that glows red. He nods at the glowing light. "How long do we have to wait, though?" he asks. "It might not even be our generation."

The woman stirs the contents of the pot with a wooden spoon. "Yes, which is why we have to stick to our set routine. Keep healthy and procreate." She glares at him, reinforcing her statement. "It isn't a matter of intimacy."

The man scratches the back of his head. "It might help if you called me by my first name," he says.

"All right, Mason, we can do that. Can we try tonight?"

"Sure," Mason says.

He wouldn't be so difficult to work with if she was a bit more human. Her choice to use his last name and her strange, cold tone of voice weren't turn-ons. He didn't even mind the shaved head—plus, shaving helped save on the limited shampoo supplies. The truth was, sex was the last thing on his mind. Of course, he understood that the interaction was only to carry on the human species. For all they knew, he was the last man on Earth, and she was the last woman. Humanity potentially came down to just them. The act of procreation was also a difficult one when it involved this automaton of a woman.

She's nothing like Chloe, he thinks. Oh, how Mason wishes to find out who those pricks in the sky were that took his girl from him. Why couldn't she be the last woman with him?

"How did you get selected again, Abigail?" Mason asks.

"For this program?" the woman asks. "No different than you."

"That's the funny thing," Mason says. "I'm not sure if I fully recall."

Abigail squints. "Your memory isn't that good. We'll have to perform more mental exercises to correct this. Hopefully it isn't a defect in your genetics." She pours the oatmeal out of the pot and into two separate bowls. "Here, eat, and we will begin our morning analysis of the surface."

"Maybe I bumped my head," Mason says, recalling driving. The mountains. Red, then white. That's all.

"Unlikely," Abigail says coldly. "We monitor our health daily. It would have been flagged in the console."

Mason takes the bowl and moves the contents around with the spoon, feeling the heat absorbed by the metal utensil. He can feel. He is alive. "Can you refresh my memory on how we got here?"

Abigail places the pot on an unused element and takes her bowl. "Well, we all took DNA tests, and then were psychologically evaluated. The results dictated who would be a suitable candidate to continue the human race."

"Right, I remember," Mason says while eating. Truthfully, he still doesn't remember the events that brought him to this underground bunker. He remembers being *told* how he got here by Abigail. Everything seems like a blur. One day he was living a normal life, had a steady job, a wife, and the next, he found himself here. There is a gap in his memory.

CRITICAL THINKING

Chloe. His last memory of his wife was that damned road trip to Jasper. That natural blonde babe was so obsessed with her job. Work seemed like a trivial thing now that he was apart from her. His life consisted of physical exercise, studying in the archives, and daily reviews of the Earth's temperature levels with the robots on the surface. They still had no answers as to what happened in Jasper. Chloe was just gone, and he couldn't remember anything else.

Mason looks up at his companion. "How many more of us do you think there are?"

"What do you mean?" Abigail asks. "Of the human race?"

"I guess I meant humans in the bunkers. There have to be more."

"Not to my knowledge. There wasn't enough time to build more before the asteroid hit."

Asteroid. A word that Mason is pondering over. He does have a chunk of memory missing, but he's sure those lights were no asteroid. "But they had enough time to do a screening process?"

"I didn't build the program. The UN did in hopes of keeping our species alive. Be thankful that you survived."

"I fear I might go insane down here."

"That is why they put the program guide together, so we have a purpose every day. I am no different than you. I signed up in hopes of surviving."

"Yeah," Mason says. "That's true. I wonder if any doomsday-preppers managed to survive through this."

"I guess our offspring will be the ones to find out about that when the ash clears," Abigail says.

Mason nods. He doesn't have any further comment.

The concept of living the rest of his life in this bunker with Abigail was not a pleasant thought. They had few to no common interests. They had been in the shelter for several months, if his memory served correctly. Then again, his mind wasn't very reliable as of late.

PLANETARY INSPECTION

The two finish their breakfast and leave the kitchen, entering a secondary room, equipped with two monitors mounted to the ceiling. Each monitor has a white office chair in front of it. Both Mason and Abigail sit down on a chair and wave at the monitors, turning them on. Each morning, after their workout and breakfast, the two analyze the latest information the drones have gathered over the past twenty-four hours. The robots are graded for space exploration and can easily survive the harsh temperatures on the surface. They are fully equipped with cameras and measuring equipment to test the planet's livability.

The monitor showcases a smaller live-cam of the drone Mason manages. The video displays an ash-covered wasteland with a grey sky. The digital interface also contains stats of the drone's health, menus, and a map outlining how far the drone has gone from the bunker. At the top right is the temperature: 148° C.

"Dammit," Mason mumbles. He'd had a small amount of hope that maybe they would see a change in temperature. But it has stayed the same for the past week, give or take a few digits.

"What?" Abigail asks.

"Nothing. The readings seem to be the same as they were yesterday, and the day before." Mason waves his hand to enhance the drone's live-cam.

Abigail turns back to her interface. "We aren't looking for hope, Mason. We are simply monitoring the aftermath for future generations."

"Right," Mason says. He merely wants to believe there is more. Each time he reviews the stats, his hope dims. Abigail and Mason are the last people on Earth.

DUTY TO HUMANKIND

Just like every day, the two move on with their routine of planetary diagnostics, studying, meditation, and eating. The activities are what the UN's program guide has instructed them to do. Abigail doesn't question it, and Mason follows, knowing if he doesn't, he would probably go crazy. He's no psychologist and has to admit the routine helps him stay focused. Even then, his mind falls back to Chloe, and he has to fight through his memories to get back into the moment.

After dinner, Mason and Abigail patrol the halls to ensure they did the daily inventory check and to review the general health of the bunker. As it is every day, everything is in order. The task generally takes a couple of hours, leaving one more task before leisure time: procreation. Great, the one task Mason doesn't want to do. The task is on the list, and he has avoided it repeatedly. But he signed up for this. It's just Abigail and Mason. The new Adam and Eve.

The bedroom lights are brought to level three of ten, creating a soft glow over the black sheets. At least the mood is right. Mason finishes showering, drying himself from head to toe. Abigail sits on the bed, hands on her lap. He wraps the towel around his waist, walks over to the bed, and sits beside her.

"Would you like to undress me?" Abigail asks.

Mason shakes his head. "You aren't good at this."

Abigail exhales and unbuttons her blouse.

Mason watches as she slips out of her shirt and pants. Her body is well-toned—hell, way better than his own. Her breasts are basically what other women paid top dollar to recreate. Abigail's physique is a frame that most men would fantasize over. In an unclear series of events, Mason has found himself as the last 'lucky' guy on the planet who gets to live that fantasy. Yet he can't give less of a damn.

Abigail leans back onto the pillows, resting her hands on her legs.

"Come here," she says.

Mason stiffly crawls over on top of her, eyeing her from her smooth legs up to her pink lips. She fits the definition of beauty, yet he doesn't feel a thing for her. Shouldn't he feel *something* for the woman who would care for his future children? Maybe it doesn't matter. They are truly the last people on Earth, and they have a duty to humanity. The act of sex was instinctual with Chloe. Why is this so difficult for him? Perhaps the concept of being the last humans is rotting in the back of his mind. Maybe he is distressed by not knowing what happened to his memories or his wife.

Abigail gently runs her hand against the back of his neck, bringing him closer. At this near distance, a red glow sheens over her iris, making Mason resist momentarily, stopping his face from meeting Abigail's. He blinks, and the blotch goes away. It's probably the stress getting to him.

"Are we going through this again?" Abigail asks.

Mason blinks a couple of times. "I can't recall what happened to Chloe." He rolls off Abigail and presses into his forehead, trying to remember something. Anything. He can't.

Abigail sits up beside him. "You're overthinking this. We've endured the impossible, being alive today when everything else is gone."

"I . . . red . . . ," Mason mumbles as Abigail takes his hand and pulls him towards her, leaning into the sheets.

Mason exhales through his nose as they kiss, pushing the thought-chatter aside for one moment. They will procreate. They will have children and continue the human race. His eyes open briefly, seeing another red shimmer in Abigail's half-open eyes. He recalls red eyes. Yes. Chrome flooring. The recognition is dismissed as Abigail's soft hands glide over his genitals. The pleasure is overpowering as their naked forms press against one another, limbs intertwining. Mason's resistance fades as she stimulates his primal desires. His thoughts are gone as he embraces the woman, melting his newfound memories for the sake of humanity.

22

The feelings of loss, misery, and sorrow dwindle. They're relatable to your situation—a lack of memory. Like Mason, you have a massive gap in your mind. Events are familiar. Feelings are familiar, yet they are all so far away. You leave the observation with empathy towards the man, but you know he wasn't you. You also can't help but wonder what happened to him and Abigail, just like you wonder what happened to many of the poor souls you've encountered through the observing. Perhaps it doesn't matter since the real you only watches these people. In the end, they all reach the euphoria and live a new life. You were robbed of it. Blissfulness is where everyone goes, and the petty problems of life do not matter when the ego and the flesh cease to be. How unfair.

"There certainly was a lot of white," you say. "Nothing jolted my memory. What was it you wanted to try out?"

Malpherities shrugs. "You mentioned white, cold, and warmth. They're common experiences when dying, but I wanted to be sure, and I knew of a particular man who was abducted."

"Wait, you knew the man I observed?" you ask.

"Yes. He is not important, but I thought I'd try," Malpherities says. "What was the one you were familiar with? Oh, yes, the ABE incident."

"Yeah, can we try that again? The All-Being Entity seemed closer.

Maybe it was just the dying again, but I'm out of ideas. These observations are getting in my head. They all seem like me, but I know they're not."

"We're distorting your memories, which is concerning," Malpherities says. "We'll try this one."

The ghoul swipes the black liquid from the bowl and drops it into your eye. Perhaps this observation will be the lucky memory to bring everything back into perspective.

PANPSYCHISM

BIG QUESTIONS

Conspiracy theories are fun. People believe some of the wildest things, which makes it so easy for the rest of us to write those folks off as crack-monkeys. Conspiracists' evidence is always contradictory or vague. Most of the time, the real answer is never found. Those conspiracy nuts sure do try, though. Some are legitimate. If you want to get into politics, a lot of stuff has been proven right. It is just tucked under the table, and life moves on. Conspiracies about the end of the world and extraterrestrial beings? Hard to hide or prove that it happened when all is dandy. Maybe it isn't the government. Perhaps there is some underlying force that keeps us together. Call it God if you'd like. Call it the universe. I honestly don't care. I do know something is gluing us together, some form of consciousness.

What is consciousness? That's an age-old discussion brought on by scientists and philosophers. Is it only humans that have consciousness, or do animals have it, too? How about a tree or a rock? I, for one, have never really worried about it. What's the point? No one has ever been able to prove it. If you dig too deep into a rabbit hole, you will never get yourself out, just like conspiracists. So, I have chosen to live my life.

Well, I used to until that damn triangle showed up in the sky. ABE. The All-Being Entity. The cosmic . . . thing has some form of consciousness that works in a two-dimensional giant triangle. Now I know. We're conscious, too. It is the underlying layer of our reality. Consciousness is in everything.

Before him, it was easy to avoid the Galactic Believers, his loyal followers. They just came across as some wacky New-Age group, believing in what some chick going by the name of The Oracle started. She foresaw humanity's bright future in the stars. Then, the numbers grew, and ABE showed up. I guess she was right. He took so many people and destroyed so much of our planet, claiming Earth was to be absorbed into the bigger picture or something.

END OF THE WORLD

If you had asked me any of this even a month ago, I would think you were shooting up smack. Today, I know consciousness can be sensed all around. ABE communicated with us for years, through the Galactic Believers and The Oracle. The whispers of millions of people that he has absorbed, speaking only in fragments. I wonder if those people are alive, or if it is just *him* manipulating us.

I remember watching with my own eyes as people were dissolved into small particles and sucked into the giant glowing triangle in a spiralling motion. People were too gullible. They couldn't resist ABE and his mindless followers. People find it so easy to give up on hope, but not all of us. ABE's Galactica Array absorption is not the end-all-be-all he claims it is. He's persuasive, and his Galactic Believers are intimidating, yet ABE is also vulnerable because he has an ego.

Still, ABE made Earth a mess. When he initiated the galactic absorption, he took his believers and those who were unable to resist him. Part of the planet tore apart. I think that something about us resisting saved the planet. I was there when my wife dissolved. Much like the other survivors, we were confronted in our homes by the

Galactic Believers. Those fools. They became some of the many particles that encompass that triangle. Not me.

Blind luck. I am no university professor; I'm just a mechanic. Odd jobs, you know? A bit of a science geek, but that's all. Thankfully, common sense isn't bound to any sort of class or trade. That is why I believe I resisted ABE. That is why others did too. I wish I could say the same about my wife, absorbed into the Galactica Array. I wanted just to give in, let ABE take every atom from my body so I could be with her again. Even after the absorption, I was positive I could hear her. For all I knew, it was ABE talking to me, wanting me to give in. Thinking about this stuff can drive you crazy, like the concept of consciousness. So, I just don't overthink it.

I hid for a couple of days. ABE remained in the sky during this time as the upward spiral of matter moved towards him. His essence—or power—crumbled all Earth and flesh. I was frightened and didn't move. I even pissed my pants, I was so scared of making any sort of movement—what a coward. On the bright side, lying under a car for days is a great method to lose weight. That didn't matter, since ABE brought humanity into a new dark era.

I had grown weak. The lack of food and lying in my disgusting filth was driving me insane. Thankfully, ABE's absorption stopped. The change was unexpected, and I got up from under the car. The spiralling particles remained stationary midair like it was on pause. I didn't believe exactly what I was looking at. I don't think anyone did. In the midnight sky, the giant glowing white triangle hovered above the planet, frozen. Well, in front of North America. I wasn't sure what the other side of the world was seeing.

THE RESISTANT

Anyway, then, I saw other people coming from under the rubble. I remember seeing one gal. Her eyes were puffy, probably from crying as much as I had. Hundreds of people started to appear from under the remains of the city. We didn't know what to say or what to do. ABE, the entity that was surely going to bring our doom, was motionless.

"Who dare prevent the absorption?" ABE's voice projected in my mind. By the look on everyone else's faces, I think that bastard was talking to them too.

We watched in awe, waiting to see what happened next.

"This planet is mine," ABE spoke. "The atoms that are treasured here must be brought into the Galactica Array."

Some guy in front of me turned around. He pointed towards the giant triangle. "He cannot absorb us! We have resisted him."

"How?" shouted a woman.

"We must be special," the man said. "Our mind, or DNA, something."

"I prayed!" a man said, his voice trembling. "God answered me. He answered us all!"

Before anyone else perked up, a pulsating wave erupted throughout the landscape. I felt it in my core, holding on to my chest as the force moved through me. I almost toppled onto the ground but managed to remain standing. Another wave pulsated, throwing me on my ass. People screamed. I didn't bother to get up because the particles falling from the sky had my keen interest. ABE's spiralling absorption began to crumble. The matter began to move back down in reverse. It was as if everything was beginning to rebuild itself. I didn't believe it. No one did. I don't even think ABE did.

BEYOND THE ALL-BEING

"Who defies me?" ABE shouted. This was the angriest I had ever heard the triangle talk. The prick was always so well composed. About time he was shaken up.

Tingling ran throughout my body. I thought I was about to get absorbed, and I got up from the ground, feeling it intensify. It was all around. My eyes were wide, watching millions of colours start to vibrate from my hand, the road, the rocks, and everything. The whole world had a translucent layer buzzing and rising up, towards the triangle in the sky.

Next, the impossible occurred. Every shadow, large and small, animated, morphed and grew—or shrunk, depending on their size—until they became a human form with arms and legs. No light touched them. They were pitch black, with millions of particles humming through them like a static TV. There wasn't a single shadow left; everything was bright with no shade as these lightless ones glided on the rising colours, like surfers, heading for ABE.

ABE's glowing form began to shake violently. Parts of the triangle began to crack like glass. All clouds blew away while the buzzing colours moved up with the lightless ones. The sky itself began to distort, rippling like water. I think. I really can't describe this to you. It was as if there were an upside-down ocean in the sky, also covered with thousands of these lightless humanoids, filled with as many translucent colours as I could possibly see outlining the ripples. Two worlds—one upright, buzzing, and the other upside down—were merging. People ran; some people stayed. I was one to watch. If we were all going to die, I at least wanted a good show.

The sky-ocean began to extend downward in the form of two massive tidal waves aiming for ABE, while the buzzing colours moved up to him. The triangle continued to shatter, violently moving back and forth, up and down—a type of speed that defied logic.

"This is mine to take. For I am the All-Being Entity!" ABE shouted.

The two sky tidal waves collided with ABE, the buzzing colours, and the lightless ones. The impact caused the triangle to dissolve like ink in a bucket of water, taking the lightless ones with it until everything was one. The forces rebounded and soared towards the surface of Earth.

I finally started to run—a little late. I wasn't sure where. I was weak, hungry, and frightened. The massive force from above engulfed the entire sky. It was faster than anything I'd seen before. I could hear millions of voices talking at once, but nothing distinguishable. The sky-ocean collided with me and sucked my body in.

I froze. Senses stopped. Black. Light. Reverse, like a VCR in rewind. Everything moved so quickly. Every sensation was backwards—try and explain how that feels, huh? I relived being under the car, ABE's arrival, pissing myself, watching my wife be dissolved (or pieced back together in this reverse-time), and the appearance of the first Galactic Believer. This continued until I was brought back to the moment before any of this happened.

RETURN HOME

I dropped my wrench, shouting, catching the attention of my coworkers at the shop. It had to be a dream. No sweat drenched me. No piss-coated clothes. A strange sense of déjà vu rushed over my being. I had been through this before. I swear to God.

"You all right?" asked a co-worker.

"Yeah," I said. "What day is it?"

"Thursday," he said.

I sighed, realizing I could answer the damn question myself. I reached into my pocket for my phone to check the time. It was exactly what I thought. I was brought years back before any of this happened. The sky-ocean from those lightless ones had rewound time. There were no special people with unique DNA, or mindsets, or God, that could resist ABE. What a foolish thought. There were only some other entities, greater than us, and greater than ABE. Something we couldn't exactly see. They took care of humanity and our planet.

It had brought me back to a time before the first Galactic Believer, so long ago. I had all this knowledge and experience in my mind, yet no one else seemed to be different from a regular day of work. I left the shop and immediately called my wife. I cried. She was confused, but lovely, as she always is. I don't think she will ever fully understand why I was crying. I didn't tell her why. No way. I just told her I missed her or something corny like that.

I took a stroll through the city, experiencing the buildings, listening to the sounds of the metropolis, and embracing the moment. There's some New-Age hokey shit, hey? When you go through an end-of-the-world experience, only to have it all be brought back, you appreciate life a bit more. Maybe those hippie-dippies were right about living in the moment. Whatever those lightless ones were that took ABE were capable of abilities that scientists can't even fathom. I can tell you that I can't look at shadows the same way anymore—or anything, for that matter. Everything is alive. I saw those humming colours vibrate.

The years went by, and the Galactic Believers never arrived. ABE was just a figment of my imagination. At least that is what sane people would say. The classic Mandela Effect. I learned I was not alone. There were others online that shared the same memories that I do. We can all discuss the destruction of Earth and the days leading up to it in immense detail. We all sound like conspiracists because there is no proof of it. It only exists as a collective story told by people who have never met. Another conspiracy theory that will drive you mad.

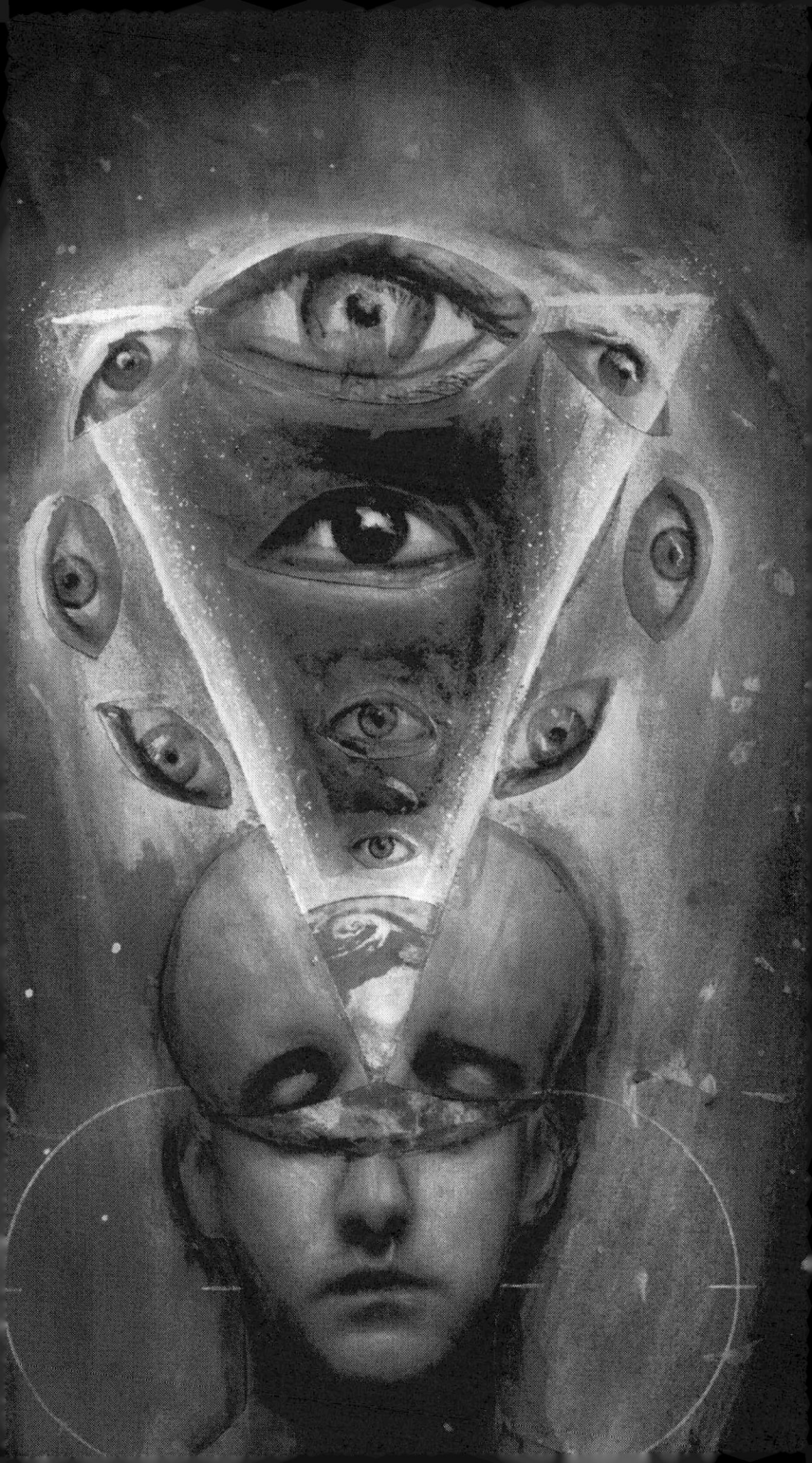

23

The Mandela Effect is a fascinating phenomenon, where memories conflict with what is supposedly real. It's like you have the opposite version and cannot remember anything. Could you have had your memory erased by some super force in the fabric of space? It certainly would explain everything that you're experiencing. Then again, Malpherities doesn't seem to think that was the case, and he is your best guide to living post-death at the moment.

"No," you say, knowing that you weren't the man you observed.

"Nothing at all?" Malpherities asks.

"There were some colours and these lightless beings that reset the planet. It wasn't anything I have seen before," you say. "Could that have something to do with me being here?"

"There is always a bigger fish."

"You have no explanation, then?" you ask.

"Just the two theories we have discussed before. I cannot say I have seen a mortal thrown into the Midway from Death's Vortex before. It's quite fascinating, but proving to be a dead end with no concerns of what I initially feared."

"You don't think anyone did this to me?" you ask.

"It's unlikely. You don't seem to be anyone of importance," Malpherities says. "It's improbable someone got their hands on that damned book and searched you out to push your soul from its transcendence. The book has been lost for a very long time, and the name has not been spoken by any tongue since. This is probably some unfortunate phenomenon, for the universe holds more mysteries than one entity could ever fathom. Every time one learns something new about it, more questions are raised than answered. So, you're not special; you're just a statistic."

The comment is a bit insulting but it does hold water. In comparison to all of the observing you have done through the black liquid—tragic events, mutated humans. trolls, knights, horse ghosts—you can't imagine your life being that eventful. It makes you wonder if you will ever find out the truth. The more observing you do, the more frustrating the whole situation becomes. Yet you haven't done enough.

In the back of your mind, you wonder how much more you must do. Can your brain take it? Are those other ghouls going to come back? By an odd chance of timing, an elongated hiss pierces your ears from the cavern entrance. It looks like one question is answered.

Malpherities shakes his head. "The Midway isn't intended for this kind of tension," he mumbles. "Let's get you observing and I'll handle this."

The ghoul dabs a droplet into your eye, sending you into a new observing state as he takes care of the unwanted visitor. This process happens one after the other. Your mind is exhausted, and you're emotionally drained. These observations vary in complexity. Strange experiences. Normal events. Dying, over and over again. When you wake, the ghoul is there, looking more impatient with each attempt. He assures you that you have the time to keep trying, despite the stress visible in his tightly gripped claws and short words.

Each new observation offers a small clue. A pencil seems familiar; so does that smell, and some tower. You remember seeing the building in one of the previous observations. Everything is getting too distorted. You try to remain optimistic that something will come out of this, but every time you enter a new observation, hope dwindles a little more.

Another dozen or so observations pass; the latest has something to do with demons and rituals, but it doesn't matter. You've lived through so many lives that they are all melding into one giant mess of nonsense. Time doesn't even line up anymore. Experiencing others' timelines makes your own, in the Midway, seem irrelevant. For all you know, you've been in this cavern for centuries, or possibly an hour. It's hard to tell, especially knowing that Malpherities is keeping the other ghoul at bay.

The memories are all mashed around in your head; it's next to impossible to keep track of which events seems familiar and which ones don't. Each observation is pushing your goal further away. You rub your head and say, "Nothing. These are starting to seem pointless, and I'm not sure what is really me and what is the person I'm seeing."

Malpherities taps his claw, growling. "We've fried your mind." He hovers down from the bowl, moving towards a dark corner of the cavern, disappearing into the darkness.

"Malpherities?" you say. "What does that mean?"

"MORTAL!" another reverbed voice booms. You see a shadow appear from the cavern entrance with tentacle hair and claws. Then another, and a third. This isn't good.

You hurry to the darkness, following Malpherities down a narrow pathway leading outside, along a path below the plateau, wrapping around the rocky shaft. You can see the outer rim of that spiralling mess of souls known as Death's Vortex. It's still just as unsettling as you remember it being when you first arrived. The ghoul stops at the edge of the rocky path, despite the fact that the path continues to spiral around and down. The ghoul stares off into the still black ocean, far out into the abyss.

"There's no point in continuing what we're doing," Malpherities says. "I've exhausted that rudimentary brain of yours. You've lived too many lives now and the memories are all melted together."

"Wait, we had a limit?" you ask. The pit of your stomach begins to twist; you have the sickening feeling that you may never find out who you were or why you're here. "What about those other ghouls?" you ask.

"Yes, there's that too."

"Can you make them go away?" you ask. "You did it before."

Malpherities shakes his head. "I can only hold them back for so long with my persuasion. We share many of the same thoughts and experiences with our connected hivemind. They know I am hiding something, and they are done waiting."

"Try one more time. I can keep going," you say.

"You're burnt; you know it. We've sent you through many eras and into the passenger seat of many souls with no verdict. Their experiences are as real to you as your lack of memory, according to your human mind. Now you question everything, overthinking any detail you see. It's counter-effective."

"So where do we go from here?" you ask.

"You don't belong in the Midway. That's why it is a *mid*, not a destination," Malpherities says.

You swallow a thick lump of saliva. "You're not going to kill me, are you?" You recall what the ghoul said about Death's Vortex when you first met.

"No. That would be a bit cruel, considering you've now established your new self. Overall, I'm not fond of doing the killing. I prefer watching. Death's Vortex will come for you eventually." The ghoul points down to the darkness below. "There's more than one way out of here." He points to the still, black ocean down below. It's the same strange liquid as found in the bowl, spanning to infinity.

"What?" You don't believe him. "You said you'd have to kill me to get me out of here!"

"I lied." Malpherities put on a devilish smile. "If I'd told you otherwise, you might have gone and done something stupid like jump into the abyss. Then how would I try and figure out why you're here?"

Your heart rate picks up as frustration and anger courses through you. Malpherities had some nerve withholding this information. He probably knows more than he is willing to share. He has his own agenda, and it's far above your own needs. Anger aside, now, after living dozens of lives, you're able to leave this damn place.

"None of this explains how I am here," you say. "I thought you needed to know."

Malpherities folds his arms. "No, it does not. Truthfully, it is not yours to concern yourself with now that you can't assist me. Nothing has occurred in the afterlife since we've started sending you into the observation states. The other ghouls haven't detected anything either, except for your presence. No other souls are breaking their natural passage, and nothing else unexplainable has happened. My worries have lessened."

"Should something have happened by now? How long has it been?"

"If it were something vindictive, I'd say so."

"What about the black rip I saw while in the euphoric state? It sent me through Death's Vortex to here."

"Yes, yes. That is what happened. You were sucked from it. That's all we know, and that is all that happened."

"And you're certain? You seemed so keen on figuring this out before."

"Seeing you observe these lives and watching your reactions tell me you aren't anyone of value or great knowledge. Like many in the universe, you're just another soul. In your case, you've just experienced a once-in-a-lifetime chance to see the other side with your conscious state intact. Consider yourself lucky."

"How is this lucky? I can't remember anything."

"Your lost past matters little, other than to feed your ego's desires. Again, you don't seem to be of importance. I'll discuss your bizarre scenario with some of the other ghouls. They'll have thoughts on the matter."

A growl roars from inside the cavern. The other ghoul is near.

"Looks like they've figured out where we went," Malpherities says.

They are near. The words are concerning for you. It was bad enough when there was only one. You are running out of ideas and ask, "Why don't I wait here, then? We can all figure it out."

"The other ghouls will be . . . less accepting of a human in the Midway, remember?"

"So that's a threat?"

"It's a chance to start anew. Since you are only an accumulation of the experiences you have, embrace the blank slate. Perhaps I will come and visit you if I find out anything more about this occurrence, but don't hold your breath."

"So that's it? After all this work we did?"

"Yes. The Midway is no place for a mortal to remain forever."

"And I am just supposed to jump into this black ocean, down there?" you ask, not trusting what the ghoul is saying. He hasn't been entirely honest with you from the beginning.

"Yes, it will send you out of here," Malpherities says. "Act fast; we'll have visitors soon."

"To where?" you ask.

"Best find out if you want to get out before my fellow ghouls arrive," Malpherities says. "And trust me, we'll meet again soon. Think of this as a second chance at life."

"You're not going to tell me where this goes?" you ask.

"Truthfully, I don't know because I know nothing about you. I know enough about the observing liquid's nature to assure you it'll be worth it."

You peek over the edge of the cliff to see a vast black ocean going on forever. The stillness of the water makes it almost look like a mirror reflection. No way. That's beyond frightening. Then again, looking around this barren wasteland, there isn't much else here. This plateau only goes so far. Or you could stay in the cavern and tempt those dimension bowls. That's assuming the other ghouls don't shred you to pieces.

The third option is to trust Malpherities's words and jump in. At this point, what else do you have to lose? Technically, you're dead. You don't know who you are or who, if anyone, loves you. The fear is real in your mind. You've embraced the unknown before coming to the Midway. You can do it again.

"Now go, Nameless One, live your life," Malpherities says, shooing you with his claw.

"Really? That's that?" you say. "It's so anticlimactic."

"That's one way to look at it. Or you could be amazed by all of the things you've observed, what you see now, and be thankful you're getting out of here."

"They're just memories."

"Yes, and they make up you. You do not need to burden your mind with what you cannot explain. It has driven many good people mad and prompted others to fabricate bogus stories to explain the unexplainable."

Malpherities brings up an interesting point. He has been shady but has yet to steer you wrong. You both worked together to try and find answers to who you are. He's been your guide. Perhaps it's worth believing him one last time. His logic makes sense. An ocean of the black liquid could do something quite exciting.

"I'm just supposed to wonder what all this is?" you ask.

"No. Appreciate it but don't obsess over it. Simply let it be."

"And I should trust you by jumping into that black liquid?"

A hiss comes from the cave's entrance about fifty paces away. Another ghoul appears from the shadows. They're thinner than Malpherities, with longer tentacles, and the extended muzzle ends in a snarl.

"Yes," Malpherities says. "Remember what a droplet can do? Think about what an ocean can offer. As I said, it will be worth it."

"MALPHERITIES! WHAT IS THIS?" booms the thin ghoul as a second one emerges from the darkness. They're bigger, plump, and have equally knotty faces. A third, finer one floats out of the cave. All three of them hover towards you, ready to tear you to pieces with those razor-sharp teeth.

"Go!" Malpherities shouts. "I've handled these three downers before."

The decision is sealed. With one deep breath, you take a step back and rush forward, jumping from the edge of the cliff and into the air. You soar for a brief moment and begin to descend; down and down you go, towards the ocean. The four ghouls and the plateau are a mere speckle below Death's Vortex, and then your body collides with a vast body of water. Your impact ripples the form for a brief moment, sending bubbles soaring everywhere as you submerge into the liquid.

There is no stinging. The water's density keeps pulling you in, accelerating far faster than terminal velocity—another mystery of this wretched place. The speed keeps increasing until you can feel your whole body begin to stretch out in the liquid. Despite not seeing anything, nor feeling any pain, you sense the body keeps stretching until it is unrecognizable and your consciousness is left in nothingness.

Stillness. Peace. A blip of light. Then a *BANG*. You fly out of blankness and curving black edges. Wait, how does this work? Those black edges are shrinking. They're . . . letters. Yes, that's an "A" and an "N." These words keep getting smaller as you're pulled away from them, seeing hundreds more, and away from a *page*. The force keeps sucking you back until you see this space in front of you and have moved into a new body . . . a familiar one. Yes. This is the real you! *You're* reading these words—another impossible. Your thoughts and actions are yours. You're not just observing. How? The black liquid held the key to escaping the Midway, and that ghoul finally shared the knowledge with you. Remember, don't overthink it. Appreciate the phenomenon, and don't go mad.

Keep reading for a little more, and then celebrate your newfound life.

You've lived so many lives, seen so much, and now you're back to your ordinary world. It can make you wonder what *normal* even means. All the dark cosmic, bizarre, and fantastic observations you had were, are, and will be—and you're the only person who knows of them. Maybe the memories themselves are what makes them real—or not. And if memories aren't real, then perhaps the only thing that is truly real is what you're experiencing right now.

The Midway . . . Death's Vortex . . . a floating ghoul . . . and a golden bowl. Try to explain this to anyone in your life, and they'll think you're crazy. These memories are yours to cherish—or squirm over. The observing states you've found yourself in will forever be a part of you, until they fizzle out, as most memories do. Until then, these other lives linger in your mind as you read these last words. You may never have an explanation for what occurred, or how you died—if you even died. Maybe it was just this book sending you into a trance. But if you had all the answers, then there would be no wonder to life at all.

The mystery of the unknown is what keeps humanity so engaged in the living world. It has led us to some truly amazing innovations, like the alphabet, which is transcribing the words on this page and into your thoughts. Who knows? Maybe you'll find out how you got to the Midway and about the black liquid in another volume. Or maybe it doesn't matter, for it is just a memory. For now, you can enjoy being alive once more. Eventually, we all reach death's door and transcend from this plane of existence. You managed to get a glimpse of the other side. Malpherities and the other ghouls are there, with the dead in Death's Vortex. You're likely to run into that mischievous ghoul in the future. Let's hope it's later rather than sooner, and you can live your life not as an observer but as a participant.

THANK YOU FOR READING INTO THE MACROCOSM.
WOULD YOU CONSIDER GIVING IT A REVIEW?

Reviewing an author's book on primary book sites such as Amazon, Kobo and Goodreads drastically help authors promote their novels and it becomes a case study for them when pursuing new endeavors. A review can be as short as a couple of sentences or up to several paragraphs, it's up to you. You can find review options on Goodreads or your preferred online distributor such as Amazon or Kobo.

ADDITIONAL WORK BY KONN LAVERY

Seed Me | YEGman | Rutherford Manor Series | Mental Damnation Series

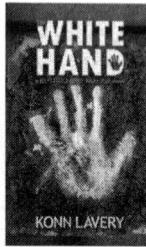

S.O.S. - YEGman Novel Soundtrack | World Mother: Seed Me Novel Score.

Find *Seed Me, YEGman, S.O.S - YEGman Novel Soundtrack* and the *World Mother: Seed Me Novel Score* at:

www.konnlavery.com

ABOUT THE AUTHOR

Konn Lavery is a Canadian author whose work has been recognized by Edmonton's top five bestseller charts and by reviewers such as Readers' Favorite, and Literary Titan.

He started writing stories at a young age while being homeschooled. After graduating from graphic design college, he began professionally pursuing his writing with his first release, Reality. He continues to write in the thriller, horror, and fantasy genres.

Konn balances his literary work along with his own graphic design and website development business. His visual communication skills have been transcribed into the formatting and artwork found within his publications supporting his fascination of transmedia storytelling.

Manufactured by Amazon.ca
Bolton, ON

23983240R00195